MAIL ORDERED

G. LOUISE BEARD

Edited by Vince Font
Cover design by Judith S. Design & Creativity
www.judithsdesign.com
Published by Glass Spider Publishing
www.glassspiderpublishing.com

I have always enjoyed reading and spent my early years thinking that I wanted to be a writer, but the necessities of life delayed my dream. I eventually returned to the idea of writing after two years of retirement. There are many people to thank for helping me through the journey . . .

Sheryl, a most amazing young woman whose vision and insight helped me to press forward when the idea of writing was just resurfacing.

Sheila M, who listened to my words, made awesome suggestions, and gave very enthusiastic encouragement. She is the one who practically tied me to her kitchen table and encouraged (demanded) that I complete my application and mail off the stories disc. After we prayed together, she then went with me and stood as I mailed the package to Washington, D.C.

WS, my husband, my friend, my partner—the one who quietly watched and prayed for me as I sat day after day, week after week, and month after month developing the stories.

Mrs. Daisy Richardson, my mother, whose wise counsel kept me on track. Thank you, Mother, for believing I had the ability and for making me believe I could do it.

Tanoka (son #1, the engine), who never knew how his bright smile, soft kisses on the cheeks, and declarations of encouragement—"You're doing good, Mom, keep it going"—helped me to press forward through the times when I was floundering.

Darius (son #2, the caboose), who never knew how his great bear hugs and his soft-spoken words—"I know you can do it, Mom"—comforted me and helped me to continue on the journey.

To the Sisters of the Women of Prayer group: Thank you, ladies, for the laughs, the tears, and the praises that we share with and for one another.

Most of all, I want to thank God for His many, marvelous, and amazing blessings.

—G. Louise Beard

CHAPTER 1

Looking into the Barnes family history, one always comes across the rather remarkable life of Emery Barnes Jr. The only child of the patriarch of the Barnes family, Emery Barnes Sr. and his wife, Lula-Mae Barnes, Emery Jr. was young when he and his parents moved to Oklahoma to build their fortune.

Emery Jr.'s own legacy included his pride and joy, his children Franklin, Sherman, and Camila Rose. Although his father was a rich man by the time he died, Emery Jr. was a much richer man by the time he himself passed away.

As a very young boy, Emery Jr. began working odd jobs to earn money while his father supported the family by setting up the town's blacksmith shop and livery stable. Emery Jr's. mother, Lula-Mae, contributed by baking specialty breads, pies, and cakes. For several years, the Barneses lived frugally and saved as much of their money as they could. While they were very cordial, they were not inclined to be very social and claimed very few if any true friends.

Samuel Jones and Emery Barnes Sr. became friends when one evening around closing time, a tired, sick, hungry white man and his pregnant wife rode into town on a worn-out nag that just about collapsed in Emery's corral.

"Sir," Samuel said to Emery Sr., "my name is Samuel P. Jones, and this is my wife, Mary-Beth. We've traveled a long way. She's in the family way, and our horse is on his last legs. We need a place to layover until the baby comes, and no one will rent us a room. Do you think you can help us? If you can, I would be forever grateful to you. As you can see, we are in a bad way right now."

Emery Sr. looked at Mary-Beth Jones and understood why they were in such a dilemma. Mary-Beth was just like he and his wife: a "Massa baby." She was half Black. Without hesitation, Emery Sr. called to his wife. "Lula, we have company."

When Lula-Mae saw the state of the two travelers, she wrapped her arms around Mary-Beth Jones without question or comment and helped her inside the family home that was just behind the smithy shop. With that, the Barnes and the Jones families became fast friends.

CHAPTER 2

Emery Sr. was a quiet man who didn't make waves. He never made any demands on anyone, and so he lived a quiet life. A life people thought was somewhat unproductive aside from his business.

Sam Jones was a college-educated lawyer from Yale University. He fell in love with and married Mary-Beth Simmons, but before the ink was even dry on their marriage documents, he was disowned by his family and then immediately and very strongly advised to leave town. Since then, wherever they went, when it was discovered his wife was half Black, they were forced out of town.

When the Barnes family took them in and helped them regain their health, Samuel decided he and Emery Sr. would be friends for life. After all, if it had not been for the unconditional acts of kindness they were shown, Sam doubted his and Mary's little girl would have been born so healthy and beautiful.

Once they were settled in, Sam set up his practice and Mary-Beth began making dresses and capes. The Jones family became residents of Checotah, where Sam and Emery Sr. became more than good friends.

The Barneses had a large amount of money saved, but they were uncomfortable using the bank in the next town over. It was well known that the bankers there would take the Black folks' money and then refuse to admit they had an account at their bank.

Emery Sr. built an underground vault, and he and Sam began doing banking business for themselves and other Black residents. After a few years, a Black man named Edward Gilmore, who had been a slave to a Southern banker and was good with numbers, moved to the growing town and helped the Checotah Freedman's Bank become a real bank connected to the United States Treasury.

The Barnes and the Jones families were business partners, so when small patches of unworkable land came up for sale, Emery would buy the property with the help of the only lawyer in town. Sam Jones, who was Emery's frontman for his purchases, would negotiate with the owners, who naturally thought they were selling to another white man. Therefore, the process went very smoothly and a fair deal was made to the satisfaction of all parties.

Some parcels of the land were used for the growing town's residents. They would build shacks and rent them to other Blacks who were leaving the South to escape the memories of slavery.

Fifteen years after their friendship developed, Emery Sr. passed away suddenly one evening after work. He had just closed the smithy and walked into the house when Lula-Mae offered him dinner. He refused, saying he just wanted to sit by the fireplace and read his Bible. Within ten minutes, his eyes closed and he was gone.

Even though Emery Sr. was gone, the family quest for wealth did not stop. Emery Jr. was just as astute with business as his father had been, and maybe just a little bit more.

When the railroad came through the growing segregated town looking for land to buy, Emery went to his father's friend and asked, "Mr. Sam, do you reckon the railroad people would be interested in those acres that we just registered and haven't begun building on yet?"

Smiling, Sam Jones looked at his partner's son and said, "The only way to find out is to ask."

They made a deal with the railroad for a settlement of four and one-half million dollars. Sam Jones accepted one million of the profits, while Emery Jr. saved two for his family and used part of one million to continue to buy land and sell it to the businesses that usually followed the railroad.

The remaining half million went to building, furnishing, and maintaining a large brick house that some referred to as a mansion.

By the time Emery Jr. was thirty-five years old, he was a very wealthy man who owned more than three-fourths of the land that the town was sitting on, and he was now receiving interest on his money from the United States federal bank.

By the time Emery Barnes Jr. passed away, he was the father of three children: two sons and a daughter. Each was left enough money to support themselves for the rest of their lives with lots more left over.

Emery Jr., realizing that his daughter had great business skills, upgraded his will when Camila had to return home to care for him and her mother, thereby giving up the opportunity to finish school, begin her own business, and become a young bride.

The two brothers at first did not know their sister was slated to inherit twice the amount they inherited. The additional monies were scheduled to be awarded to her one year after her marriage, or on her twenty-second birthday if she chose not to marry.

CHAPTER 3

Camila Rose Barnes walked into the Checotah Freedman's Bank and stepped up to the window manned by the teller George Henry. "Good morning, Mr. Henry," she said with a smile. "I'd like to get my monthly allotment, please."

George Henry looked at Camila, his eyes filled with remorse. "Miz Barnes," he said, "I'm really sorry, but there's a situation, and you'll have to speak to Mr. Gilmore."

With her eyebrows drawn, Camila went to a door marked *Private* and knocked lightly. When the door finally opened, a haughty-looking Lincoln Gilmore stood, lightly scrutinizing her.

"Oh, Miss Barnes, it's you," he said. "I wasn't expecting you this early." He opened the door wider, stepped back, and waved his hand. "Please come in." Then he summoned the young floor sweeper and message runner to "go over to the Barnes Mercantile and have Mr. Barnes to come to my office."

"Mr. Gilmore," Camila said, "what's going on? All I wanted to do was get my monthly allotment and leave. I have some dresses to collect from the dressmaker and a pair of shoes to get from the shoemaker. Is there a problem with how I use my allotment? I have never been overdrawn, and I'm certainly not a careless spender."

If the truth would be known, Camila was very frugal with her spending. She used her monthly allotments wisely. She never spent more than seven or eight of her thirty dollars. Sometimes, she didn't use any at all and would put the entire amount or the remaining amount in a reticule she kept hidden at the bottom of her large carpetbag. No one knew that most of the monies she spent usually went to purchase supplies to make carpetbags that she would sell. She would then deposit her profits in the reticule along with her leftovers from the monthly allotment. Unbeknownst to anyone, Camila Rose Barnes had a stash of cash that was well over $24,000.

Just as she finished her complaint to Mr. Gilmore, her brothers Franklin and Sherman arrived. Franklin was not wearing his grocers' apron. Instead, he was dressed in his double-breasted vest and matching day coat. He removed his bowler as he walked in. He looked at Mr. Gilmore, put his thumbs in his vest pockets, and nodded his head.

Sherman followed him in, still wearing his blacksmith apron, pulled up a chair beside Camila, took her left hand in his hands, and asked, "How you doing, baby sister?"

Franklin took a breath and began. "Cammie, Willa and I are expecting a child, and we need more room."

She looked at her brother and took a deep breath. "Congratulations." Then she turned to look at Lincoln Gilmore and asked, "What does this have to do with my monthly allotment?"

Franklin stood over his sister, looking down into her upturned face. "Basically," he said, "it does have quite a bit of something to do with your allotment."

Confused, Camila gazed up at her oldest brother and asked, "What are you talking about, Franklin?"

Franklin pursed his lips and huffed like having this conversation with his sister was a waste of his time. "There's no reason for you to be there in that big house by yourself, Camila, so we are moving into Mom and Dad's house."

"Oh, really, Franklin? I still don't understand. What is your point? Why are we all here?"

"Well, little sister, as you can well imagine, there can only be one mistress in any household, so you will be moving."

Camila looked at Franklin. She looked at Mr. Gilmore and then at her brother Sherman. She snatched her hand out of Sherman's and stood. "What do you mean, I'm moving? That house was left to me. How are you going to just take over, move me out, and move your wife in? Where am I supposed to live?"

"Sit down, Cammie," Franklin said condescendingly, "there's no need to get dramatic. You will be well taken care of. Linc, Sherman, and I decided that since you turned down Lincoln's proposal and you are too old to catch the eye of anyone else here in the Checotah area, we would send you off as a mail-order bride. And just so you know, you are going to be living in a town called Alamosa in the Colorado territory. Your husband's name is Garrison LaRue, and he's waiting for you. You have three days to pack your belongings. You can only take your clothes and other personal items. All of the furniture stays in the house."

Lincoln Gilmore stepped up to Camila and offered her some papers. "You need to sign these documents. They give your brothers the right to your inheritance. Since you are about to be married, you won't be needing your allotments anymore. Besides, your brothers are businessmen, and they need money in reserve just in case they have business problems. This way, they won't have to use their own personal funds."

"I'm not signing anything," Camila snapped. "This is not legal. You can't take my inheritance away from me. Wherever I go, if I go anywhere, it goes with me. No! I'm not signing anything, and I'm not moving. You forget that I am a one-third owner in the store and of the smithy. I'm also a one-third owner of the largest deposit in this bank, as well as a one-third owner of the land this town is sitting on. I will sell my portions to the first white man I see for a dollar if you try to force me to sign those papers, and you better not try to get someone to forge my name, because I will send you to prison and take *your* businesses and *your* inheritances."

Lincoln Gilmore looked at Camila, saw the anger in her eyes, and leaned forward to whisper in her ear, even though it wasn't in her ear nor was it a whisper. "I bet you wish you had accepted my marriage proposal now, don't you, Camila Rose? I bet you wish that you had taken your brother's advice and said yes. Don't you? You see, you're just a woman, and you have no rights. We can do whatever we want, and you can't do anything about it." Then he stood up straight and smiled at her like a weasel about to enter a chicken coop.

Camila's eyes darkened, and her mouth became a hard line. "Get out of my face, Lincoln!"

Recognizing the signs of her mounting anger, he cautiously stepped back and returned to his desk, still holding the papers he'd tried to force her to sign.

Camila turned slowly, looking at the other two men in the room. "Franklin? Sherman? How dare you two try to do this to me? What have I ever done to you that would make you turn against me like this?"

Both brothers looked at the floor. When they did not answer, Camila smiled, and as she was walking out of the room, her last act was to say, "I dare you to try me. I promise I will make your lives a living hell. Good day!"

When she walked out of the office and slammed the door, Lincoln Gilmore handed the papers to Franklin. "Barnes, we have a contract with that cowboy, and my daughter is all excited and anxious about moving into that house. You better do something and do it fast. I don't want my daughter to be unhappy for any reason! You told me that you could control your sister. Well, you better be good to your word, or I'll hold back your allotments!"

He went to the door and, opening it slowly, he watched Camila Rose Barnes walk determinedly through the bank and up to the teller's window as her brothers left without looking at her.

CHAPTER 4

Camila was angry, almost too angry to remember that she was a lady. She approached George Henry's window. "Hand over my allotment, Mr. Henry. Please!" she demanded.

George Henry looked over at his boss, and when Lincoln Gilmore nodded his head, he counted out her allotment, smiled, and said, "Have a good day, Miz Barnes."

After collecting her money, Camila placed it in her reticule, but before she left the bank, she returned to Lincoln Gilmore's office and poked her finger into the bank president's chest. "I know this whole thing was your idea. You are a low-down snake in the grass, and if you try to stab me in the back again, I promise I will do more than make your life miserable. I will make you wish you had never met me! Furthermore, I'll make you wish you never proposed to me."

Smiling pretentiously, she stepped closer to him, and when she spoke next, she whispered, "I will kill you slowly and painfully. The first thing I'm going to do is cut off your man-parts! I'm sure you remember that I carry a very sharp knife and a gun in my reticule at all times, don't you?"

The smirk on Lincoln Gilmore's face quickly faded, his eyes grew large, his heart rate increased, and he began to sweat.

In a very ladylike fashion, Camila reached up and straightened Lincoln's necktie, feeling happy when his eyes grew large and he flinched. Afterward, she stepped back, winked, and smiled in his face. Turning around, she squared her shoulders and exited the bank.

The fresh air outside soothed Camila's hot face. She stood breathing slowly, letting the gentle breeze minister to her heated body and frayed nerves. She walked to the dressmaker's shop and retrieved her dresses. Then she went to the shoemaker and paid for her shoes. With all of her business done, she climbed into her carriage and drove herself home.

By dinnertime, Camila was still too upset to eat. Even though she had prepared a light meal, she threw it away and went to the parlor to sit in her rocking chair and watch the sun as it slowly set and the dark of night took over the light.

Two days after the incident, at the noon hour, Camila saw her brothers, Lincoln Gilmore, and her sister-in-law Willa being helped from a carriage that had regally delivered them to the front door of her home.

Franklin stepped onto the porch and attempted to open the front door. When he realized it was locked, he banged on the door and yelled, "Camila, you know we are out here, open this door!"

Almost right away, a softer knock sounded, and Willa said, "Camila, it's us. Would you open the door, please?"

After a few moments, Camila stood with the door open, not stepping back. She looked at her family members. Finally, Sherman spoke up. "Cammie, we came to apologize and see if we can come to a compromise. Let us in, please."

Not trying to hide her displeasure, Camila stepped back. As they stepped into the house, they could see the signs of her sadness. Her eyes were swollen and red. Her mouth was pressed into a thin line, and her hair was loose and resting on her shoulders.

Lincoln Gilmore hesitantly spoke first. "Uh . . . Cam . . . um, Miss Barnes. Your brothers have revised their requests and, uh . . . they want to present the new terms of their proposal to you."

Franklin was next. "Look, Cammie, maybe I was a little too aggressive the other day, but believe me, what I did I was doing for your own good. I don't want to see you spend the rest of your life as a spinster. And we definitely didn't want you to go into a marriage and sooner or later have this unknown man take all your money from you."

Sherman offered, "I was against it from the beginning, but Franklin insisted, and Lincoln threatened to shut down my allotment and sell my shop out from under me if I didn't go along with their plans. I'm sorry, Camila Rose."

"They are just silly men," Willa said. "They don't know how to respect a woman." Willa stepped forward and tried to hug Camila, but when she rejected the gesture and stepped away, Willa dropped her arms and said, "Come on, Cammie, we've been friends since we were little girls, and you know that I wouldn't do anything to hurt you. Franklin was out of line when he threatened to take this house from you. If your marriage doesn't work out, then you know that you can always come back here. We'd be more than glad to have you live here with us."

Camila looked at Willa and frowned. "Marriage? Live here *with* you?"

Lincoln Gilmore stepped forward and said, "If you hear us out, we can explain everything and answer all your questions." He stretched out his hand to take her elbow, but she moved away from him.

Camila went into the parlor, intending to listen without interrupting, but when she spoke, her voice was little more than a croak. "I'm really not up to another argument with you all. But I do want to know why you thought it was acceptable to treat me like you did. What makes you think I wanted to be married in the first place? How dare you plan my life for me!"

"We thought we were doing something for you for your own good," Lincoln Gilmore ventured cautiously.

Giving him a look of disgust, Camila threw at him, "Putting me out of my own house, taking away my inheritance, and shipping me across the country to marry some unknown man is for my own good? How stupid do you think I am? You are truly unbelievable."

Franklin was getting impatient. "Look, Cammie, here's the deal. We are willing to let you keep the house and your inheritance if you would agree to abide by the contract to be a mail-order bride."

There was silence in the parlor for several moments. Then Camila turned to Sherman. "Manny, what's going on? Doesn't this sound as ridiculous to you as it does to me?" She moved to the large glass windows of the parlor and stood before them. "How are you going to be willing to *let* me keep what was willed to me in the first place? I read the will before Daddy died, remember? I even have a copy of the will, remember? So why are you trying to do this to me?"

Sherman looked at his brother, his sister-in-law, and the bank president, then stood in front of his sister. "In total honesty, Cammie, Franklin has gotten us into some trouble. He has overextended himself in the mercantile, and people are demanding to be paid. So instead of asking you to help him, he decided to listen to Linc here and try to lord over you."

Franklin looked at his brother and said, "Manny, that's none of her business."

"It *is* her business, Frank. You should never have overspent yourself thinking that you could grab Cammie's inheritance to cover your shortfall. You should have done like I said and asked her for help. But instead, you listened to someone Dad told you to never trust, and now look at the mess you've gotten yourself into. I told them that it wouldn't work, but they wouldn't listen to me. So now here we are." He turned his attention back to Camila and handed her two pieces of paper. "Here, read these."

The first piece of paper was a telegraph message that had been sent to a Garrison LaRue. It read: *Sister changed her mind STOP Need to cancel contract STOP Will return train ticket and travel allowance STOP F. Barnes.* The second sheet of paper was a return message that read: *Will not relent STOP A contract is a contract STOP Expect her as soon as possible STOP G. LaRue.*

Camila walked back to her chair, looked at Manny, and asked, "So?"

"So they offered this LaRue guy a dowry and promised that if the contract fell through, he could keep the total amount. Frankie figured that if he and Linc could get you out of here, they could use your allotments to pay off the overdue bills. That way, Frank could keep his own allotments and continue his high-society lifestyle."

"Look, Cammie, I'm sorry," Franklin said. He stepped forward and knelt before his sister. "I should have been upfront with you about the whole thing. I want to ask you to at least think about this. I want to ask you if you would consider helping me out. We've made . . . that is, *I've* made a contract with this man, and if we don't make an attempt to fulfill it, we could get a bad name with him as well as the other business owners that I owe money to. Can you at least go out there and see what he has to offer? It's a contract that covers a time period from six months to one year."

When Camila said nothing, Franklin felt he should explain the details of the time period.

"Cammie," he continued, "if you get there and he wants to send you home within six months, he gets to keep the whole dowry. If you stay for up to a year and he decides to send you back, he can only keep half of the dowry."

"How much was the dowry?" she asked with a huff.

"A full two years of your allotment," Sherman said.

Lincoln Gilmore stepped forward. "Miss Barnes, Camila, we could have to pay him almost $1,500 or more when you add in the cost of the train ticket, your clothing, and food allowance for that time. So you see why we don't want to go back on the contract?"

Camila regarded her guests then focused on her oldest brother. "I need your new proposal in writing. And I want it by Wednesday afternoon. It will include the fact that I grant temporary living privileges to you and your wife concerning this house from six months to a year. You will send me a bank draft every month for $15, from your account, for the first six months. Then, for the remainder of the time I am there, you will pay me $30 a month for the privilege of living in my house until I return.

"I want it stated clearly and specifically that you have no rights at all to any part or parcel of my inheritance. And that you will never again involve Lincoln Gilmore or anyone else outside of our family in the attempt to limit the dispensing of my allotment. Before I leave, I expect each of my brothers to issue a bank draft for six months of an allotment from their personal accounts to me. And I want it stated that no part of my inheritance can or will be used without my spoken *and* written permission. You will sign it with your official signatures. I will review it and then sign it before I leave next week *if* the changes meet with my approval.

"Also, you will make a copy to be taken with me so that if you try to make any changes, I will always have a copy of the original agreement. The last thing that I'm demanding is that this proposal be filed with my lawyer and be stamped with the seal of Oklahoma."

Franklin stood and pointed his finger at his sister. "Now who's being ridiculous, Cammie? You can't be serious. You better act like you have some good sense. We can do anything we want with your inheritance and this house. After all, you don't have any rights, you're just a woman."

Standing from her chair and stepping close to her oldest brother, Camila drew herself up to her full height and looked into his eyes. "Our father's will gave me rights, Franklin. When he registered the will, I gained as many rights as you and Manny. Daddy's intent was to make us equal partners in the empire that Granddaddy Emery began and he built on. So now that you done messed up, you want to all of a sudden take over. Well no, Franklin, I'm not going to let you run me down like a herd of wild horses and take what was willed to me."

Franklin stepped back and looked her up and down. "Look at you, you run around this town all hours of the day and night dressed any kind of way. People see you out in the mornings at the smithy, at the post office carrying boxes back and forth. Then you're seen in the afternoons and the evenings walking around town unescorted. You live in this big house by yourself with no servants, doing all the cleaning and cooking and the maintenance yourself. No wonder you're an old maid. There's nothing dainty about you. You're as tall as most men, and you're as strong as a horse. You're not as attractive as most girls, and you don't even try to fix yourself up like a lady. To be honest, Camila Rose Barnes, you are an embarrassment to this family."

Sherman stepped up to his brother. "That's enough, Franklin, you don't speak for me. Stop talking to her like that." He turned to his sister and touched her shoulder. "I'm so sorry about all of this, Camila Rose, I don't feel that way about you. He's just mad because he thought he could bully you out of your money. He forgets that you are a very strong-willed woman and a very smart person."

Camila gave Sherman a half smile and patted his hand. Then, turning to Franklin and lifting her chin so that her oldest brother couldn't see how his words hurt, she spoke in a steady voice. "So, Franklin, that's it, huh? Because I'm not willing to change who I am to fit into some man's idea of what a woman should be you are embarrassed by me? Are you saying that I'm too ugly to be treated like a proper lady? Or am I just too ugly for you, for Lincoln Gilmore, and your wife to look at? Did you sell me to some man, sight unseen, so you wouldn't have to look at me anymore while you're trying to steal my inheritance?"

She stepped close to Franklin. Then, with all of her strength, she punched him in his gut. When he doubled over and fell to the floor, Camila watched as Willa screamed and knelt on the floor beside her husband. "Oh, no! Honey, are you alright?"

Camila smiled. "My terms will be met, or the deal is off. And let me suggest that you read Daddy's will again. There are some things there that you must have missed." She pursed her lips. "You know what, big brother? You embarrass me. You're not only a fool but also a pompous ass."

Camila walked out of the parlor and stood beside the staircase, her hand resting on the banister.

"You all can let yourselves out of my house," she said, then lifted her skirts and walked up the stairs to the second floor. Stepping into her bedroom, she slammed the door closed behind her.

When she heard the front door close, she stood at her bedroom window and watched them leave. As soon as their carriage had rolled out of the front yard, Camila crumbled to the floor and wept.

CHAPTER 5

Within a week, all of Camila's demands had been met, and she began packing her travel trunks for the trip to Alamosa, Colorado, to meet her husband. The day of her leaving, Sherman was the only one at the station to see her off.

The ride across country was full of adventure and angst for Camila Rose Barnes. She had never traveled more than fifty miles from her home in Checotah. The train ride, which took almost a week, gave her a lot of time to watch the landscape change from lush, green plains to almost desert-like lands. The place where she was going was completely foreign to her. It was nothing but high, jagged mountains covered in scrub brush and tall pine trees that looked to her like they could crumble at any moment. Even with the ominous appearance of the mountains, Camila found it exciting when she saw the large herds of bison, elegant-looking deer, and magnificent wild stallions spread across the land.

On the afternoon of the last day of travel when the train stopped for supplies, Camila took the time to stand and walk around after sitting on the hardwood bench in the Negro section of the train.

She emptied her slop jar off the side of the train like the conductor directed her to, then she poured some water from the water bucket onto the towel she used to keep the cinders from her clothes to refresh herself as much as possible. Then she ate her last biscuit, hoping silently that Garrison LaRue was a nice man who didn't think very unfavorably of women.

Garrison LaRue was pacing the loading dock, waiting for the train to arrive. "I don't have time for this," he grumbled to himself. Then he went to the ticket window and asked, "Is that train really on time, Joe?"

The ticket agent looked up and smiled tightly. "Garrison, I told you it was on time ten minutes ago, and it's still on time. Relax, Sheriff, your horses will get here, and they will be in good condition when they do."

In the distance, the train whistle sounded and the smoke from the train's smokestack could be seen. On the train, Camila Rose Barnes had just tried to refresh herself from the long train ride. She had run out of food a half-day earlier, and sitting in the car at the back of the train on those wooden benches had long ago gotten to her. It had been a long, uncomfortable trip, and she was feeling worn out.

"I hope Mr. LaRue's homestead is not very far from the train station," she said to herself. "I don't think I can take too much more traveling."

Fifteen minutes after the train pulled into the depot, Camila was standing on the platform surrounded by two trunks and four carpetbags. She looked around and did not see anyone.

I hope he remembers that I was to arrive today, she thought.

It had taken thirty minutes for Garrison LaRue to get his horses unloaded, signed for, and tied to the back of his wagon. When Garrison heard Joe call his name, he looked up to see the ticket agent running down the platform in his direction. "Sheriff, there's a woman on the platform that says you were supposed to pick her up. Says her name is Barnes."

In all the excitement of his horses arriving, Garrison has forgotten all about Camila Rose Barnes! She had been contracted through her brother to be his mail-order bride. But for right now, he had some important business to take care of.

"Okay, Joe, tell her I'll be back. I got to get these horses over to the vet to make sure they're healthy. Tell her to sit tight. It won't take very long."

An hour after she had arrived in the town of Alamosa in the Colorado territory, Camila was still sitting on a wooden bench just inside the Union Pacific ticket office. She had long since given up trying to be understanding and had made up her mind to give Garrison LaRue a tongue-lashing when they finally met. Here she had traveled for four days bundled in her travel clothes on that uncomfortable train, and now after all of that, here she was, sitting in a room that was getting warmer by the minute, forced to wait for a man she didn't know. A man for whom she was rapidly losing any kind of basic respect by the minute. When the waiting room got too hot for her to remain inside, Camila stood and went to the platform waiting area.

Leaving Doc Hales' office and returning to the train station, Garrison pulled his wagon to a stop at the end of the loading platform and stood looking at the woman that was supposed to be his wife.

He chuckled to himself. "She's dressed like one of those proper eastern educated women. Look at what she's wearing. I'll bet she's about ready to burn to ashes in those high-society clothes. And that hat! It looks like a couple of birds had a fight and left their feathers behind."

He was inclined to stand watching her for a while longer until she was approached by two men who began talking to her and trying to touch her. Garrison was surprised when she quickly pulled her parasol from the side of her carpetbag and started beating and poking the two men with it.

Laughing, Garrison climbed down from his wagon, took the steps two at a time, and ran across the platform to rescue those poor men. "Whoa, whoa," he said holding up his arms and stepping between the men and the parasol-wielding woman. "What's going on here?"

One of the men dropped his arms and stepped behind Garrison. "Sheriff, all we did was ask the lady if she needed help getting her stuff over to the saloon."

Garrison looked at the men and smiled. "Slim, why would you ask her something like that?"

"Well, look at her. Look how she's dressed. The only time fancy ladies like her come to town is to work in the saloon or at Miss Annie's House of Comfort."

"Well, guys, I'm afraid that this time, you are wrong. Now, apologize to the lady. And then take her trunks and baggage and load them into my wagon."

The men mumbled some words in Camila's direction and quickly began to take her trunks and bags to a wagon at the far end of the loading platform.

Camila was still standing with her parasol in her hand, ready to defend herself again. "Wait . . . um, Sheriff? What are you doing? Why are you taking my things?"

Garrison stepped closer to the woman and relieved her of the parasol. "My name is Garrison LaRue, and I'm assuming that you are Camila Barnes. Welcome to Alamosa." He walked away, still holding her parasol in his hand, and looked back over his shoulder. "Let's go. I have better things to do than stand around this train station all day."

Camila looked at his back. "One would think that there would be a little more courtesy in your voice, and maybe even a little more respectful behavior from an officer of the law," she said.

The only indication that he heard her comment was an almost imperceptible hesitation in his step, a slight raising of his shoulders, and stiffening of his back.

CHAPTER 6

Garrison LaRue and Camila Barnes were sitting on the seat of a high-sided buckboard wagon loaded with her belongings, traveling through the town of Alamosa, and neither was saying a word.

Camila looked at the profile of the rude, ill-mannered man that had come to her rescue at the train station. Her first impression after noticing his grumpy and crabby attitude was that he was very handsome. His skin was smooth pecan-brown with red undertones. His long, coal-black hair, pulled back and tied at his neck, was so black that in the sun it looked dark-blue. And if she remembered correctly, he was tall. Taller than average. He had a broad chest, wide shoulders, narrow hips, and long arms and legs. But his eyes were hard, his jaw was set, his well-shaped full lips were pressed together tightly, and he acted as though he was being put to some kind of test.

Camila felt that if this man was intended to be her husband, she needed to know something about him. Holding onto the seat of the wagon so that she wouldn't tumble off, and using her other hand to hold on to her hat, Camila looked at the man driving the wagon. "So, you are Garrison LaRue."

Without looking at her, he said, "Yep."

She asked, "And you are the sheriff of this town?"

"Yep," he said again, and before Camila could ask another question,

Sheriff LaRue pulled back on the horse reins. "Whoa, boys!"

The wagon halted outside of a building that was labeled Alamosa Courthouse.

As he climbed down, Garrison said, "Well, don't just sit there, let's go. We have business to tend to. Then I need to go check on my horses before we go to the ranch."

As Garrison walked around the back of the wagon, Camila said, "If you expect me to come with you, I'm going to need some help."

Sighing loudly, Garrison came up to the side of the buckboard where Camila was sitting and reached up for her hand. He had a solid grip on her until her feet touched the ground. Then he dropped her hand as if it were a hot poker and walked to the entrance of the courthouse.

Following him down the hall, Camila's heart began to pound, wondering what kind of legal affairs they needed to take care of. Pushing through some doors at the end of the hall, Garrison held the door for her then said, "Judge Anderson is going to marry us."

When Camila looked at the short round man standing behind the desk, he smiled and said, "Well, good afternoon, Miss Barnes. Welcome to Alamosa. Just so you'll know, this ceremony binds you and Garrison LaRue together in a civil marriage. Do you have any questions?"

Garrison quickly answered, "No."

But Camila presented her question without hesitation. "Yes, I do," she said. "What is a civil marriage, and why is a judge performing a marriage ceremony?"

Garrison looked at her. "This is not going to be a marriage in the biblical sense. We can't live under the same roof if we don't have a marriage certificate, according to the law. I need a cook, a housekeeper, and a woman to help look after my children, nothing more. It's all in the contract."

"Well, that's all well and good, Mr. LaRue, but I, as of yet, have not seen the contract. I have no recollection of signing any type of marriage contract."

Garrison looked at her and shifted his weight from one foot to the other. "Nevertheless, the contract is signed and has the Oklahoma seal on it. So it's a lawful, binding agreement, Miss Barnes."

She looked from him to the judge. "Lawful? How?"

Slapping his gloves against his thigh, Garrison said, "It has your name on it, and it is signed. You are here. What more is there to say?"

"Well, I want to see that contract, because I didn't sign it!" Camila said strongly.

Garrison huffed. "The person who signed the contract, I believe, is your brother Franklin Barnes."

Judge Anderson looked at Camila with sympathetic eyes. "Miss Barnes, the law doesn't state specifically who has to sign the contract. It just requires the contract to have an adult's signature and a witnessing signature. And when the mail-order contract was shown to me, they were well within the law. Are you willing to enter into this contract with Garrison LaRue, Miss Barnes?"

Camila took a deep breath then nodded her head; she didn't trust her voice. She felt like chattel. She couldn't believe that her brother had deliberately put her in a situation like this just because he wanted to get not only the house from her but also her inheritance.

Judge Anderson looked at Camila like he was waiting for her to change her mind. Then Garrison cleared his throat and blurted out, "Let's get this over with, Judge, I have important things to do today and I need to get back home."

Judge Anderson turned back to Camila. "In that case, raise your hands and repeat after me: I, state your name, hereby agree to enter into a civil marriage. And I do hereby agree to abide by the rules stated in the marriage contract."

After Garrison and Camila repeated the oath, Judge Anderson said, "I now declare that you are joined in a civil marriage. All properties and belongings remain separate from the spouses. When and if the union dissolves, you will maintain ownership of what you legally owned before the civil marriage ceremony was performed."

Garrison and Judge Anderson signed the piece of paper, and then

Camila was handed a pen to sign her name. It wasn't until she laid the pen down on the marriage license that she realized there was another person in the room.

Judge Anderson said, "Now my wife, Mrs. Anderson, will sign as a witness, and everything should be nice and legal." A short, slightly plump woman stepped forward. She offered Camila a quick smile then picked up the pen and signed her name.

Garrison was given the marriage license and contract after it was sealed in wax with the state seal, folded, and placed in an envelope. He shoved it into his inside vest pocket, turned, and walked out of the office.

Camila looked at Garrison LaRue and then at the judge, and in as calm a voice as she could, said, "Judge Anderson, if it's possible, I would like to have a copy of those contracts for myself also, please."

Garrison was standing at the door holding it open when he said gruffly, "Let's go! I have one more piece of business before we get home. You can look at this one when we get there."

Before she turned to leave the office, Camila looked at Judge and Mrs. Anderson then repeated her request. "I would like to have a copy of the contract, Judge Anderson. I'll pick it up the next time I'm in town, or you can have it delivered to me. Thank you."

Mrs. Anderson smiled and winked at the feisty young lady while the judge nodded his head.

"Thanks to both of you for your kindness," Camila said with a faint smile.

Garrison snatched his gloves from the back pocket of his Levi's, slapped his thigh, and stormed down the hall of the courthouse toward the front entrance.

The next stop was at the veterinary hospital near the end of town, which was nothing more than a large barn with a corral. Garrison, without looking at Camila, said, "You stay here. I'll be right back." Then he jumped down and disappeared into the barn.

When ten minutes had passed and he still had not returned, Camila climbed over the seat and lowered herself to the bed of the wagon to get out of the sun and the wind. She was tired and was becoming very uncomfortable in her traveling clothes. She removed her hat, unfastened her cuffs, and unbuttoned the collar of her jacket and blouse. It did not help ease her discomfort, so she sat down in the bed of the wagon, scooted herself between the trunks, lay against her carpetbags, and promptly fell asleep.

Garrison tried to hurry through the business with Doc Hales, but he had to be absolutely sure that his new horses were indeed strong and healthy and ready to work. After he made arrangements for them to be delivered to his ranch the next morning, he went back to the buckboard.

When he didn't see Camila sitting where he left her, he slapped his gloves on his thigh and growled, "Damned woman! I told her to stay here. Well, I don't feel like wasting my time going to look for her."

Old Sam, the stable keeper, spoke up. "Sheriff, you ain't got to go lookin' fer that there girl, she in back o' the wagon. She done fell asleep a good while ago. Why'd you leave her sittin' in the sun and wind like that, son? I know you, boy, you wouldn't even leave your horse tethered in weather like this. Why would ya treat that woman like that?"

"Hey, Mr. Sam," Garrison said, greeting the old man. "I didn't think it was going to take this long."

He stepped to the back of the wagon and looked at Camila, watching her sleep for a few moments. She was a nice-looking lady, and there was a look of peace on her face. He didn't want to, but he had to awaken her. She couldn't ride back there all the way to the ranch or she'd be a black-and-blue sack of sore bones by the time they arrived.

Garrison reached into the wagon, grabbed her ankle, and shook her leg. "Wake up, we're heading for the ranch now."

Camila gasped loudly, sat up quickly, and snatched her ankle from his grasp. She looked around, and almost immediately when she looked at him, the scowl was back on her face.

CHAPTER 7

arrison thought about the reprimand Old Sam had laid on him back at the stable and figured he owed Camila something of an explanation. "Listen . . . .uh . . . Miss Barnes. My ranch is called LaRue Crossing, and it's five miles west of town, so we should be there fairly soon. Then you can rest for the remainder of the day and be ready to take over the household chores in the morning."

To Camila, those were the first civil words he had spoken to her since her arrival in Alamosa. They also sounded like music to her ears. These were the last five miles of a long journey. It was still a long ride, but she had been traveling for four days. The thought of arriving at her destination brought some kind of comfort to her.

Since the journey was now almost over, she prayed it would be one well worth the trouble. In the long run, all she wanted to do was to help her brothers get back on their feet. But for right now, all she wanted to do was get to wash her body and get in a bed. She had never been so dirty and so tired in all her life.

Several long miles from town, Garrison LaRue broke the silence between them and spoke quietly to her. "Here we are, Miss Barnes, just a quarter mile to go."

Camila looked up as the wagon rolled through a huge arched pergola that had a sign attached to it that read *LaRue Crossing, Brand LX.*

As they pulled into the front yard of a large two-story ranch house with an upper and a lower veranda, Camila was in awe. The house stood out against its background of rolling foothills, dark sparkling green grass, tall budding trees, and majestic pines.

The sturdy, well-built house looked as though it had been recently given a fresh coat of white paint. The red-clay tiled A-frame roof was neatly done, and all of the windows had black storm shutters. The house looked neat and well-kept, at least on the outside. In the distance, she saw two barns, a corral, and what looked like a bunkhouse with a small lawn, a tree-shaded porch, and a hard dirt yard.

Garrison slowed the wagon as they approached the main house. "Just so you know," he said, "I have one rule for you. That is that you never leave my children alone, you never leave them with someone else, and you never go into town unless I know about it and you have my approval! Have I made myself clear?"

"Sounds like three rules to me, Mr. LaRue," Camila said softly.

Garrison looked at her dismissively and his lips thinned, but he made no comment.

When the wagon pulled up to the front porch of the big house, two people were standing at the front door. They were a handsome older couple with welcoming smiles on their faces. When they saw the wagon draw close, they stepped from the front door of the house to the edge of the porch followed by two little children.

As Garrison LaRue pulled the wagon to a complete stop, four men walked around from the back of the house, and the oldest of them stepped forward and started giving orders. Garrison LaRue jumped down from the wagon seat, and the children ran up to him. He immediately scooped them up in his arms and walked into the house.

Following the older man's instructions, the three young men began unloading the wagon. The older man offered Camila a hand and helped her down from the wagon. "I guess you's the new Miz LaRue," he said. "My name's Roy, and these here fellas is Jarrod, Todd, and Wesley."

Each man tipped his hat, and when the wagon was empty, the young man named Todd jumped onto the seat and drove it away. The man and woman who had been standing on the porch walked down the steps and presented Camila with a smile. The man offered his hand.

"Hey there, little lady, welcome to LaRue Crossing," he said. "I'm Thaddeus, and this here is Anna Wolf. We're Garrison's parents."

Camila took his hand and offered a tight smile. But before she could return his greeting, Camila was bundled into an unexpected but comforting hug by Garrison LaRue's mother.

Anna Wolf LaRue whispered, "Don't worry, young one, our son seems to be a tad cantankerous right now, but he'll come around. Don't take nothing off him. Stand your ground, and things will work out just fine." Anna Wolf gave her daughter-in-law another quick hug and stepped back.

The other two men stood looking at Roy, the older ranch hand, until he ordered, "Jus' take 'em in and leave 'em in the front hall, then go help Todd curry the team and secure the wagon. After that, y'all may's well git yur hands and faces washed. Supper's ready!"

Camila followed Mr. and Mrs. LaRue up the three steps that led to the front porch of the house where she would be living for the next six to twelve months. She stepped through the front door and looked around. The house smelled like a combination of old food and dust. She could see that the rugs and the floors were caked with dried mud, the corners of the ceilings and walls were full of cobwebs, and the furniture needed cleaning.

The LaRues were standing beside her, and Roy was standing behind her. Anna exclaimed, "Oh, if I had known this place was in this kind of shape, I would have come down here and done something about this!"

Roy said, "As you can see, Miz LaRue, there ain't been a woman in here for quite a while now. I'm afraid ya got yur work cut out for ya."

Garrison LaRue was standing at the top of the staircase. "Well, that's why she's here, Roy. Take her things to the rooms off the kitchen."

When Roy grabbed one of her trunks, Mr. LaRue grabbed the other one. Mrs. LaRue and Camila picked up her carpetbags and practically dragged them as they followed Roy through the house to the rooms by the kitchen.

As she stepped through the door at the far left end of the kitchen, she was surprised to see what looked like nice, well-kept miniature living quarters. There was a parlor with a small fireplace, a bedroom with a warming stove, and a separate water room also with a small warming stove.

The parlor had a settee and a rocker sitting in front of the small fireplace, and a writing desk and chair across the room in front of the window. To the left of the parlor was a door that led to the bedroom. That room was furnished with a four-poster bed and a double-door chifforobe.

The last door straight ahead through the bedroom was the water room, and it was equipped with a marble-top washstand with a sunken washbasin, shelves for linen, and a commode closet with a small skylight and a drawstring above the commode chair.

To her great pleasure, those rooms were cleaned, and it smelled like the windows had been opened to freshen the air. Anna Wolf stood in the doorway with her hands on her hips. "Well at least they made this place look livable," she said and shook her head, whispering to herself, "My, oh my, oh my."

Thaddeus LaRue took Camila by her shoulders. "Welcome to the family, young lady. Anna and I just came down to deliver the kids to their father. We're going to leave and let you get settled in. Hope to see you again soon." He kissed her cheek, turned, and took his wife by the hand as they left the house by the back door.

After Roy had checked to see if the last of her bags had been taken into the bedroom, he returned to the housekeeper's parlor, lightly touched Camila's shoulder, and said, "If you pardon my being so forward, but I hope your being here can bring some happiness to this house, Miz LaRue. Things been down for a long time here. This here place needs some happiness."

With watery eyes, Camila looked at the sweet older man. She smiled, reached up, and touched his face, then while rubbing her hand over his scruffy beard, whispered, "I'll do my best, Mr. Roy, thank you."

Roy turned and walked out, closing the door just as the first tear rolled down Camila's cheek. She let the tears go unchecked for a few moments then pulled her handkerchief from her sleeve and dried her eyes, saying to herself, "I'm here now so, as Momma would say, I may as well make the best of the situation."

As Camila began to unpack her clothes, she could hear movement in the kitchen. Then she heard a knock at the door. She crossed the small parlor and opened it. It was the young ranch hand named Jarrod.

"Pardon me, ma'am," he said shyly. "Mr. Roy thought you might want some hot water for your bath." He walked into the water room and set two buckets full of steaming hot water on the floor. "Have a good night."

The water room warming stove had been stoked, and the room was thankfully warm. Camila took a sleeping gown and a jar of lavender oil from her travel bag and walked into the water room. Water never felt so good to her as she was finally able to cleanse her body. It felt so good that she sat soaking herself until the water became cool.

Just before going to bed, Camila took the contract she had with her brothers and the banker, as well as her copy of their father's will, from her carpetbag and placed them in the bottom drawer of the chifforobe where her unmentionables were being placed.

"Just in case I have a need to review them from time to time," she whispered to herself. After everything had been unpacked and put away, she eased onto the bed and immediately fell asleep.

Morning seemed to come quickly. Before she knew it, the first light of day was breaking through the window. She got up, did a light toilette, and put on a thin house gown. She knew she had some heavy-duty housework to do today.

Entering the kitchen, she stopped short. Garrison LaRue was sitting at the table. "We start early around here, Miss Barnes," he said. "Me and my ranch hands like coffee first thing in the morning. I made it this morning, but I don't intend to do it again."

She looked at him. "You will if you keep getting in the kitchen before I do, Mr. LaRue."

With that said, she walked across the kitchen and looked in the cabinets. She pulled out some flour and meal and was looking for eggs when Roy walked in with a basket of eggs, a slab of bacon, and a small pail of milk.

As she began breaking eggs, Roy skimmed the cream from the milk and took it to the cooler. Then he came back to the kitchen worktable with a crock of butter.

Garrison sat watching Camila for a moment or two. He couldn't believe she had just spoken to him as she had. It was only because Roy had walked in that he decided to hold his tongue until they were alone again. After giving Roy a wary stare, Garrison turned and left the room. He decided to go to the corral to wait for the call to breakfast.

Camila and Roy set about preparing breakfast. "If you don't mind, Mrs. LaRue, from now on, I'm gonna let you take care of the meals. I'll be sure that you have eggs, milk, and butter every morning. I was only cookin' 'cause nobody on this ranch can cook but me. Now when you gets ready to do the chores, give me a call, and I'll help ya with the heavy stuff."

Breakfast was a joyful occasion at LaRue Crossing this particular morning. Camila made a breakfast that was special for the men. They had eggs mixed with crispy chopped bacon, and potatoes fried with hot peppers and onions. The meal was topped off with big, fluffy, buttery biscuits that were completely unlike Mr. Roy's flat hardtack biscuits.

The three young ranch hands complimented and thanked Camila for their breakfast as they stood scraping their plates into the slop bucket and put them in the dishpan before leaving to begin their chores for the day.

Just as Roy was about to leave, he said, "Listen, little lady, you's a real treasure. And I believes that you gonna do real fine around here, yes ma'am, real fine."

"Mr. Roy, I believe you and I are going to become good friends," Camila said, smiling at the sweet old man.

Her smile quickly disappeared when Garrison LaRue cleared his throat and said, "Roy, don't you think the boys could use some instructions on what needs to be done today?"

Not getting upset about being put out, Roy smiled. "Sho 'nough, boss!" Smiling, he patted Camila on the shoulder and walked out of the kitchen.

"I don't accept back-talk from anyone, most especially from you, because you are my housekeeper," Garrison said. "So don't talk to me like you did earlier this morning ever again."

Camila put her hand on her hip and looked at Garrison. "Since we are setting boundaries around here, you need to know that I won't let you be rude and disrespectful to me, either. We're both adults, Mr. LaRue, and we should treat each other as such."

Instead of waiting for him to comment, she walked to the stove, picked up the tea kettle of boiling water, walked to the sink, filled the dishpan, and started soaking the breakfast dishes. Then she walked across the room right past Garrison, who was standing with his arms folded across his chest, to put the remaining eggs and butter in the cooler.

Garrison watched her with narrowed eyes, then he dropped his arms to his side, snatched his gloves from his back pocket, slapped his thigh, mumbled, "Damn obstinate woman," and stomped out of the kitchen. As he was walking out, he said, "I'll be back later when you have some control of yourself. There are things we need to discuss."

Not wanting him to have the last word, Camila offered her last words to his back. "You'll find me in the same frame of mind when you return, but I hope you are in the frame of mind to show me around this place since I didn't get a 'welcome to the ranch' tour yesterday. That is, if you are not too busy . . . *sir!*"

As she smiled, Camila thought she heard Garrison LaRue growl before the front door slammed shut.

CHAPTER 8

After the dishes had been cleaned, dried, and set up on the sideboard hutch, Camila refilled the two large pots of water on the stove so they could boil, wiped down the worktable, washed the caked-on dirt from the two windows, and swept the floor. After she finished those chores, she felt she needed to take a break, so she grabbed a cape from her bedroom, went outside, stood on the back porch, and looked around.

She was surprised to see that LaRue Crossing appeared quite large. She could see several buildings, lots of fences, animals, crops, and wide-open spaces.

Roy saw her and crossed the yard. "Kin I do somethin' for ya, Miz LaRue?"

Smiling Camila, asked, "Do you have time to give me a quick tour?"

Roy nodded his head and said, "Follow me, young lady."

On returning to the house, Camila gathered some sagebrush sprigs, and when she got to the kitchen, she tied them together and started swiping at the cobwebs on the baseboards and the walls throughout the rooms on the first floor.

Roy came into the hall just as Camila was dragging a kitchen chair to the main parlor to get the cobwebs from the corners of the high ceiling.

"Miz LaRue, I thought I told ya that I would help do the heavy stuff. Now git down, little lady, and tell me what ya wants done."

Camila's plan was to concentrate most of her attention on the parlor, formal dining room, staircase, and hall. While she cleaned the ashes from the fireplaces, washed the hearths, and dusted the furniture in both rooms, Roy took down the drapes, took them outside, and shook the dust out of them. Then, following more of her instructions, he rolled up the rugs from the parlor, dining room, and hall and took them to the back to beat the dust out of them. The last part of the cleanup was to wash the windows and scrub the floors of the parlor and dining room.

Just as she finished pushing the furniture back in place in the parlor, Camila turned and saw two sets of eyes staring at her through the railings on the staircase. A little boy stood up and looked over the banister. "My name is Garrison LaRue Jr.," he said. "I'm six years old, and you are not my momma."

Camila smiled. "Well, hello, Garrison LaRue Jr., it's nice to meet you. And you are quite right, I am not your momma. I'm just here to help your poppa take care of you."

"We don't need your help. I already know how to dress me and my sister."

"Well," Camila said, "since you've done such a good job dressing yourself and your sister, how about something to eat? Are you hungry?"

Little Garrison crossed his arms over his chest and shook his head, but before he could say anything, a little girl stood up. "My name is Ella Grace, I'm this many." She held up four fingers. "I wants sumfing ta eat."

Smiling, Camila stretched out her hand, and the little girl took it as she walked down the last four steps.

When Roy returned to the house, Camila asked him to rehang the drapes while she and Ella Grace went to the kitchen holding hands, her brother trailing behind.

"What do you want for breakfast?" she asked. The children started talking at the same time. Stopping just inside the kitchen, Camila stooped down, smiled at the two chubby-faced children, and said, "Okay, little GJ and Miss Ella Grace, why don't you go to the table, and I'll surprise you."

Camila warmed the biscuits, fried some bacon, and scrambled two eggs for the little ones. While they were eating, she cleaned the pans she had just used and left the children at the table.

"Okay, you two stay here and finish your breakfast, and I'll be right back."

She returned to the front of the house, rearranged the furniture in the parlor to make it more spacious, and wiped down the staircase. Then she ran outside and pulled some dried blossoms and leaves from one of the newly budding, highly fragrant lilac bushes, ran back in the parlor, and threw some blossoms into the fireplace. Then she did the same in the dining room.

By this time, it was ten o'clock, time to start preparing the noonday meal. She remembered that the cream she used this morning was turning sour and the potatoes in the vegetable bin were beginning to grow roots and one or two of the onions were about to get soft, so she returned to the kitchen to check on the little ones and decide what to fix.

The children were still sitting at the table. They had eaten all of their food and were just finishing their cups of milk. Camila pumped out a half bucket of water and threw in the potatoes. Then she took the bucket to the summer workroom, set it on the low table, and had little Garrison and Ella Grace break off the sprouts and wash the potatoes.

She asked Mr. Roy if he would run to the smokehouse and pull down some beef while she whipped the sour cream. She had the beef soaking so that she could chop it and the onions then fry them together in the dutch oven pan before adding the potatoes, which she later mixed with the sour cream.

The noonday meal was served to five hungry men, and while they were eating, Camila took the little ones into her parlor and taught them their lessons.

"What kind of meal was that?" the voice from the doorway rang out.

Camila turned to see Garrison LaRue filling the space in the open doorway. "It's called sour cream potato and beef casserole, boiled cabbage, and hot water cornbread," she said. "I didn't know what else to do. I fixed that because the cream was turning sour. I don't like to waste food, and the cabbage was in the garden at the side of the house. If it had stayed there any longer, it would have split open and been almost too tough to cook."

"It was good and the parlor looks nice," Garrison said. "Do you want the rugs put back down?"

"No, thank you," Camila said "I'll do that myself. I know just how I want them placed."

Garrison looked at her, and as she steeled herself for a biting retort, he simply asked, "Are the children finished with their lessons?"

"They could be if you say so."

He held out his hands, and the children jumped up from the floor and ran to their father. Garrison Jr. sighed and said in a loud whisper, "I don't like lessons, Daddy. And I don't like her, she's not our momma." Holding her father's hand, Ella Grace looked back, smiled, and waved goodbye.

With a couple of hours before she had to begin the evening meal, Camila decided to do a little more housework. After placing the rug in the parlor in front of the fireplace and dragging the high-backed chairs onto each end of the rug, she pushed the settee across the room to rest on the long side of the rug. Then she ran back to her room and slid her largest empty trunk to the parlor and positioned it like a table between the fireplace and the settee. She took one of her fringed shawls and draped it across the top of the trunk. The final touch was to get a bowl, fill it with blossoms from the lilac bush, and set it on the top of the trunk.

After standing back to admire the room, she turned her attention to the walls in the hall. She used her sagebrush broom again and finished pulling down the cobwebs in the entry hall then took down the front-door curtain and washed it and the window. The only thing left to do was to dust and polish the furniture in the dining room and scrub the floor in the hall. While waiting for the floor to dry, Camila went to her room to take a nap.

For dinner, Camila made shredded pork in gravy oven rice, spring greens, and creamed corn. After dinner, she put water on the stove, filled the tub with water, and bathed the children. By seven o'clock, the house was settled and she was very tired. It was all she could do to take the last of the heated water to her water room and bathe herself before she fell onto the bed and slept soundly.

On the Saturday two weeks after her arrival at LaRue Crossing, Camila asked Roy what time they left for church. He looked at her. "Uh, Miz LaRue, no one 'round here's been to church since Miss Grace, the first Mrs. LaRue, died." When she asked why, he told her, "You prob-lee wants to talk to Mr. LaRue 'bout that."

After supper that night, Camila asked Garrison as he was leaving the kitchen, "What time should I be ready to leave for church tomorrow? I've been here for two weeks, and we haven't gone yet."

Without turning around, he said, "We don't go to church!"

"Well, I do. So what time should I be ready?"

He turned and looked at her. His eyes narrowed, and he slowly repeated himself. "I said: We. Don't. Go to church!"

Camila put her hands on her hips. "And I said that I do!"

Leaning forward, he said, "Look, woman, this is not something I'm going to discuss with you. We don't go to church, and that's that! This discussion is over, and we won't be going over it again, ever!"

With that said, he turned and stormed out of the kitchen. Camila heard him stomp up the steps, down the hall, and into his room. The bedroom door slammed, and then there was silence.

On Sunday, Camila served breakfast and the noonday meal, then after she put the children down for a nap, she put on a cape. Being early April, there was still a chill in the air, so she also took a quilt from her trunk. Then she picked up her Bible and walked out of the house.

She went to a place across the front yard where there was a big tree with a nice bench under its wide branches. She sat down and spread her blanket across her legs and leaned against the tree trunk, reading her scriptures.

Garrison stood in the parlor and watched her. "Damn stubborn woman. She can sit there until the cows come home for all I care."

A week later, on Thursday morning right after the men had come in and gotten their morning coffee, Garrison looked at Camila and said, "You need to follow me."

"For what?" she said before thinking. Then she modulated her tone, smiled, and asked, "Where are we going, Mr. LaRue?"

Garrison leveled a look at her that was meant to put her in her place, but when she didn't move, he added, "For the tour of the ranch, of course."

She gave him a fleeting look. "No, thank you. Roy already showed me where everything I need is located, and I plan to find out for myself the rest of what the ranch has to offer." She turned back to the worktable to concentrate on preparing the food for breakfast.

That exchange ended with him snatching his gloves from his back pocket and slapping them on his thigh as he was storming out the back door.

After breakfast, Garrison said to Camila, "Listen, Miss Barnes, I'm going into town, and as you know by now, I won't be back until Monday morning. Take care of my children, and remember, don't leave them with anyone, don't take them anywhere without my permission, and don't go into town or take my children into town for any reason without me."

Camila didn't like his tone of voice or his authoritative manner, but she understood that his job was intense and dangerous, and she felt he shouldn't have to worry about his family while doing his duty, so she intended to follow his instructions to the letter.

CHAPTER 9

After three months, Camila was settled in and had clearly made quite a few changes in and around the ranch house. She had made up her mind that if she was going to live on the ranch for up to a year, she was going to make it look like a woman actually lived there, so she had taken on projects around the house, and Roy had become her accomplice.

Even though Garrison LaRue usually had little or nothing to say to her, Camila and Roy were becoming friends. He seemed to always be there when she needed some help with the heavy-duty chores. He seemed to be around when she needed some meat from the smokehouse, and he was always more than willing to take her list and go to town to get the items she needed from the mercantile every Friday.

Roy would hand the list to the mercantile owners, and they would send back with him what they had in stock, or they ordered items and delivered them to LaRue Crossing when they arrived.

Camila instructed Roy to tell the store owners, Mr. and Mrs. Anderson, to send the ordered items to the ranch when Garrison was in town working. Using her charm—although it didn't take much doing—she swore the older man to secrecy and paid for everything from her own cache of money.

One particular Monday morning, Garrison rode into the side yard of his ranch and saw that a new building had been constructed. "What is that woman doing to my place now?" he asked himself in a one-sided conversation. "I don't mind too much what she does to the inside of my house, but I do mind when she starts adding buildings. Damn busybody woman!"

He wanted an explanation, so he went looking for his foreman, and when Roy told him it was a laundry shed, Garrison quelled his annoyance and walked into the house, mumbling, "Well, that's one place she can have to herself. I'm not going near that building. I hate doing laundry."

When the front parlor, the main hall, and the staircase had all been made presentable, she turned her attention to making the formal dining room look more elegant. Camila gave Roy a list of items that included a chandelier, drapery material, lace, and a large flower design rug. Had she not had Roy and the ranch hands to build her a laundry shed, it would have been difficult to hide the materials and supplies that she ordered for the house from Garrison, but because he hated doing laundry, she had everything put in and behind the shed. She knew he was not going to go near that place for any reason.

In the weeks that followed, as she finished with the dining room, Camila turned her attention to the summer room. While taking almost an entire week to clean it from top to bottom, she happily ordered a rug, a heating stove, material to make curtains for the windows, and a set of café doors for the doorway that led from the summer room to the kitchen. The last of her order included two padded rocking chairs, two large lamps with colorful cut-glass covers, and a long side table.

On another particular Monday morning, as he was getting home from his weekend working in town, Garrison stepped through the door from the back porch into the summer room and stopped short. He looked around the room. It smelled fresh and looked different, much different than it looked when he'd left four days ago.

The walls were white at the bottom and covered with flowered wallpaper from the ceiling down to the newly installed dark-stained chair rail. There was a heating stove installed in the far corner of the room in front of a wall that was now covered with stone, the windows had curtains, and most of the floor was covered with a big fringed rug.

Centered under the three new narrow side-by-side windows sat a long table covered with a crotched tablecloth, and there was a lamp sitting on top of each end of the table. Angled at both ends were matching padded rocking chairs. Finally, he noticed the low table with benches that he had made for the children sitting in the middle of the area of the rug-covered floor.

Seeing the changes to the room made Garrison a little angry. He pushed through the café doors, which were also new, and stepped into the kitchen. He noticed that these walls were also covered with fresh paint, the table was covered with a bright-red oilcloth, and there were two sets of shelves built into the wall on each side of the cooler. The final touch was the flowery new set of curtains at the windows.

Garrison stormed through the house looking for his housekeeper. When he found her, she was in the dining room dusting the corners. Standing in the doorway of the dining room, he was again taken aback. He looked around at the room and saw that it, too, had been transformed into a place that looked very different from its previous makeup.

The upgrades included a three-globe oil lamp chandelier hanging from the ceiling over the dining table, the walls were papered from floor to ceiling, there were new drapes at the windows, and the floor was covered with a very large fringed flowered rug. The chairs had been padded and covered, and the table was topped with a lace tablecloth. The final upgrade he noticed was the fireplace with a brightly painted cinder screen in front of it.

When she saw him step into the room, Camila smiled. "Hello, Mr. LaRue, welcome home. How do you like the changes?"

"What's going on with that summer room?" he snapped. "I don't remember talking to you about making any more changes to my house. You have even had buildings put up on my property! You had no right. And this room, look at all of this! Where did all this stuff come from? Who do you think is going to pay for all of this? I'm definitely not going to. You may as well pack all this stuff up and send it all back!"

As he turned to walk out of the room, he heard her say, "No. I won't send anything back. This is my home now too, and I want to live in a place that looks like a lady lives here."

He spun around and looked at her with disbelief. "What? What did you say to me?"

She took a deep breath. "I said no. No, I'm not sending anything back. No one asked you to pay for anything. I happen to have some money of my own, you know. I don't have to depend on you for anything. Everything new that you see in and around this house has already been paid for."

They stood looking at each other for several moments. "Woman, do you really want to push me on this?"

"Push you? How is making this place look clean, organized, open, and inviting pushing you?"

Not waiting for an answer, she moved to step past him just as he took in a deep breath to try and calm his temper. He put out his arm and grabbed the doorframe so that she couldn't leave the room.

Camila stopped short and looked up at him. He saw that her eyes were glistening, and when she blinked, a tear coursed slowly down her cheek. "Excuse me," she said softly.

"Wait, Miss Barnes. I'm sorry, I just wasn't prepared for these changes. It looks . . . the house looks . . . very different. I'm not used to change, and as a matter of fact, it seems lately that every time I come home, some changes have been made, and . . . well, it's hard to keep up with so many changes."

Camila pulled a lace handkerchief from her sleeve and dabbed the tears from her cheeks and eyes. "Mr. LaRue, I'm sorry. I didn't think that I was doing anything wrong. I realize now that I really should have discussed these things with you, but I thought that as the housekeeper it was my duty to make your house comfortable for you and the children, as well as looking presentable to your guests. I never meant to make you angry. I just wanted to surprise you."

"Well, this is quite a surprise. Um . . . thank you. I can see that you've worked very hard over the last few months. I appreciate it."

Garrison dropped his arm, and Camila walked down the hall toward the kitchen. Garrison snatched his gloves from his back pocket and walked up the steps slapping his thigh.

After several months of deep cleaning and upgrading the house, there were still several rooms she had not yet touched. Two of those rooms were labeled off-limits to her. She was, by strict orders, not to go into Garrison LaRue's office, and she was not to, under any circumstances, ever enter Garrison LaRue's bedroom.

The compromise that was made was that he was to bring out any and all dirty dishes from the office for her to wash, and he was to bring down from his bedroom his dirty clothes and bed linens every Monday so she could clean them.

By the end of six months, things had fallen into a comfortable, workable routine. Monday through Saturday, Camila would get up early and make the coffee. Garrison LaRue and his crew would get their coffee before they would do their early chores, and then they would return for breakfast. After the men had eaten, Camila would feed the children, teach them some lessons, prepare the noonday meal, clean up, do some more housework, and prepare the evening meal.

Monday and Tuesday were laundry days, and she would wash and iron the family's clothes on those days. Wednesday was baking day, when she made loaves of bread and usually two cakes or three pies. Thursday was the day she scrubbed floors and washed windows. Friday was the day she made butter. Saturday was spent getting ready for Sunday.

It was Saturday again, and Camila was bathing the children. Little Garrison was grumbling and demanding to know why they had to take a bath.

"So we can go to church in the morning," Camila replied. "Your daddy didn't work in town this weekend, so maybe he would like to go to church."

"We don't go to church," the little boy said. "Daddy's mad at the church, so we don't go. And that's why I don't have to take a bath."

Smiling, Camila said, "You still have to take a bath so you can smell nice and clean whether you go to church or not. And your daddy is not mad. He's probably just really sad."

"Well, why is he sad?"

"Oh, I don't know, but what I do know is that when people are really sad, they need some hugs and kisses. So go find your daddy and make him happy before you go to bed."

Camila shooed the children out of the kitchen, emptied the tub, and mopped the floor. While she was waiting for the floor to dry, she decided to take a walk. She took a light shawl from the hook in the summer room and stepped out the back door.

She didn't get very far before Jarrod ran across the yard to talk to her. Garrison was standing in the upstairs hall outside of the children's rooms looking out of the window when he saw his young cowhand and his wife meet in the middle of the side yard. Immediately, he was angry. He watched them talking and laughing. Then he saw them put their heads together and hold hands.

Garrison watched as Camila reached up and pulled a pin from her hair and let it unfurl to just past her shoulders. He was furious as he walked away from the window, ran down the stairs, and left the house by the front door. But by the time he got outside and around to the side yard, Jarrod was gone and Camila was standing in the middle of the yard with her eyes closed, letting the breeze blow through her hair.

CHAPTER 10

Garrison snatched Camila by the arm and started pulling her toward the front of the house.

Her eyes flew open. "Ouch, stop!" she cried, trying to pull her arm from his grip. "What are you doing? Let me go, you're hurting me."

"Stop resisting before you really get hurt. Just get inside the house."

"No!" She swung her free arm at him. "Get away from me. Let me go," she demanded.

They stopped at the base of the front steps.

"What's wrong with you, woman? Is this what goes on when I'm in town? Are you so desperate for a man's attention that you have to try and seduce a young boy? Don't you have any respect for yourself?"

The words cut to Camila's heart, and she stepped away from Garrison, lifted her chin, and took in a shaky breath. "What are you talking about? Why did you grab my arm? How dare you speak to me like that!" She folded her arm across her body and rubbed it with her other hand.

"I saw you and Jarrod meet in the middle of the side yard, and I saw you holding his hands. I also saw you shake out your hair in his face."

Before Camila could say anything, Jarrod jogged around from the side of the house. "Oh, there you are, Mrs. LaRue," he said. "I went and put some liniment on it like you told me to. It feels better now, see." He held out his hand palm up. "Ma'am, I don't know what I woulda done if you hadden'a took that splinter out. Thanks a lot for helping me."

When Jarrod walked away, Camila looked at Garrison. "I am not now nor have I ever been desperate for a man's attention." She went up the steps and disappeared into the house. Garrison stood looking at the door that she left standing wide open.

By the time he went inside, she had already gone to her rooms. Garrison stood looking down the empty hall that led through the kitchen to the back of the house. He had no idea why he'd just talked to her that way or even why he'd acted the way he just did. He decided that he needed to apologize to her.

When he got to her living quarters, the door was ajar. Garrison pushed it open and walked through the little parlor to the bedroom where Camila was pacing the floor and mumbling to herself.

He stood listening to her angry mumblings, and so instead of going in to apologize, he turned away, feeling like he needed to give her some time to calm down before he spoke to her again.

The next morning, the coffee was prepared, but Camila wasn't there to serve it. When it was breakfast time, everyone showed up to find the meal cooked, but they had to serve themselves. The other meal of the day was served the same way. Things continued that way for the entire week and through the next weekend.

Sunday, Camila cleaned the kitchen after the noonday meal then gathered the children, picked up her quilt and her Bible, and again walked to the big tree across the yard.

On Monday, the men again found their meals cooked but had to serve themselves. After dinner had been eaten and the cowhands had gone to the bunkhouse, Garrison put his children to bed and returned to the kitchen.

Camila was washing the dishes. When she saw him come in, she dropped the dishcloth and ran toward her rooms, but he got to the door first and blocked her way. "Miss Barnes, can we talk?" When Garrison reached out to touch her elbow, she took a quick breath and jerked away from him.

He dropped his hand and sat in a chair beside the kitchen table. She went to the stove, picked up a cloth, and removed the kettle from the back burner. She poured some of the hot water into a china teapot and covered it with a cozy so the water stayed warm while the leaves were steeping. She set the kettle on the stove, and with her back to him, said, "So talk."

Suddenly finding himself unable to find the words he wanted to say, Garrison watched Camila wash the dishes. When she started drying them, he stood and began putting them away. After a few minutes, she poured tea into the cups. They sat at the table and sipped the sweet orange-flavored drink.

"This is good," Garrison said.

"Thanks," Camila pushed out through pursed lips.

Garrison looked at the dainty little cup in his hand and smiled sadly. "Near the end of our time together, my wife and I didn't get along. She was no longer interested in me." He shifted in his chair, cleared his throat, and continued. "Grace and I were happy for a while, but then she decided she didn't want to be a rancher's wife anymore. She started sneaking into town while I was working in the fields or out on the range with the guys."

When he stopped talking Camila didn't say anything. She could see that this was difficult for him.

"She was nothing like you," Garrison said. "She was small. I guess some would call her dainty. The only time she had a full shape was when she was pregnant. I did everything I could think of to make her happy. I even built her a weekend house in town so that we could be there together when I was on duty as the sheriff. We would leave here on Thursday afternoon. She would shop, order the groceries for the week, have tea with the Ladies' Missionary Society, and on Sundays she would go to church. Then, after I got off work, we would come home together.

"For a while, it seemed she was happier and we began to get along better. Then one Sunday afternoon, Mrs. Johnson, the pastor's wife, came by the office to drop off little Garrison and Ella Grace. She told me she and the pastor had to visit a family outside of town, and they couldn't find Grace anywhere. As it turned out, she wasn't at Mrs. Aires' dress shop having tea like she told Mrs. Johnson she was going to do.

"When I asked Mrs. Johnson why she had little Garrison and Ella Grace, she looked surprised and told me that she watched them every Sunday while Grace claimed she was having tea with Mrs. Aires and some of the ladies from church. I found out that Grace had been having lunches with the deacon, and that particular Sunday, she and the deacon had decided to run away together. Later that afternoon, they were found on the road by Old Sam from the livery stable.

"From what it looked like, the carriage wheel probably hit a rock and the carriage turned over. The deacon was thrown from the wagon. He had a lot of injuries, including a broken arm, a back injury, and his leg was broken in two places. Grace was crushed when the wagon landed on her."

Camila's hand was shaking as she set her cup on the saucer. But still, she made no comment.

"After the funeral," Garrison continued, "the doctor told me that Grace was pregnant." He put his face in his hand then moved it back to smooth over his hair. "I haven't been back to church since the funeral. Those people knew what was happening, and no one told me. They continued to smile in my face and pat me on my back when all the while, their deacon was having an affair with my wife. I refuse to be among those hypocrites. I'm never going back there again."

Camila felt strong compassion for Garrison, but she still felt compelled to offer, "You don't go to church for the people. You go to be in the presence of the Lord."

Garrison snorted. "I'm in the presence of the Lord right here on this ranch."

"Well, don't you miss the fellowship of your friends?"

Without warning, Garrison slammed his hand on the table and stood. "I don't have any friends. I don't need fellowship, and I'm telling you for the last time I'm not going back to that church, and I don't want my children to be there either."

"Children need to be in church. They have to be taught about the Lord early so that they will be able to accept Him as their Lord and Savior when they are older. How can you deny them the opportunity to get to know who God is? That's just wrong."

Garrison stood over her. "Don't push me on this, woman! I'm not going to argue this with you anymore."

Before he could exit the room, Camila asked, "What does all of that have to do with the way you treated me a few days ago?"

He opened his mouth to say something but closed it quickly and expelled a sigh of exasperation.

CHAPTER 11

Seeing the determination on Garrison's face, Camila decided she didn't want to argue about church or anything else. If he thought he had a good reason not to go to church, then who was she to change his mind? If he wanted to stay angry with the world because of his deceased wife's behavior, so be it. But she had to make him understand her position on certain things.

Therefore, she couldn't resist saying, "You know, Mr. LaRue, I'm not Grace. I'm Camila Rose Barnes, and I'm new to this place. I have not met anyone in the town other than the judge and his wife. Being on this ranch all day, every day, is very difficult for me. I would like to at least see, talk to, or have tea with another woman every once in a while. I've been here for more than six months, and I haven't made any friends. I'm sure it doesn't even concern you that there's no one here for me to talk to. Have you ever considered that I'm the only woman on this ranch?"

It had never crossed Garrison's mind that she was lonely. It never seemed important to him that she was the only woman on the ranch. "Well," he said, "I'm going back to work next weekend, and you can have Roy drive you into town on Sunday morning. I'll let you have one Sunday morning a month in town. But as soon as church is over, you need to bring my children to the office, and Roy will pick you up from there and drive you back home. That's the best that I can offer."

Camila stood and collected the teacups and teapot. When she finished washing everything, she dried them and put them back into their storage box. She looked at Garrison. "Would you empty the dishpan, please? I'm tired," she said, then went to her room and closed the door.

The next morning as he and his crew were returning from repairing fences, Garrison told Roy about allowing Camila to go to church once a month.

Roy looked at his boss curiously. "Excuse me, Garrison, but why you punishin' that gal in there for somethin' Miz Grace done?"

Glaring at the older man as if he had just cursed him, Garrison said, "You don't know what you're talking about, Roy. I'm not punishing her. Grace is gone. What does she have to do with this? Miss Barnes is my housekeeper, and I need her to keep my house in order and take care of my children. That's all. And she can't do that if she's out running back and forth to town."

Roy read the strain on his boss's face. "Have you stopped to look around your house?" he asked. "Have you noticed how clean that house is? Have you even took notice of the changes she done made to that house since she been here?"

Roy waited a moment for the younger man to answer his questions. When Garrison made no attempt to speak, Roy shifted his weight to one leg, looked directly at his boss, and continued.

"Well, I have, and I got to admit that it's cleaner now than long before the first Mrs. LaRue died. Do you even 'preciate the changes that's done been made inside that house? That there gal has worked hard to make your house more of a home for you and your li'l ones."

Feeling like he was on a roll, Roy kept pointing out the attributes of the new woman of the house. "That's a good woman in there. She makes sure that the little ones get the best of everything. She treats them like a mother, like they is her own natural-borned childrens. She spends all her time doing for everybody on this ranch, and she does it very well. So why shouldn't she have some time to herself and go to church if she wants to?"

Garrison blew out a breath. "That's just it, Roy. She's beginning to act as though she's a part of my family. Like she has some say-so about what goes on inside my house. She was relentless about getting her way with going to church. Even when I told her no, she pressed the point. She even put the children into it. Claiming that children need church. And now here it is she has wormed her way into getting into town and going to church."

Watching Garrison, Roy could see he was getting a little upset, but he still said, "She should be acting like she's part of your family, Garrison, because you married her. I would like to point out to you one simple fact. She's more than a housekeeper and a babysitter. She's your wife! And let me say somethin' else to you. If you don't start treatin' her better, she's goin' ta be gone. And this time, it will be all your fault that you done lost another wife. Even if you don't treat this one like she is a real wife, that's a good woman in that there house, and you needs ta start treatin' her better."

Still not waiting for a comment from his boss Roy continued. "You just remember, she's a beautiful woman. Even though she don't know it. And one day, someone's gonna come along and make her believe it, then she'll be gone."

Roy turned away from Garrison, and as he was walking back to the bunkhouse, he added, "Here's somethin' else to think about . . . She ain't nothin' like Miss Grace. She ain't one of your childrens. She don't need to be raised by you, she already grown."

Stopping in mid-stride, Roy turned to look back at his boss. Raising his hand to rub the scruffy hairs on his chin, he chuckled and offered his final comment: "Just in case you ain't noticed yet, boy. She is a bona fide full-growed-up woman. I wouldn't mind having a body like that warming my sheets every night. If ya gets my drift." And with a broad smile on his face, Roy winked and walked away.

Garrison stood with his thumbs in the belt loops of his Levi's, listening to his oldest employee. He wanted to dispute what the older man was saying, but he couldn't. So when Roy walked into the bunkhouse and closed the door, Garrison snatched his hat from his head, reached up with his other hand, and smoothed it over his hair.

Then he smacked his hat against his thigh and said, "Damn!"

CHAPTER 12

On the following Sunday, Camila went to church and showed up in Garrison's office right around twelve o'clock with his children in tow. Much to his pleasure, she seemed to have done exactly what she was told to do.

With a secret smile, Garrison asked, "Did you meet any of the ladies at the church today?"

Camila replied immediately, "No, I didn't meet anyone. I did as I was ordered. If you can remember you demanded that 'after service, don't stop to socialize, just get yourself and my children over to the office.'" She gave the last part of her statement a mocking tone, and her lips were pulled tight while her arms were folded across her chest.

Garrison saw that she was flushed, and the indent between her collarbones at the base of her throat was throbbing. Her breasts were rising and falling as she breathed deeply. He knew she was angry, but he told himself he really didn't care. He was pleased because he felt that Camila was finally going to start acting like a good, obedient wife.

The next few weeks were interesting. Garrison and Camila didn't have much to say to one another; they only spoke when it was necessary. They both tried very hard not to be alone in the same room together, and when they were together, they were overly polite to each other.

All of this strained behavior did not go unnoticed. Roy held his tongue, watched, and smiled saying, to himself, "Thank you, Lord. She just what the boy needs."

During those weeks after what he called "The Great Church Incident," Garrison began to pay closer attention to Camila's interactions with his children. He began listening to her as she taught them and was surprised to hear Ella Grace call her Mommy. He heard Garrison Jr. laugh and answer questions with confidence. He saw how the children enjoyed being around her. It seemed to him that since he'd put his foot down, she was less opinionated and followed his instructions without question, just replying, "Yes, sir" and "No, sir," which made him very happy. Or so he thought.

Just when Garrison thought things were going well, he came home one warm, sunny late-September afternoon to find Camila and the children gone.

He checked the inside of the house thoroughly. Then he went outside and checked the side yards and the vegetable gardens—he even looked for them behind the hay barn and the corral, but he didn't see them.

He was furious. As he was stomping back toward the big barn to get the wagon and search for them, they came strolling into the backyard. Camila was carrying Ella and almost dragging Little Garrison as they walked together, holding a picnic basket between them.

Without saying anything, Garrison quickly made his way to the back of the house. He was determined to let her know just how unhappy he was with her right now.

But when Camila raised her head and saw him standing on the back porch outside the summer room with his arms folded across his chest, she asked, "Can you help us out here, please?"

Garrison lifted his son into his arms and carried him to his room while Camila set the basket on the kitchen table. Then she carried the sleeping little girl up the steps to her room, undressed her, and laid her in bed.

Meeting Garrison in the hall, she offered a quick smile. "Thank you. I didn't know how we were going to make those final few feet to the house. As you could see, they are both very tired."

Garrison looked down at her smiling face, then frowned and grunted.

"Is there a problem?" she asked as they walked down the steps.

"Didn't I tell you to never take my children anywhere unless I knew about it first?"

"What are you talking about? We didn't go anywhere."

He grabbed her arm. "You were not here in this house when I got here. I didn't know where you were. You took them away without my permission."

Before he could see it coming, Camila slapped him. "You only get one time to manhandle me. I won't let anyone—but most especially, *you*—touch me like that. Don't ever touch me again!"

Garrison's eyes registered extreme disbelief and instant anger, but Camila didn't see that. She stalked into the kitchen, washed her hands, checked the stew, and moved it to the middle of the stove where the heat was the highest. Then she took the light towels off of the dough that she'd left rising in their pans and put the three loaves into the oven. Finally, she emptied the picnic basket, wiped it out, and put it away on a shelf in the pantry.

"He really knows how to take the fun out of a good time!" she grumbled to herself.

When she turned, she saw Garrison LaRue standing in the doorway. They stared at one another for a few moments. He saw sadness in her face. She saw anger in his eyes.

As she turned her back to him, Camila's thoughts immediately went to *I've finally gone too far. He's probably going to send me home. And if that's the case, then so be it.*

"Are you staying, or are you leaving?" he asked gruffly.

"Isn't that up to you? If you don't want me here anymore, I can pack my clothes and be out of here by morning," she huffed.

"Miss Barnes, I don't think we are on the same page." He pointed at her. "I'm talking about the way you are dressed."

Camila looked down and realized she still had her shawl on. While she removed it and hung it in the summer room, Garrison walked into the kitchen and sat at the table. She poured him a cup of coffee and set it on the table in front of him with a little more force than she intended.

"I'm sorry," she offered as she quickly wiped up what had sloshed from the cup. Then she began to explain. "We really hadn't gone anywhere except to eat our lunch down by the stream. I was wrong for not letting you know, but what was I to do? You weren't here, and I didn't want to miss the opportunity. I didn't leave a note because we didn't leave the ranch."

"Well, maybe I did overreact a little. It's just that today is Ella's birthday, and I have a present for her, and when I realized you all weren't here . . . I didn't know what to think. I never thought that you went beyond the front and side yards." Garrison's voice had lost any trace of harshness that was there just a few minutes before.

Camila laughed lightly. "Oh, my, we have traveled to many points beyond the yards. At least one day a week, we spend the whole day outdoors. We call them our nature days. They are lots of fun. And today, we celebrated Ella's birthday outdoors. That's what she wanted to do. She asked if we could sing happy birthday to her in the flowers."

Garrison looked over at the worktable at the last thing Camila had taken from the basket. It was the remains of a small cake. He also noticed that a bigger cake was sitting on the hutch, waiting for the evening meal.

He lifted his hand and rubbed his cheek. "No need to apologize. I was wrong too. But you know what? That was quite a wallop, Miss Barnes. I believe I've learned my lesson. I promise that I will never touch you *like that* again."

Without thinking, she stepped to him, stood between his knees, and touched his face. They smiled at each other. Then he reached up, touched her hand, and held it to his face. He liked the way it felt. He liked the way she smelled. He liked the way she looked.

At that moment, Garrison noticed that her golden-brown skin shone like it was polished. Her off-black hair with reddish-brown sun-enhanced highlights had begun to unwind itself from the bun at the base of her head, and some curly tendrils had fallen and were framing her face.

Her eyes were dark-brown with light-brown flecks, and they were framed by long, thick lashes that curled up slightly. Looking up at her,

Garrison could see a distant pain and sadness in her eyes. But her voice never seemed to have the tone of anger that his had from time to time. Her full and well-shaped lips seemed ready to be kissed.

There were things about Camila that intrigued him. She was tall for a woman, but it didn't seem to hinder her. She was not fat but was of good size, with a body that was curvy and made of solid muscle. Her face was not what you would call beautiful, but she was pretty.

Beautiful, he thought, *is not real. You have to use makeup and do special things to be beautiful, but pretty is natural, like her.*

As a matter of fact, Garrison believed the more he looked at her, the prettier she seemed to get.

He became so aware of her that he was uncomfortable in her presence. Removing her hand from his face but still holding it, he stood and looked down into her eyes. "I hope you can forgive me. I promise to never grab you or be forceful toward you again."

Without warning, he leaned forward and pressed his lips to her temple, released her hand, stepped around her, and left the house.

The next time Garrison was on duty as the sheriff. he left the ranch earlier than usual. Before leaving, he took some time and reminded Camila, "Take care of my children, and do not leave them with anyone or leave this ranch for any reason, especially to go into town."

Instead of saying what was on her mind, Camila nodded her head and went into the formal dining room to begin her dusting chores for the day.

As soon as Garrison got to town, he went straight to the mercantile. When he opened the door, Contessa, the store owner's wife, ran to Garrison and kissed his cheek. "Hello, little brother, what brings you here this morning?"

"Can't a man come see his sister? I missed you and wanted to see you, that's all."

Contessa smiled at her brother. "You are such a liar. Why are you here? Where's my niece and nephew? And why haven't I met my new sister-in-law yet?"

"Well, I guess you could say that's part of the reason I'm here. You haven't seen the children in a while, and you also haven't met Miss Barnes yet."

Tessa looked at her brother. "Sooo?"

Garrison reticently asked, "Do you mind going out to spend some time with them on Saturday or Sunday? I know you usually spend your weekend time off from the store with Mom and Dad, but could you do this for me as a favor, please?"

"How 'bout I spent Saturday night and Sunday with them?"

Garrison gave his sister a bear hug. "That sounds good to me. Thanks, Tess."

As he was leaving the store, Contessa called, "Garrison?" When he turned to look at her, she asked, "Why do you call your wife Miss Barnes?"

He shrugged his shoulders. "That's her name," he said and left the store.

CHAPTER 13

It was early Saturday morning as Camila was working on the vegetable garden, collecting the ripe vegetables and pulling weeds from the greens, when she heard what sounded like a carriage coming into the front yard. By the time she had the dirt brushed from her clothes, washed the dirt from her hands, and came around to the front of the house, she saw a very pretty woman climbing out of a carriage.

"Hello," Camila said, "how can I help you today?"

"Mrs. LaRue?" the woman asked.

"No, I'm. Uh . . . Um, yes," she stammered uncertainly. "I'm Camila."

The pretty woman laughed. "Hi, Camila. My name is Contessa Anderson. My husband and I own the general store in Alamosa, and your husband, Garrison, is my younger brother." Contessa threw her arms around Camila and hugged her tightly. "I'm so glad to finally meet you."

"Oh, it's good to meet you too, Mrs. Anderson. Are you related to the judge and his wife?"

"You should call me Tessa, and Judge and Mrs. Anderson are my in-laws. I'm married to their son Hank."

Camila stepped back. "And I see that they are going to be grandparents soon."

Contessa smiled and rubbed her slightly rounded abdomen. "Yes, in about five months. Hank and I can hardly wait."

Camila looked longingly at the woman and smiled. "Congratulations.

Come inside, let me get you some tea. Do you have time to eat a meal with us before you return to town?"

"I told Garrison that I would stay until tomorrow afternoon, if that's okay with you."

The ladies had two hours to talk before little Garrison and Ella Grace woke up and occupied their aunt's attention.

"It certainly looks different in here," Contessa said as she came through the front door. "How did you get my brother to do all of this?"

Laughing lightly, Camila offered, "He didn't do this. I did this, with a lot of help from the ranch hands. Let me show you the changes that had been made. I've only had time to do some things to the first floor of the ranch house. I have a lot more planned."

After the quick tour, the children came rumbling into the kitchen, so while they were talking to their aunt, Camila finished preparing breakfast. While everyone was eating, she went upstairs and started putting Ella's room in order as the guest room.

Just as she was putting the quilt on the bed and fluffing the pillows, Contessa walked in, "I wish I had known what you were doing," she said. "I usually sleep in the rooms off the kitchen when I come out."

Camila smiled. "Well, that's where I sleep, but you are more than welcome to sleep there, if you choose."

Contessa stared at her sister-in-law. "You don't sleep in the master bedroom?"

Camila looked at the floor and smiled sadly. "No. We don't have that kind of marriage. You see, I'm just the cook, housekeeper, and babysitter. I think he is still in love with his wife. He's still mourning her."

When Tessa saw Camila's eyes welling up, she offered her a smile and winked. "Don't worry, this is our secret. I promise. Hank and I had a rocky start when we first married. We weren't in love from the beginning. We were just two lonely people who were looking for companionship so we wouldn't have to grow old alone. It took us a while to get together too. Don't worry, sister-in-law. It's going to happen. You just keep doing all that you are doing, and he's bound to come around." She hugged Camila.

"Listen, I came bearing gifts. Let's go get them. They're in the carriage."

When the sacks and boxes were opened, the children were overjoyed with their bags of broken peppermint sticks and new toys. Little Garrison played nonstop with his wooden horses and train, while Ella Grace was very pleased with her life-size rag doll and alphabet blocks. Camila was grateful for the hand lotions, the combs, and the oils for her hair.

After the children were in bed for the night and sound asleep, the two women had tea in the main parlor. Tessa took Camila's hands. "Okay, now that it's just you and me, please tell me how are you, really?"

Camila gently pulled her hands away, stood, and walked to the windows. "I . . . I'm fine. I've just been a little lonely." She turned back to face her sister-in-law, offered her a weak smile, then continued. "And that's why I'm so glad you came all the way out here to see me. Thank you."

Tessa wasn't convinced that Camila was happy, but she didn't press the issue even though she thought she saw Camila's eyes well up with tears that she blinked away.

Rather than make an issue of the situation, Contessa made herself content with becoming a friend to the pretty lady who was married in name only to her brother. She also made a mental note to talk to Garrison. She had more than once looked at Camila's hand and noticed with sadness that the woman didn't even have on a wedding band.

"Has my brother told you anything about his life?" Contessa asked.

Without hesitation, Camila replied, "No. We don't have conversations. He's a private person."

Contessa held out her hand and invited Camila to sit with her. "Listen, Camila, I like you, and I want my brother to be happy. So let me tell you a few things about him that might help you understand him."

The ladies sat together as Contessa settled back against the cushions of the settee.

"When we were young," she began, "being colored and Indian was difficult. When our mother fell in love with the son of freed slaves, the tribal leaders didn't accept the relationship, and the tribe turned their back on her. As a result, our parents left and came to Colorado territory, and this house is sitting on part of the land that our parents homesteaded.

"When I was born, Mother sent word to the tribe, but they didn't answer. Then, when Garrison was born, they finally replied and asked her to send him to them so that he could learn their ways and help rejuvenate the tribal nation. Of course, our parents didn't honor that request, and so my brother and I grew up with each other as our only relatives. The other people in and around town who were former slaves that settled here and their children became our family."

A slight smile crossed Contessa's face. "As you can see, Garrison got more of the native looks than I did, and as a result, he had a harder time in school and around town. The white boys would tease him. They called him names like savage, half-breed, and renegade. In school, when he would react to the taunting, he got into trouble as long as we had the white teacher. But when Mrs. Aires became our teacher, she made us feel proud of who we are and how we look. She saw through the mean acts and helped Garrison control his anger and look for another solution to the problem.

"It was George Tate, who is half-white, that led the bullying, and as we grew older, most of the other boys stopped following him and became friends with Garrison. Instead of stopping, George became more determined to continue."

Camila was watching her sister-in-law share those childhood memories and wondered out loud to the other woman about the young Garrison's ability to withstand such torment. But her doubts were quelled when Contessa continued.

"Well, one day, Mrs. Aires turned her back and let Garrison beat George to the ground. Since then, everything George has done has been sneaky, underhanded, and behind the back. He still tries to this day to upset Garrison by using other people to do his dirty work. Right now, that person is Mildred Horn, so watch out for her. She is mean and likes to talk down to other women. A while back, she wanted my brother to marry her. But he let her know he wasn't interested. So you may become her next target."

Contessa sadly recounted, "The final straw came when Garrison's wife

Grace and George Tate's affair became public knowledge. It was then that I saw my brother change. I thought he was going to lose his mind. He became even more quiet, solitary, and hard. His smiles are few and far between, and when you do see one, the joy doesn't fill his eyes. After the funeral, he shut himself away. He wouldn't leave this ranch and wouldn't let anyone come to visit him. It was Roy who kept me up to date about him and the children. If it hadn't been for little Garrison and Ella Grace, I think my brother would have killed George Tate."

Contessa touched Camila's shoulder. "When you came to Alamosa, I was hoping that he would let himself become human again. I was hoping that you could get him to let down his guard."

Camila smiled sadly. "I know that you want your brother to become the man he used to be, but that may not be possible. He is a result of his experiences. He has to decide how they make him feel and act. Maybe one day he will let someone into his heart again, but I'm sure that this is not the time, and I know that I'm not that someone."

After a few moments of silence, Camila smiled at Tessa and said, "It's getting late. You and that little one need to get your rest. I made up the bed down here for you, so goodnight."

After receiving a hug from Contessa, Camila climbed the staircase and went into Ella Grace's room, where the little girl was sound asleep on her bed. Camila smiled down at her angelic-looking stepdaughter.

"Sorry we're not sharing my bed tonight, Little One," she whispered. "Maybe another time."

Camila lay down and slept on the pallet she had made up on the floor.

When Sunday afternoon rolled around, Camila hugged her sister-in-law and helped Tessa into the carriage.

"Thank you again for coming all the way out here to spend time with us, and thank you so very much for our gifts," Camila said. "I enjoyed having you here. It was nice sitting with and talking to another woman. Hopefully, we can get together again soon."

Contessa smiled at her sister-in-law and led the carriage away from the house with Wesley on his horse trotting beside her. He was going to see that she arrived home safely, and then he was going to return to LaRue Crossing early in the morning.

Camila and the children stood on the front porch waving until the carriage was out of sight. She enjoyed the visit from Contessa but was once again feeling isolated and lonely.

With a heavy heart, Camila offered the little ones a smile and said, "How about we go into the summer room and I'll read you a story while you have a piece of pie?"

Little GJ and Ella Grace cheered and ran into the house. As Camila followed them, she thought that if she busied herself with entertaining the children, the cloud of sadness wouldn't come back to engulf her again so quickly.

When Tessa Anderson arrived back in town, she realized she was very anxious to get back to her home to see her husband and tell him about her new sister-in-law. So after dropping the wagon off at the livery stable, she thanked Wesley for riding with her then quickly walked down the street and stepped into the parlor at the back of the store. After she greeted her husband with a long hug and a deep kiss, she began telling Hank about her trip as he sat and listened intently.

She told him how sad she was for her sister-in-law. "Hank, they sleep in separate rooms. As a matter of fact, they sleep in different parts of the house. He's banned her from his bedroom. She doesn't know this, but I know that she slept on the floor in little Ella's room last night. Usually, she's down in those rooms off the kitchen. The worst part of this whole thing is that she doesn't even have a wedding band. I'm so mad at my brother right now I don't know what to do."

Hank looked at his wife and smiled. "Well, baby, let's mind our own business for now. Maybe they have to figure it out for themselves like we had to do five years ago."

"But Hank, I have to do something. Even if they didn't have a Christian wedding, she's still his wife and she should at least have a wedding band to prove it."

"Look, Tessa, baby, calm down," Hank said. "Let me take care of that. One day, when your brother comes into the store, I'll just ask him if he wants to get his wife a better ring and show him the catalog."

CHAPTER 14

Garrison usually visited his parents one morning a week before going to work. On this particular morning, he felt more than ever that he needed to talk to them. About how he and his housekeeper kept bumping heads. He was not happy about what he considered her lack of respect, and especially how she would make decisions that affected the family without asking him first—like the changes she was making to his house.

When he rode into the yard, his father, Thaddeus, stepped out onto the front porch. "Well, hello, son," he said, "how are you doing this morning?"

Dismounting, Garrison tied his horse to the hitching post and, accepting his father's hug, said, "Dad, I'd like to say that I'm fine. But Miss Barnes is driving me crazy. She is the most willful woman I've dealt with in a long time. I don't know what to do with her."

Thaddeus LaRue laughed and put his hand on his son's shoulder. "Come on inside and let's talk with your mother about it."

Anna Wolf LaRue hugged her son. "Hello, darling," she said, looking into his face, knowing immediately there was a problem. "Oh, my, look at that face. What is it? What's the matter?"

"Mom," Garrison said, "that woman is a handful. She doesn't listen, doesn't want to abide by any of my rules, and she argues everything that I say. I'm going to have to send her back to where she came from."

Anna smiled. "The way I heard it, son, she's a breath of fresh air, a welcome addition to that place of yours. I understand that she's turning your house into a palace. I can't wait to see it."

"Oh, I guess you've been talking to Tessa, huh?"

"Well, yes, and she tells us that Camila is a wonderful young woman. I also understand that the children already love her."

Thaddeus spoke up. "What's the real problem, son?" he asked.

Sitting around the kitchen table drinking coffee, the trio discussed the "problem" with the new housekeeper/wife at LaRue Crossing.

Leaving his parents' home, Garrison felt as if his parents had turned against him. They seemed to believe that Camila Barnes hadn't done anything that could be considered willful or disrespectful. As a matter of fact, according to his mother, "It seems that your *Miss Barnes* is doing her job. And it seems that she's doing it quite well."

Before he left, Garrison's mother told him, "Son, you need to let that woman be who she is. You can't hold a butterfly too tight, or you'll crush its wings, and a butterfly that can't fly will soon die."

For the entire time he was fulfilling his duties in town, Garrison would reluctantly let his imagination wander to what could be happening with his family. More than half a dozen times, he found himself thinking, *I bet Miss Barnes and the children are having breakfast now.*

I'm sure they are doing their lessons now.

It's nap time. What is she doing? Could she be taking a bath?

That final thought caught him off guard and caused things to happen with his body.

"Damn!"

Garrison jumped up from behind his desk strode across the room, strapped on his gun, snatched his hat from the wall peg, and stormed out of the office.

He walked through town, going in and out of the shops and other businesses, talking with the owners and other workers just to keep his mind on his job and off of that woman at his house. He didn't like what was happening to him. Most of his weekend was spent trying to convince himself that he wasn't feeling things. Things he swore he would not allow himself to feel again. Those feelings were all centered around Camila Rose Barnes.

He loved to watch her without her knowing he was watching her. He liked how she moved around the kitchen; he enjoyed the sound of her voice as she sang to herself while she prepared the meals. The one thing he noticed about her the most was that she was pretty and always smelled good.

"This is not happening to me," he said. "I won't allow it. She's not going to get to me." Garrison continued talking to himself. "You better get a grip on yourself, then, man. That woman is a wife in name only. You don't need any complications in your life from another woman ever again."

When he arrived home on Monday afternoon, Camila and the children were in her parlor doing their lessons. He had a letter for her, but rather than hand it to her, Garrison laid it on the kitchen table.

He went straight up to his bedroom and didn't come back downstairs until everyone had eaten dinner. Garrison told himself that he was only going downstairs to get the children so that he could spend time with them before they went to bed.

CHAPTER 15

During his time with the children, Garrison chose not to have a conversation with Camila, so later, after little GJ and Ella Grace were in bed, and when she had finished cleaning the kitchen, Camila came to his office door and knocked.

"Come in," Garrison barked. He wasn't very happy to be looking into her pretty face. "What?" he threw out gruffly.

"I'm so sorry to disturb you, Mr. LaRue, but I wanted to thank you for your kindness."

Garrison glared at Camila but said nothing.

She cleared her voice and continued. "For bringing my brothers' letter to me. And . . . umm, your sister told me that you asked her to come visit me and the children. I was glad to meet her."

Garrison nodded his head and offered a half smile/half scowl as he said, "As for the letter, I was already in town, and as for my sister, she's a busybody. She said she wanted to get to know you. Which really means she wanted to get into your business."

"Well, thank you anyway," Camila said, then added, "do you have any dishes in here?"

Looking at her, Garrison couldn't help but notice that she was even prettier when she was happy. Her eyes didn't have the look of sadness that seemed to always be there. He noticed the dress she was wearing, and how it hung close to her body. And he noticed, not for the first time, that she had a lush, full body.

Even though she was modest and around the house wore loose, unappealing gowns, they did nothing to hide the fact she had a supple, inviting, curvaceous body. He was looking at her, and it gave him thoughts about how it would feel to pull her close and hold her to his chest, next to his heart.

He sat behind his desk as if glued to the chair. Camila's voice interrupted his thoughts. "Is there anything I can get you?" she asked, and when he didn't answer her, she offered, "Well then, if you get hungry later, just know that I left a plate in the warmer for you."

He softly replied, "Thank you."

Then, just to get away from her, he stood, walked around his desk, and stepped out of his office. Camila looked up at him and stepped back. Stopping just in front of her, Garrison reached out and touched her face. Then, almost as if he had been shocked, he quickly snatched his hand away.

He moved past Camila into the hall and then climbed the staircase to his bedroom. For several hours, he paced the floor, trying to get her and his desire for her off his mind and out of his heart.

After a while, he stopped pacing and sat on his bed. For the first time, he noticed that his room had been cleaned. The bed was fresh, the floor had been scrubbed, and the windows had been washed until they were so clean you almost couldn't see the panes. He also realized the curtains had been washed, starched, and pressed. His clothes were put away, his shoes and boots were lined against the wall, and the refreshing scent of crushed pine needles filled the room.

Garrison smiled, and instead of being angry that Camila had disobeyed his orders to not enter his bedroom "at any time for any reason," he was grateful.

During the night, the weather turned stormy. Garrison got out of bed to look in on the children. As he was standing in the hallway outside their bedroom watching the storm, for some reason, Roy's words began playing through his mind: "If you don't start treatin' her better, she's goin' ta be gone. And this time, it will be all your fault that you done lost another wife.

Even if you don't treat this one like she is a real wife, that's a good woman in that there house, and you needs ta start treatin' her better."

Then Garrison heard his mother's voice repeat one of her tidbits of sage advice: "You can't hold a butterfly too tight, or you'll crush its wings, and a butterfly that can't fly will soon die."

With the flashes of lightning, the blasts of thunder, the sound of the heavy rain pelting the windows, and the roaring winds whistling, Garrison hoped maybe this display of God's awesomeness would take his mind off of Camila Rose Barnes.

As he stood praying, thanking God for His grace and beseeching God for His mercy, a bright flash danced across the sky, accompanied by a loud burst of thunder. Garrison thought he heard another sound and went to the top of the staircase, where he saw a low light coming from the main parlor below.

At the bottom of the staircase, he looked into the parlor and saw the object of his turmoil. She was sitting in the high-backed wing chair by the fireplace, wrapped in a quilt with her face in her hands. He could hear her soft sobs and see her trembling shoulders.

Before he could think it through, Garrison had crossed the hall and entered the room. He stood in front of the chair and, reaching down, took Camila's wrists in his hands. When she looked at him, he could see the tears on her cheeks, and his chest grew tight. He pulled her gently to her feet, walked to the settee, lifted her, sat down, and settled her on his lap.

Using his thumb to wipe away her tears, Garrison held Camila's chin and whispered, "It's just a storm. You're fine. I'm here with you."

She lay her head on his chest, and after a few minutes he felt her breathing settle down, and he knew she had fallen asleep. He kissed the top of her head, stood, and carried her to her bed.

Just as he laid her down, she whispered his name. "Garrison."

For some inexplicable reason, when he returned to his room he realized he was experiencing a feeling of contentment. And as a result of that serenity, Garrison lay in his bed and slept peacefully until the morning sun shone through his windows.

CHAPTER 16

At breakfast, neither Garrison nor Camila met each other's gaze. He was remembering how soft and supple her body felt in his arms, and he could still smell her alluring lavender scent and hear her voice whisper his name. She was remembering lying against his solid chest, thinking of how comforting it was to hear his soothing words and how being in his arms took away her fears.

For several weeks after the incident, Camila's dreams were filled with images of Garrison LaRue as he'd comforted her during the storm. Her dreams, however, took on a life of their own when they became filled with things more intimate than being comforted during a storm.

It became a habit for Garrison to sit in the kitchen with Camila before the children were up and give her instructions for the day and sometimes the upcoming week, depending on his work schedule. On Tuesday morning during their conference time, Camila said to him, "I want me and the children to go into town with you tomorrow, and maybe we can stay through the rest of the week and the whole weekend."

"No!"

"Why?"

"Because I said, no."

"Well, I need to go. There are some things I need to get."

"Make a list, and I'll get them and bring them back Monday afternoon."

"No."

"Then you will have to do without . . . *those things*," he said, his lips pressed tight.

"Then I will go into town and get them myself."

"No, you will not! You won't take my children into town, or anywhere else that I don't approve."

"Who said I was going to take them with me?" Camila said. "They're your children, and you can at least take care of them yourself sometime. And oh, by the way, you only have two children, not three. I'm a grown woman and I will not be told what to do. I will no longer accept being hidden away on this ranch like a bad secret or settle for being treated like a child. You need to think about your desire to always be in control. I don't like it. I don't like it at all. Especially when you are trying to control me!"

Camila turned, went into her living quarters, and closed the door. She spent the rest of the day doing her chores and preparing the meals, but she had nothing else to say to Garrison LaRue.

The next morning, Camila woke at her usual time, and when Roy brought in the milk, she asked him to hitch up the buggy for her. "I need to go into town this morning."

Roy looked at her and smiled. "Sure thing, little lady, it'll be my pleasure." Roy thought over her request. He knew she was going against Garrison's wishes, but he smiled and said to himself, "Good for you, young lady. Don't let him corral ya."

Immediately after breakfast, Camila started cleaning the kitchen, and as soon as she finished, she changed her dress, put on her cape, her hat, and her gloves, then went out to the buggy. Before she rode away, she asked Roy to give his boss a message. "When he comes out of the den," she said, "let Mr. LaRue know that I'm on my way to town and I'll return in time to prepare the noonday meal, please. Keep an eye out for the children. They're still asleep, and I left their breakfast plates in the warming oven."

"Sure thing, Miz LaRue," Roy smiled. "You just be careful, don't let Old Sue here get away from ya. Don't worry none, I'll take care of them young'uns."

A while later, Garrison left the den and stopped short when he saw the children at the table being served their breakfast by Roy. "What's going on here? Where is Miss Barnes?" he asked Roy as he bent and kissed his children on their cheeks.

When Roy gave his boss Camila's message, he could see Garrison was not very happy. And when Garrison asked, "How long has she been gone?" Roy could hear the anger in his voice.

"Round 'bout sixty minutes now, Boss."

Snatching his gloves from his back pocket, Garrison threw out an order. "Let me know the minute she gets back here." Then he slapped his gloves on his thigh and left the house in a huff.

When she arrived in town, Camila wasted no time. She went directly to the bank, then to Mrs. Aires' shop, and finally to the mercantile, where she and Contessa talked as Hank filled her order. Camila paid for her items and decided to get some extra supplies to make something special for tonight's dessert.

It felt good to have some time away from the ranch. Camila looked around the town and took in the weekday activities. Later, when she climbed into the buggy to head back to LaRue Crossing, she was genuinely smiling for the first time in a long while.

Turning off the road onto the path that led to LaRue Crossing, Camila saw two figures on the front porch. One was sitting on a rocking chair. The other was standing at the edge of the porch by the steps. She could tell the man standing was Garrison.

As she came closer, she saw that he was now standing tall with his legs parted and his arms folded across his chest. As she rode even closer, she saw that he was annoyed—no, more than annoyed. He looked irate. She could almost see smoke coming out of his ears.

When she pulled to a stop at the steps of the front porch, Roy eased himself from the rocker, walked down the porch steps to the side of the buggy, helped Camila down with her packages, then quickly drove the buggy to the barn.

"Where have you been, Miss Barnes?" Garrison demanded.

"As if you don't know. I went to town, of course. I asked Roy to let you know."

"He did tell me, but I couldn't believe it. Do you remember I told you that you could not go into town without my permission?"

"No, but I do remember that you said that I couldn't take your children into town without your permission."

"You left them here all alone while you went galavanting all over town. That is, if you even went to town."

"Of course I went to town," Camila said, "and I was most definitely not galavanting. I told you yesterday that I needed to do some shopping."

"And I told you that you couldn't go!"

"And I told you that I am not your child!" Camila stood toe to toe with Garrison, her shoulders squared, her chin raised, her eyes boring into his.

"You are more trouble than you are worth," Garrison replied. "I'm ready to send you back to where you came from. I'm ready to hire another woman. One who's not so cantankerous and pigheaded."

"Well, as soon as you find someone, you be sure to let me know, and I will pack my belongings and be gone. Maybe you can find someone this time who doesn't mind being treated like a child!" Camila stepped past him and marched up the steps, through the front door, down the hall, through the kitchen, and into her rooms without looking back.

What followed was another day of silence from her, and it didn't go unnoticed by the ranch hands.

Early Thursday morning, Garrison went into the barn to check the animal supplies. He was going to do an inventory so he could give a list to Doc Hales, the vet, to put in an order for him. Todd, Jarrod, and Wesley didn't hear their boss enter the barn, and they continued talking.

"Miss LaRue cooked good but didn't serve us our meals last night, or this morning, either," Jarrod said. "Wonder what Mr. LaRue did this time. She was looking real sad this morning when I took the eggs and milk in for Roy, and I could swear she had been crying."

"He may not have done anything," Todd said. "You know it's hard to figure a woman out. They get sad at times for no reason at all. Sometimes, it could be because the wind is blowing in the wrong direction. Who knows? Like I said, women are hard to understand."

"Well, I got her all figured out," Wesley added. "She's a woman, and all women want is for a man to bed them every once in a while. And with her living in the housekeeper's quarters, I'll bet she ain't been bedded, at least not by Mr. LaRue, anyway. But you know what? If he don't know what to do with that fine specimen of a woman, I can tell him a thing or two."

"Shut up, Wes," Jarrod said. "That's disrespectful. Miss LaRue is a nice lady. It's not fair the boss tries to keep her here on this ranch like she's his prize heifer or something. I feel sorry for her. She's getting a raw deal being married to the boss. That man has a cold heart."

So that they wouldn't know he had heard them, Garrison walked back to the entrance of the barn and kicked the milk bucket. Then he went into the tackle room where the guys were sitting. They all looked at him when he entered.

"Don't you men have something to do?" Garrison snapped. "Or am I paying you to sit in this tack room all day?"

The surprised men all jumped up and scattered, leaving behind comments like, "Oh, hey, Boss," and "You know, I think I'll go check that new foal," and "Let me see how Roy is making out over at the smokehouse."

When he returned to the ranch house, Garrison looked into Camila's parlor and stood listening as she read a story to the children. There was a lilt to Camila's voice that was not there when she talked to him. He also heard her laughing with the children.

He stood taking it all in until Ella Grace noticed him and said, "Hi, Daddy." She jumped up and ran to him.

Then Camila closed the book and said, "Storytime is over. Go with your father." She stood and left the parlor quickly, went into her bedroom, and solidly closed that door.

CHAPTER 17

On his Sunday off, when he saw his housekeeper put on her cape and leave the house, Garrison joined Camila at her tree. "What are you reading?" he asked her.

"Matthew 6:14. It says, 'If you forgive those who sin against you, your heavenly Father will forgive you.'" She looked up at him.

His eyes were focused on her. "Do you need to be forgiven, or is there someone you need to forgive, Miss Barnes?"

"Both," she said.

"Is it me, Miss Barnes? If it is, then I want to offer you my apology."

"I accept your apology, Mr. LaRue."

He dropped down to kneel beside her. "So, what have you done that you need to be forgiven for?"

"I'm asking that I might be able to forgive my brother Franklin."

"Why? If I'm not getting too personal."

When she looked at him, he saw pain flash through her eyes. Before she could respond, Garrison stood and took her hands as he guided her to her feet to stand in front of him.

"Go inside and tell Roy that we are going to be gone for a little while," he said. "Tell him to listen for the children. Put on a bonnet, then meet me at the front door."

Before he walked away, he picked up the quilt, shook it, and rolled it under his arm.

Roy had been standing in the summer room watching the younger man and his housekeeper, cook, babysitter, and bride. He whispered to himself, "She's a good woman. Better than ya deserve. Don't mess it up, boy."

When Roy saw Camila coming, he stepped out onto the back porch to meet her.

"What's goin' on, Miz LaRue?" he asked.

Camila gave him Garrison's message then went into the house and up the steps to check on the children. Afterward, she came back downstairs, put on her bonnet, tied it under her chin, and stepped outside through the summer room, where Garrison had pulled up in a one-horse carriage.

Before she could lift her skirts, Garrison came around and lifted her onto the running board, holding her elbow as she stepped into the carriage and sat down. When he climbed into the carriage, he reached back and picked up the quilt and laid it across her lap. "Just so you don't catch a chill before we get back."

"Where are we going?" Camila asked.

Garrison smiled and said, "To a special place."

They rode in silence for ten minutes. Then Garrison stopped the carriage. He looked at Camila and said, "Listen. Can you hear that?"

She turned her head and looked around. "Is that a waterfall?" she asked, smiling.

"Yep, it is. And when I need to get away, I ride up here and sit and listen to the water. Then I ride around the bend and watch the water rush over the edge of the rise and let the mist blow over my face."

They sat for a few moments, listening to the water. Then Garrison spoke to her. "I want to ask you a question, Miss Barnes." He looked at her, and when she said nothing, he pressed forward. "What did you need to get in town last week?"

"Nothing that would concern you," she answered guardedly.

"But you did want something, and you wanted it so badly that you drove yourself to town against my wishes to get that thing. So, what was it?"

When she only looked at him instead of answering his inquiry, Garrison posed another question: "Was it a some*thing* you wanted, or was it a some*one*?"

The intensity of his vocal tone took her by surprise, and in his eyes she recognized the darkening of his gaze as low-grade anger. Camila sighed deeply, stared down at her hands, and stammered her answer. "I . . . umm . . . I needed to see the dressmaker to get measured for some new undergarments. I also needed some cloth and cotton for my monthly. I needed some shoes and a pair of boots that fit my feet, along with some material to make new dresses for Ella and new shirts for GJ."

Although she was not looking at him, Garrison could see her face flush as she was giving him her list of needs. "Well, why didn't you tell me that?"

With intensity in her voice, she said, "I'm a grown woman. I don't feel I have to tell you about my personal needs. Why do I have to report everything I do to you? It's clear that you don't share your personal wants, needs, and desires with me."

Their eyes locked for several moments.

"I don't owe you any explanations about what I do!" he threw at her.

"So why do you expect me to tell you anything about my personal affairs?" she threw back.

His voice was louder than normal when he responded. "Because you're my wife, and a man is supposed to be the head of his wife, and that means she answers to him for everything."

"I am not your wife. I am your cook and your housekeeper, as well as your children's teacher and babysitter. We were joined by a civil ceremony. I'm a wife by contract. Which, by the way, I've never been allowed to see. I'm just someone who works for you without pay. I'm not your wife. You call me Miss Barnes. So don't pull that 'you're my wife' stuff on me."

Garrison was incensed. "You are the most confounded woman I've ever met!" he said. "Why are you so contrary?"

"Confounded, contrary, obstinate, stubborn. You've called me many things, Mr. LaRue. And now you want to know why I'm so out of sorts. Well, let me ask you something. How would you feel if you were a twenty-year-old spinster who was contracted into marriage without your knowledge or permission so that your family could try to rob you of your inheritance, shipped across country, and married in a civil ceremony so that you could live under the same roof with a bullheaded, mulish man who treats you like an indentured servant and blames you for his dead wife's indiscretions? How would you feel? Tell me!"

Camila threw the quilt from her lap, turned in the carriage seat, and jumped out. She quickly walked away, wanting to get as much distance between herself and Garrison LaRue as she could. But before she was able to get more than a few steps, she was lifted from her feet by a hard, muscular arm that felt like a vise around her waist, hauled back to the side of the carriage, and set on her feet.

"Is that why your brother answered my ad instead of you?" Garrison asked. "He told me you were interested but that you were too shy to contact me. He told me that he was authorized to represent you in settling the contract. As a matter of fact, he told me that you preferred a civil marriage in case it didn't work out. And since I didn't know anything about you, I thought it would be smart to sign a contract that said if it didn't work out between us, we could annul the marriage and you would go back to Oklahoma."

She looked at him. "When I found out what Franklin had done, I refused to honor the contract, but he and the owner and manager of the bank, his father-in-law, Lincoln Gilmore, tried to force me to sign the contract they had negotiated with you. When I refused, he said that if I didn't agree to go through with it that I would be sorry. Franklin and his father-in-law threatened to have me declared unstable and dangerous to myself. He also said that you had demanded a dowry that represented two years' allotment of my inheritance. And that you could ruin his reputation with other business owners if I didn't come out here and marry you."

"So," Garrison sighed, "what we have is all built on threats and lies."

Camila started at him, somewhat surprised. "What we *have*? What do we have, Mr. LaRue?"

Looking a little jolted, he stammered, "We . . . well, we have a . . . Umm. A contract. A contract of marriage."

"Oh, really?" Camila said. "What does that mean? What kind of responsibility do we have to each other under the rules and regulations of that contract?"

"We," Garrison continued to stammer, "well . . . under the terms of the contract, you . . . are responsible for taking care of my house and my children. And I am . . . I am responsible for your safety, and . . . I'm responsible to provide you with a place to sleep, clothes to wear, and food."

"I had all of that and more before I met you," she informed him.

"More? What do you mean you had more before you *married* me?" Garrison insisted.

"I have my own home. I have my own money. I had independence, and, Mr. LaRue, I made my own decisions. I didn't have to report to or answer to anyone but God and myself. I even had my own business. *That's* what I mean by more."

Taken aback, Garrison looked at the woman standing before him. Then he asked, "Were you happy. Miss Barnes? Were you at peace with your life?"

"Of course I was happy, and yes, I was at peace. I had the freedom to come and go as I pleased. I went where I wanted to go when I wanted to go. I even went to church when I wanted to without having to ask permission!"

"Well, if you were so happy and free, what are you doing here? You didn't have to come, you know. You could have stayed in Oklahoma in your big empty house, living your big empty spinster life."

Camila recoiled from him like she had been slapped. When she turned her back, he quickly stepped up close to her.

"I'm sorry," Garrison said. "I didn't mean to say that." He took off his hat and rubbed his hand over his hair. "Some of the time, I don't know when to back down. I never meant to say those things to you. Please forgive me, please."

He was standing so close behind her that she could feel his breath on her neck. He could feel her body heat and smell her lavender scent. It seemed natural for him to fold her in his arms, lean forward, and rest his chin on her shoulder.

They stood that way for several minutes, experiencing the moment. Camila had never had the occasion of resting her body against a man, much less a man such as the one holding her at that moment. When she felt her body relax, she slowly closed her eyes, enjoying the experience. But when a moan of contentment began rising in her throat, she quickly removed herself from the man's dangerous embrace.

Garrison was grateful for her decision to move. He felt himself begin to enjoy the feel of her warm, plush, full body in his arms. After a moment to collect himself, he dropped his arms, stepped back, cleared his throat, and touched her elbow to help her back into the carriage.

Camila removed her bonnet, lay her head back on the carriage seat, and closed her eyes. "That sound is so peaceful," she said, "and the sun feels good on my face."

Garrison stared at Camila. Her eyes were closed, and the pale morning sun had added a golden glow to her skin. He could see the shadow of her lashes on her cheeks. Garrison felt a twinge in his chest, and he almost reached across the carriage to caress her face.

But instead, he gripped the reins and urged the horse forward. Then, after a few moments, they stopped again, this time in a place where they were able to see the falls. Camila sat up and just stared at the water rushing down to the pool surrounded by rocks large enough to lay on and feel the mist settle over you.

Garrison saw her eyes were bright and shiny and that she was actually smiling. He liked that. Something inside urged him to touch his lips to hers. Something inside of him desperately wanted to feel her body pressed to his again. His hands tingled with a desire to see if her hair felt as soft as it looked.

"You never accepted my apology, Miss Barnes. Do you forgive me?"

Camila didn't answer but instead asked, "Are you ever going to say such mean and hurtful things to me again?"

Looking into her eyes, Garrison said, "I promise to do my best not to."

"Then I will try to forgive and forget," Camila said with a gleam in her eyes.

Garrison took her hands in his. He didn't speak for a few moments. Finally, he asked, "What do you think? Should we complete the contract? Or would you rather I release you and send you home?"

"That's totally up to you, Mr. LaRue. You are in charge. You're the man of your house. I don't make any decisions. Except you won't have to send me anywhere. I will just leave."

"So are you saying that, if I want you to, you will stay?" he asked quietly.

She softly inquired, "Are you asking me to stay?"

Garrison looked at his wife and offered a half smile. "Yes. At least for another year or two, for my children's sake." He wrapped the reins around the brake lever and stepped down from the carriage. "Come on," he said to her as he lifted the quilt from the seat.

He helped her down and they walked closer to the waterfall. He spread the quilt on the ground. And sitting on the coverlet, watching the water flow over the cliff, he gave in to the desire to kiss her.

She was sitting beside him with her legs stretched in front of her, leaning back on her elbows. Her head was back, and her eyes were closed. She looked so peaceful.

Garrison reached over and touched her cheek. Then his hand moved to the back of her head and pulled three large pins from the tightly wrapped bun. As her hair tumbled loose, she opened her eyes, and he looked for a sign of approval. He saw no resistance. He leaned forward slowly and gently touched his lips to hers. Still no resistance. As a matter of fact, he thought he felt some participation.

Her mouth was soft, and her sweet lavender scent was rising from her clothes. He let his hand travel to her shoulder and gently pressed her back.

She was lying on the quilt, and he was leaning over her. He rolled fully onto his side and moved his hand across her collarbone to the loops that fastened her jacket and her blouse.

Opening her blouse, he could see her breasts rising and falling under her camisole. She looked at him, and he lay his head on her partially exposed breast. She was so soft and warm, and her scent was even stronger. He closed his eyes.

Camila knew that she should resist Garrison LaRue's advances, but he was her husband, and she was experiencing something she had only heard other women talk about: passion. She wanted so desperately to feel a man's lips against her own. She wanted to feel a man's hands caressing her. She wanted him to teach her how to make love.

When he partially exposed her breasts and lay his head on her chest, it seemed so natural for her to fold her arms around him. When she did, she heard him exhale a moan.

Garrison heard himself moan and quickly lifted his head, pushed himself away, and stood up. So that she wouldn't follow him, he said, "You better stay here. I'll be right back."

Confused, Camila sat up and began to button up her blouse and jacket. She had no idea what had happened. Immediately, she started to wonder what she had done wrong.

Camila was feeling a sense of loss as she tried to get her emotions under control. She could see Garrison pacing back and forth in front of the falls. She wanted to go to him and ask what she had done to make him leave, but he didn't look very happy.

When he returned a few minutes later, he helped her to stand, snatched the quilt from the ground, and helped her into the carriage. He climbed in beside her, took the reins, and urged the horse into motion, turning the carriage toward home.

Camila could tell Garrison was angry. She touched his arm. "I'm sorry."

He snatched his arm away like her hand was a hot iron, and without looking at her, he replied, "So am I, Miss Barnes. So am I."

CHAPTER 18

Garrison couldn't get Camila's scent out of his nose, or the look and feel of her out of his mind. Every time they were in the same room, he felt as if he might lose control, and his body had a definite reaction to her presence. Every time she looked at him, her cheeks got warm. She enjoyed the gentle, sensual way he had touched her when they were at the falls, and she unashamedly wanted to feel those hands on her body again.

With all of the awkward thoughts and feelings between them, they kept their distance from each other for several days.

The following Wednesday after breakfast, Garrison followed the ranch hands outside. "Listen, guys," he announced, "my family and I are going to be gone for the next few days. We'll be back Monday morning."

After the noonday meal, when the ranch hands finally left the house and Camila began to clean the kitchen, Garrison said to her, "You need to pack for several days for you and the children. We are going to town this evening, and we'll be there until Monday morning. Take a trunk, because you need to go shopping."

"Really?" she asked, then looked at him tenderly. "Thank you."

In the late afternoon after dinner, Garrison pulled the carriage around to the front of the house. He loaded the empty trunk and two packed carpetbags under the back seat. After helping Camila into the front seat and the children into the back seat of the carriage, they were off.

When they reached Alamosa proper, he turned toward the courthouse and passed it. He drove to a section of town where there were quite a few one-level houses with two, three, and four rooms. They stopped in front of a house with a freshly painted picket fence around the front yard. The house had a red front door and red shutters at the windows. At the end of the street, you could see a churchyard.

"This is the weekend house," Garrison said in a flat tone.

Inside the small house was a large room furnished with a settee and two high-backed cushioned rocking chairs in front of a fireplace. Sitting farther in the depths of the room, on the other side of a short wall, was a small dinner table with four chairs. At the far end of the room, through an arch, was the kitchen.

The house had two separate bedrooms, each with its own warming stove and water room. The first room was furnished with a large bed, big enough for two people to sleep in and still have room. The other bedroom had two smaller beds on opposite walls.

Garrison carried the trunk and the smallest bag into the large room then put the large carpetbag in the smallest of the bedrooms. Then he went outside to carry in wood for the stoves and fireplace.

Camila brought a picnic basket to the table and laid out a late snack. After they had eaten, Garrison reported, "I have to go to work. You and the children go to bed, and tomorrow morning, I'm going to show you where everything is in town. Don't wait up for me. I sleep at the office when I'm in town. I'll be back in the morning."

After she had cleaned the kitchen and gotten little GJ and Ella Grace washed and settled in bed, Camila went into the sitting room and sat in front of the fireplace. She was enjoying the quiet of her new surroundings.

After a few minutes, her mind began to wander. She imagined making some changes to this house the way she had done with the ranch house. Camila looked around, smiling and thinking about what she would have to order, when she heard footsteps and saw a shadow pass slowly by the window. This happened several times, and because this was her first time in the weekend house, she was unsettled.

She recalled that when they first met, Contessa had told her some of the history of the weekend house. She told Camila that Grace had been suspected of entertaining a gentleman there from time to time, and when someone told Garrison, he had the house boarded up. A short while after that, Grace was killed in the accident.

I certainly hope no one thinks something like that is still happening in this house, Camila thought to herself.

She stood and shook her head; she was scaring herself. Her mind went to how she would protect the children if someone tried to enter the house. After the figure walked past the window for a third time, Camila got up, pulled the drapes tighter, and engaged the night latch on the front and side doors of the cottage. After that, the walking stopped.

In the morning when Garrison returned, he had to knock on the door several times before Camila opened it.

"What's going on in here?" He stepped into the house looking around and asked loudly, "Why are the doors latched and the drapes closed?" He snatched the drapes on the windows back open. "Open these things."

She wanted to tell him why everything was like it was, but the children were watching her closely and she didn't want to frighten them or show disrespect to their father in front of them, so she simply said, "It's a new place for me. I was a little uncomfortable about sleeping in an unfamiliar place."

"Really?" he said. "A grown woman afraid of a new place. Come now, Miss Barnes."

She saw his shoulders rise and fall as he chuckled, and all she wanted to do was punch him in his gut. She snatched up her reticule and opened the door. "If we're going shopping, we should be going, then." As he walked past her, Camila said softly to him, "I don't appreciate being made fun of in front of the children."

This time, instead of a chuckle, he laughed outright. "Yes, *Miss Barnes,* please excuse me, *Miss Barnes.*" His smile faded, and he walked out of the house holding his children's hands. "Let's go shopping," he said with a mirthful lilt to his voice.

CHAPTER 19

It only took five minutes to walk to the center of town. When they got there, Garrison explained, "I'm sure you remember, but across the street, there's the bank, the general store, the dressmaker, the milliner's, and the shoemaker. As you can see, on the other side of the street is the restaurant and saloon. At the far end of the street is the freight office, and of course my office and the jail. While you're shopping today, tell them you want to put your purchases on my account, but don't go crazy. Those bills have to be paid at the end of the month." He looked down at Camila and stepped back. "I have to get to the office."

He walked Camila and the children to the mercantile. Leaving them there, he felt as though he were making a mistake.

"I'll be back in a few minutes. I have to go check on things at the office," he said, then walked away.

When Camila stepped into the store, there were two older women looking at material, and when they realized she was with Garrison LaRue's children, they looked at her disapprovingly. One pointed to her and the children, and the other one whispered something to the other.

Contessa walked over to Camila. "Hello, Camila, glad to see you and these two little ones today." Contessa looked at the man behind the counter and waved him over. "Hank, here she is. Our sister-in-law is here."

Hank smiled. "Hello, Camila, it's nice to see you again. Welcome back to Anderson's Mercantile. When you're ready, let me know what I can get for you today?" Then he stepped back and regarded the children. "Say, don't I know these little ones? Could it be? Are you my nephew and my niece?"

He bent down and scooped Ella Grace up into his arms. Then he grabbed Little Garrison's shoulder and took them over to the cracker barrel, giving them three crackers apiece and letting them sit on the bench by the window.

Camila smiled. "Hank, I'd like to get a pair of shears, some material, needles, thread, ribbon, and lace, if you have some, please." Raising her hand, she added, "I may as well have you fill this grocery list, as well as this notions list."

While Camila was waiting for her order to be tallied and wrapped, Hilda Anderson, the judge's wife, came into the store. She saw Camila and said, "Hello, my dear. How are you doing today?"

She and Camila talked for a few minutes until Hank Anderson interrupted. "Excuse me, ladies," he said, then hugged his mother. "Hello, Momma." Looking at Camila, he said, "I already know the answer, but I have to ask so he won't get upset." With a sheepish grin, he then asked, "Do you want me to put this on Garrison's account?"

Smiling, Camila replied, "No, Hank. This doesn't go on his account." Then she added, "I'm going to pay cash for everything."

Hank raised his eyebrows as gasps were heard around the room. The storekeeper stepped to the counter and presented her with the tally sheet. Slowly taking her money, the surprised man wordlessly laid the bills in the cash drawer just as Garrison was returning from his office. The two older ladies still in the store began to whisper almost feverishly when they saw him, moving their eyes from the sheriff to his mail-order bride in anticipation of something to gossip about later.

They were more than taken aback when the sheriff looked at them with a quirky smile, grabbed Camila's hand, and brought her over to them. Touching the brim of his hat and dipping his head in a greeting, Garrison said, "Mrs. Giles, Mrs. Mayes. Good afternoon, ladies. I know you two busybodies are wondering who this is. Well, she's my wife. Yeah, that's right. I've gone and done it again . . . finally. Now, go on about your business and start spreading that and any gossip you are going to add to it. Just be sure to tell them that her name is Camila Rose, and tell them how pretty she is."

Camila tightened her grip on Garrison's hand and looked up at him. When he looked down at her, he gave her a quick wink and kissed her cheek. Tessa Anderson laughed behind her hand as the ladies huffed and stormed out of the store.

Garrison turned to Camila and pointed to the boxes and packages. "Is this all ours?" When she nodded, he picked up the smaller parcels, looked at Hank, and said, "Can you have the rest delivered to the weekend house later this afternoon?"

As soon as his brother-in-law confirmed his request, Garrison and his family walked out of the store. A few steps down the street, Garrison turned to Camila.

"Leave the children with me," he said. "I'm taking this to the house, and we'll meet you at the dressmaker's."

Inside the dressmaker's shop, when Camila came out of the dressing room, five women were sitting in the waiting room. None of them wanted anything. They were just there to see Garrison LaRue's new wife. Word had spread around town, and women were coming from everywhere. Some were even standing outside of the dressmaker's shop looking in the window.

Inside the shop, one of the women stepped forward. "So you're the mail-order bride? Oh, aren't you different from the first Mrs. LaRue? I would even venture to say that you and she are total opposites of each other."

Camila smiled pleasantly. "Who are you? And, just as a point of interest, I don't remember asking you for your opinion."

"I'm Mildred Horn, and these ladies are members of the Ladies' Mission Society, of which I am the president. And just so you know, I am also the nurse to the town's doctor. So how does it feel being married to a man who has been scorned and shamed by the actions of a whorish wife?"

Camila's smile waned a little but remained. "Hello, ladies, and, uh . . . Mildred Horn. Let me first say this to you: Even though we have just met, I can tell right away that you are the town gossips, because to me 'The Ladies' Mission' *Society* means town busybodies, and 'president' means that you, Miss Horn, are the busiest of all the gossiping busybodies in the whole town. And since you had the nerve to ask, let me tell you something about my husband. Garrison LaRue treats me like a queen. I don't want for anything, and that includes his love and affection. When he wraps me in his strong, muscular arms and holds me close, I lay my head on his broad, solid chest and feel comforted and protected. I couldn't ask for a better husband. Now, if there's anything else you want to know, like what happens during our private time . . . well, that's none of your business. But let me just repeat something I said earlier: As the wife of Garrison LaRue, I don't want for anything!"

The other ladies in the shop gasped and huffed. Two ladies began to fan themselves furiously while Mildred gushed, "Well, I have never! How dare you be so forward?"

"Maybe I can ask you the same thing, *Mildred*," Camila said with a voice full of scorn. She slowly looked the woman up and down then continued, "What makes you think you can get into my business?"

Before Mildred Horn could answer, Garrison, who had been standing in the lobby of the shop from the beginning of the conversation between the two women, spoke up. "Good afternoon, ladies. I see you've already met my lovely wife." Looking from the array of women in the shop to his wife, he smiled and asked Camila, "Are you ready?"

When she smiled and nodded her head, Garrison tore his gaze from his wife's alluring eyes and tipped his hat for the second time that day. As his lips replicated a warm smile, he gently took Camila's elbow, but as they were walking toward the door of the shop with GJ and Ella Grace in tow, Mildred Horn stepped forward and began to verbally challenge him.

"Why a mail-order, Garrison? What's wrong with the women of Alamosa? Do we know too much of your business? Does she know about the first wife? Does she know about the fallen angels that you visit up on the hill at Miss Ann's House of Comfort? Does she know that your wife was a fallen woman and was running away with . . ."

Camila stepped up to the woman. "Listen, *Mildred Horn*, you are much too mouthy. Don't you see these children standing here? You need to shut that mouth of yours before I shut it for you."

"Shut my mouth? Shut it for me? Who do you think you're talking to?" Mildred spat, stunned.

"I know exactly who I'm talking to. I'm talking to you, a pitiful woman who apparently has no business of her own so she gets into other people's business. And if I didn't know better, I would think that this attack was because he is my husband and not yours."

The two ladies stood looking at each other. Camila raised her hand and pointed her finger into Mildred's face.

"Just let me tell you something, Mildred Horn," she continued, "when it comes to me and my family, from now on you better mind your own business. Doesn't the scripture say, 'Let he who is without sin cast the first stone'? Are you without sin, Miss Horn? Are you so pure that you can sit in judgment of others? I don't think so, because you've just been caught in the sins of gossiping, passing judgment, and oh, yes, coveting." Camila stepped back and smiled. "Now I hope you have a wonderful day, and I'm looking forward to seeing you in church on Sunday afternoon."

Garrison opened the door, guided the children out of the dress shop, then put his hand on the small of Camila's back and guided her outside. Tipping his hat again, Garrison said, "Ladies," and closed the door.

Once outside, Garrison smiled ear to ear. "Well," he said, "I certainly don't think you made any friends in there today, Miss Barnes."

Before they could get too far down the street, someone called out, "Sheriff, Mrs. LaRue. Yoo-hoo! Mrs. LaRue, Sheriff . . . you forgot your order form."

Mrs. Aires, the dressmaker, was quickly walking after them, waving a piece of paper. When she got close to them, she laughed.

"Thank you so much for your business," she said. "Your merchandise will be ready in a week. And thank you for being the one to finally stop that woman's mouth. For a little while, at least." Then she took Camila's hands in hers and pressed lightly, looking at Garrison, and said, "I like her, Garrison. She has spunk." Then, turning her eyes back to Camila, Mrs. Aires said, "Welcome to Alamosa, Mrs. LaRue."

CHAPTER 20

Church on Sunday afternoon indeed was interesting. Mildred Horn was in attendance, but she refused to look at Camila as she sat with the LaRue children.

However, periodically during the service, Camila would look up from her Bible to see one of the familiar-looking men seated on the deacon's bench looking back at her. Once or twice he smiled and nodded his head, so she smiled and nodded back politely. After the service, several women introduced themselves to Camila, invited her to tea, and promised to visit her very soon at LaRue Crossing.

As soon as they could get away, Camila and the children walked from the church to the center of town, where they were soon sitting on the restaurant side of Miss Kit's Restaurant and Saloon, waiting for Garrison to join them.

After they were seated and the children were settled, Camila looked around the restaurant and noticed a man watching her intently. She recognized him as the same man from church. Out of courtesy, she offered him a quick smile and again began attending to the children.

When she looked up next, she realized the man was walking toward them. Not knowing what else to do, Camila watched him move close. She noticed that the man had a limp and was using a cane to navigate his way across the large table-filled room. She didn't know why, but something about the way the man walked made her uneasy.

Before she could dwell too long on the reason for her discomfort, the man stopped beside the table and introduced himself. "Good afternoon, Miz LaRue, my name is George Tate. I'm the deacon at our fine church, and I'm also a teller at the town bank."

Camila nodded her head in recognition. She also recognized him as the same man who had been in a guarded conversation with Mildred Horn after church service ended. "Since it seems that you are alone," he added, "do you mind if I join you?"

"Good afternoon, Mr. Tate," Camila said. "Thank you for stopping, but *we* are waiting for my husband."

George Tate smiled at Camila. "So the sheriff finally allowed you to come view our fair town, did he? My hope was that one day he would stop hiding you on that ranch and formally introduce you to us town folk."

When she made no attempt to answer him, George continued, this time leaning forward and invading Camila's space. "Mrs. Horn and I are friends. I believe that you and she have spoken. And I see that she was quite wrong, you're a sweet young thing, aren't you? And I understand that you have quite a sassy mouth, too. I like that in a woman."

Camila pulled her elbow away from the man and slid her chair closer to the children. Before she could speak, she felt a flood of heat engulf her body.

Just then, Garrison arrived, stepping between George Tate and his family. "Tate, I don't ever want to see you talking to my wife again."

"Is there a problem, Sheriff? I saw this young lady in church this morning all alone with these children. She doesn't have a ring on, so how am I supposed to know she's your wife? Can't a man talk to a lady and let her know he's interested?"

Taking a deep breath and leaning forward, Garrison's eyes became stony and his voice dropped. "Walk away, George, while you still can."

George Tate smiled uneasily and took one more quick look at Camila. Then he defiantly touched his hat, said, "Miz LaRue" and slowly walked away.

A few uneasy steps later, he was entering the saloon with Garrison's cold eyes locked on his back. Once there, the smaller man ordered a drink, slowly released his breath, and quickly sat at a table before his legs failed him.

Garrison turned his attention back to his family. Looking at Camila, he barked, "We're not staying here. Get up. Let's go."

He reached out to help the children from their chairs left Miss Kit's restaurant, almost dragging the little ones.

As the four of them headed toward the weekend house, Garrison said, "I don't ever want to see you speaking to that man again. I don't ever want my children in his presence. Never again! Ever! do you understand?"

When Camila didn't answer him, he stopped, faced her, and leaned down close to her.

"Did you hear me? I asked you a question, and I expect an answer, Miss Barnes!"

The tone in his voice, the strained look on his face, and the depth of his breathing warned Camila not to comment but to just agree to honor his request. She slowly nodded her head. This was a side of him she had not seen to date. She imagined this was probably the same attitude he exhibited when working as the sheriff.

When they got to the house, he opened the door, picked up the children, and carried them through the door. Then he took them to their bedroom and set them down. "You guys take a nap," he said, "and I'll see you when I get home from work."

After kissing GJ and Ella Grace on their cheeks, Garrison returned to the main room and trained his gaze on Camila.

"Lock this door," he said. "Don't answer it no matter what. Be ready to go back to the ranch by nine o'clock in the morning. And don't ever talk to that man again!"

"Garrison?" Camila asked. "What is this all about?"

"Just do as you're told!" he threw out at her.

Taking in a deep breath, Camila asked, "Why are you angry at me?"

"That man was out of line. He was trying to get close to you. Don't you know when someone is flirting with you, woman?"

Camila saw the nerve in Garrison's jaw jumping. She didn't know why he was being so mean, but instead of getting pulled into an argument, she drew another deep breath before speaking. "We didn't get to eat," she said, "and the children are hungry."

"Well, do your job and cook something!" Garrison snapped shaking his head. He stepped out of the house, closed the door soundly, and didn't walk away until he heard her engage the lock.

On Monday morning, they rode home in silence, and nothing was mentioned about George Tate again.

CHAPTER 21

That Tuesday morning, Garrison noticed Camila wasn't acting her usual self. He thought maybe she was angry about what had happened on Sunday afternoon, or that maybe she was tired and needed some time off. Whatever it was, he had no intention of getting pulled into a discussion with her at the moment. So, after breakfast, he followed the ranch hands out to the corral and worked with the horses the entire morning.

At the end of the noonday meal, he came into the kitchen but she wasn't there. He looked out of the kitchen window and saw her wrapped in her cape, headed in the direction of the tree where she studied her scriptures when it was still warm enough to sit outside.

Garrison quickly left the kitchen and caught up with her. Camila heard him coming and turned around.

"I'm going into town," Garrison said. "Do you want to come with me?"

"No," Camila answered in a flat voice.

Garrison touched her shoulder. "Is something wrong? Do you feel sick?"

But Camila only repeated her two-letter answer: "No."

Still, Garrison wouldn't relent. "Something is wrong. What is it?"

Camila stepped back and away from his warm hand on her shoulder. "I've been here for over seventeen months," she said. "I want to go visit my family. My brother Sherman wrote to me he got married, and I would like to meet Athena, my new sister-in-law."

"You can't go," Garrison said. "It's almost too late in the year to take that kind of trip."

"I miss my family."

"If you were to go, how long do you think you would be gone?"

"Two months."

Looking surprised, Garrison said, "What am I supposed to do with my children for those two months?"

"I can take them with me," Camila offered.

Garrison couldn't believe she had just said that. "No! My children don't go anywhere without me. You can't go. Besides, in that time the weather will take a turn and you won't be able to get back before the spring. You'll be gone for the holiday season. That's just inconvenient."

Camila's face was drawn, and her eyes were piercing. "Did you treat your wife like you're trying to treat me?"

Garrison stepped close to Camila, leaned over, and almost touched his nose to hers. "You won't talk to me like that. What happened between me and my wife is none of your business. Don't you ever talk about her again."

Throwing her hands on her hips, she asked, "Why?"

Garrison huffed. "You have no right. Besides, what happened in my life before you arrived is none of your business."

"Really? So what you are saying is that I don't have a right to know what I've gotten myself into by becoming the replacement wife?"

"You have a right to know what I want you to know," Garrison retorted.

Not backing down, Camila countered with, "And you have no right to treat me like I belong to you, like your livestock." Her voice rose. "You have no right to force me to stay here with no friends and no social life. You have no right to steal my life from me!"

"You're my wife, and you are under my rule," Garrison said with an edge to his voice.

"A wife in name only," Camila said, squaring her shoulders. "We never had a night in the marriage bed. And I don't have to stay here if I don't want to."

Garrison huffed loudly. "A night in the marriage bed? Is that what you're mad about? Because we don't sleep together? It's not that kind of marriage, lady! Don't flatter yourself, you are not the kind of woman I desire."

"Don't flatter *yourself*, Mr. LaRue. I would never let a man like you touch me. I have a family, and I want to see them. I wouldn't expect someone like you to understand family loyalty."

"Someone like me? Not understanding family loyalty? Just what does that mean? What are you trying to say?"

"I'm saying that you are a self-centered, bullheaded, pompous horse's butt! Is that plain enough for you?"

The two stood toe to toe, Camila with her hands on her hips, Garrison with his arms crossed over his chest, neither one blinking.

After a very long moment, it looked as if a light turned on in Garrison's eyes, and he smiled. "If you leave," he said, "you owe me $650."

"Oh, really?" Camila said. "You just stay right here, then, mister!" She turned and stormed into the house. When she returned, she slapped an envelope against his chest and said, "Here. I hope you enjoy it."

Surprised, Garrison snatched the envelope, opened it, and pulled out two bank drafts for $325 each. He looked at them and then at Camila, but she was walking back to the house. He ran up behind her, circled her waist with his arm, and lifted her off the ground.

"Stop!" she said. "What are you doing? Put me down."

Garrison carried her back to the tree, set her on her feet, and turned her around to face him. He held up the envelope and shook it. "Where did you get these?"

"They each represent a year of my allotment. I know that you were promised two years, and if you feel that they are not enough, I will give you the rest when I leave."

"I don't want your money," Garrison declared.

"Well, then, what? What do you want?" she asked, trembling.

"I . . . don't want you to go," Garrison said.

The air was still, and all that could be heard was their deep breathing.

Garrison took his hat off and smoothed his other hand over the leather strip holding back his blue-black wavy hair. "I'm afraid you won't come back."

"If I take the children, I'll have to come back."

"The children? Why do you want to take my children? You are not their mother."

Camila turned her back to him. "I may not be the kind of woman that a man would want as a wife. And I may not be the natural mother of your children. But after being here all this time and being with little GJ and Ella Grace, I know that I can love a child like a real mother can. I want to prove to my family that I'm not worthless as a woman. Especially one they consider to be no good for anything in this world. Even if a man will never love me, at least those sweet, innocent little children love me. And I love them. I want to show my family the two precious little ones that make me happier than I've ever been in my whole adult life."

Garrison's stern look waned, and his hard voice softened. "It's too late in the year to travel that far. Can you wait until the spring?"

She lifted her apron and wiped her face, then turned and looked at her in-name-only husband. "Excuse me," she said and stepped past him back in the direction of the house.

Once inside, she snatched off her wrap and flung it onto a peg on the wall, stepped into the kitchen, laid her apron on the back of a chair, and quickly entered her rooms. She lowered her body onto her bed and tried to collect herself. A few moments after she settled down, she felt some weight at the foot of the bed. Looking up, she saw the children kneeling near her feet.

Ella Grace spoke first. "What's the matter, Mommy? Are you sad?"

Not waiting for Camila to answer, little GJ asked, "Why are you sad? Do you need some hugs and kisses like Daddy when he's sad?"

Camila sat up, and the children scrambled to sit with her. Ella sat on her lap, and GJ sat leaning into her side under her arm. "I'm not sad, I'm happy," she said. "I'm happy to be your new mommy. I love you so much."

"And Daddy," Ella said. "Do you love Daddy, too?"

Camila snuggled the children to her and whispered, "Well, little lady, he is your daddy, and I love him for that." She tightened her hold on the children and kissed them both on their cheeks, then tickled each one.

Garrison watched the interaction between Camila and his children. He listened to their conversation and enjoyed hearing their laughter. As he stepped away from the door, Garrison thought, *I can't ever remember Grace spending that kind of time with them.*

With his head down and his heart full of emotion, he went back outside to the barn, saddled his horse, and rode away from the ranch.

CHAPTER 22

It was after dark when Garrison returned home. He walked through the summer room into the kitchen and saw Camila sitting at the table.

"Why didn't you ever get married?" he asked as he pulled a chair out to sit down.

"No one that I liked ever asked me," she said honestly.

"Why?" he asked softly as he looked into her eyes.

Camila hunched her shoulders, and after a few moments, she said, "I guess it's because earlier in my life, my oldest brother was very protective, and so there were not many young men who could get to know me well enough to court me. Then I spent a year in finishing school, and after that, I went to a women's college. Near the end of my second year, my parents were injured in a fire started by lightning, and I had to return home to help them try to recover from their injuries. I spent two years taking care of my mother and three years taking care of my father."

"What about after they were gone?" Garrison asked curiously.

"Well, by then I was nineteen years old. I went back to school and finished my last year. Since I had no suitors, there was nothing else to do but go back home. I was living in my parents' home, and I started working in the bank, but when a man needed a job, they released me and gave him my position. So I began to help my oldest brother in his store.

"After a year, I noticed that he was chasing away anyone who showed interest. When I asked him why, he said that I was good for business and he didn't want to lose me. Then he said that since I was a spinster, he was afraid I would meet someone who would be after my money. So he thought it was his duty to be the one to find me a husband. Then he got married and his wife started helping him at the mercantile. He claimed he didn't need me anymore and insisted I should get married. But by then, all the young men in my age group were already married."

Garrison looked perplexed. "So you have never been asked by any man to be his wife?"

"I didn't say I had never been asked," she replied. "I said that no one I liked ever asked me."

"Who were they?" Garrison asked. "Why didn't you like them?"

With a sour look on her face, she answered, "His name is Lincoln Gilmore. My sister-in-law's father. I don't like him because he's a money-hungry, low-down snake in the grass. He didn't want me, he wanted control of my inheritance. Just the thought of him touching me makes my skin crawl."

"So, you turned him down. What about the others?"

"There were no others," Camila said softly, her hands folded in her lap.

Garrison moved to the edge of the chair and leaned forward, touching her hands. "I don't know why you would want to go back there. Sounds to me like the men in Checotah are fools."

Camila raised her head and looked at Garrison but said nothing.

After a few moments, Garrison released her hands and sat back in his chair. "After you had no job, what did you do?"

Smiling wistfully, Camila said, "I started my own business. I made carpetbags and sold them. I shipped them to different mercantile and general stores across the country. My brother Manny would cut the wood to make the handles for me, but I would sand, decorate, polish, and attach them to the bags. And by then, in the town and surrounding areas, I had gotten the reputation of being a free-spirited, free-thinking, independent woman."

Garrison smiled but didn't comment.

"Besides," Camila continued, "I've never been the kind of woman a man wants as a wife. Like my brother Franklin often took great pleasure in telling me: Rather than being dainty like a real lady, I'm big-boned. I'm too tall. I don't know how to fix myself up like a lady. I'm too opinionated. I'm as strong as a horse, and I have more education than most men. Those are not attributes that men look for in a wife."

"Well," Garrison said, "I see you as an intelligent, resourceful, open-hearted, giving, loving woman who would make the right man a good wife someday."

"That day will probably never come," Camila replied with a sad smile.

"Why do you think that way?" he asked, surprised.

Camila looked into Garrison's dark eyes. "By the time you find a woman you want to be married to in the biblical sense and she comes to take care of the children and takes over cooking and doing the housework, I will truly be too old to get married."

She stood and walked across the room to go into her parlor. When she turned to close the door, Garrison was standing behind her, filling up the doorframe. He put his hand on the door so she wouldn't close it in his face, then said, "About your trip to Oklahoma. I'll let you go. I'll let you take my children. I'll let you be there for a month. But if you are not back here after that, I'm coming after you. No matter what the weather is like."

Without thinking, Camila threw her arms around Garrison LaRue's neck and kissed him. It was meant to be a quick thank-you kiss, but his arms quickly wrapped around her waist and pulled her close. Close enough for her to feel more than his belt buckle.

He broke the kiss, looked down into her eyes, and smiled. Then he kissed her again, and this time, it could not be interpreted as anything other than an "I want you" kiss.

Forcing himself to end contact with Camila, Garrison looked at her with hooded eyes and said, "Woman, every time I'm near you, you make me think about doing things I'm not supposed to do."

Tightening his hold on her, he leaned in, pressing his forehead against hers, whispering her name, and kissing her slowly and gently.

Abruptly, he broke the kiss, dropped his arms, stepped back, and said, "Close the door."

As the door was closing, she could hear him stomping through the kitchen toward the staircase. She also heard him growl.

CHAPTER 23

By the time she got up to make the coffee the next morning, Garrison was already gone. He had, however, left a note for her on the kitchen worktable.

I'll be back on Monday. Take care of my children. Don't forget the rules. Even though I think it's too late in the season to be traveling, start packing for the trip. I'll get the tickets. The sooner you all leave, the sooner you all will return. Garrison.

This particular morning, after his weekly visit to his parents' house, the ride to town was somber. Garrison's mind was in a jumbled state. So many thoughts were rolling around inside of him that he had a hard time keeping them under control.

He thought about how his life had changed in the year and several months.

He thought about the person who was responsible for those changes: Miss Camila Rose Barnes.

He thought about how good it was to once again hear joy come back into the voices of his children.

"And now she wants to take my children back to visit her family. Like they are her children, and I guess that somehow, her family has become their family."

He was not feeling like letting them go was the right thing to do, mainly because she would be gone, too. And with her would go the delicious meals she cooked every day, the bright, clean, dust-free house, and the sound of laughter from his children. But most of all, her fresh lavender scent would be gone too.

Just as he rode into town, Garrison saw George Tate. "Great," he mumbled under his breath, "that's all I needed to start my day."

Tate had been Grace LaRue's secret lover. He had also been the one driving the carriage when the accident that took her life happened. By now, Tate had recovered from his injuries, but he had to use a cane and would have to for the rest of his life.

The accident had killed Grace, the mother of Garrison's children. Leaving them to grow up without the love of a mother, and forcing him to take on a mail-order bride in order to get some consistent—and hopefully, permanent—help in raising little Garrison and Ella Grace.

As luck would have it, Tate was standing outside the bank, which was where Garrison was headed. Not wanting to deal with the man's snide remarks just yet, Garrison decided to wait until later to do his banking.

As he rode down the street toward his office, the two men locked eyes.

George Tate looked at Garrison LaRue and smiled. "Morning, Sheriff."

Garrison didn't acknowledge the greeting. He just stared at George Tate and continued down the street.

After the noonday mealtime, when the businesses on Main Street reopened for the afternoon, Garrison entered the bank and went directly to the president's office.

Mr. Aires greeted Garrison heartily. "Well, hello, Sheriff. How can I help you today?"

Garrison gave the man the bank drafts that Camila had shoved at him during their argument. "Mr. Aires," he said, "I want to use these to start an account for my wife. It has to be in her name only. And she'll be the only one who can deposit or withdraw funds."

Mr. Aires looked at Garrison confusedly. "Sheriff, this is a lot of money. Why does a woman need this much money?"

With a straight look, Garrison replied, "Mr. Aires, this is her money. Her brothers contracted it to me as a dowry, but I don't want or need it. She should have some money of her own in the bank just in case something happens to me. Besides, I have no rights to her money. So will you do this for her, please? I'll tell her about her account when I get home on Monday afternoon."

The bank president cleared his throat. "Uh, Sheriff, your wife already has an account at this bank. She makes a $30 deposit every month. Do you want to add this to her account, or start a new one?"

Even though he was not supposed to be involved in the transaction that was taking place, George Tate insinuated himself into the situation anyway. He stood outside of the partially closed door to Mr. Aires' office and listened, overhearing the sheriff tell the bank president to add the two bank drafts to his wife's already existing account.

Isn't that interesting? he thought to himself. *She has money of her own. I wonder if she's as needy for a man's attention as his last wife was?*

When he heard a chair scrape across the wooden floor, George Tate scurried like the rat he was back to his teller's window. He pretended to be restocking his drawer for the afternoon business when the two men exited Mr. Aries' office.

With his head down, he watched Garrison cross the bank to the exit door. But before he left, he turned around, and the two men's eyes met.

Tate smiled wickedly. "Have a good afternoon, Sheriff."

Garrison didn't miss a step as he closed the door behind him, even though he wanted to punch George Tate in the face.

Camila worked hard the next two days. She mended, washed, pressed, and packed clothes in the trunk. She was excited thinking about the trip back home. She wanted her brothers to see that her life was going well in spite of what Franklin had done to her.

Even though it's not a real marriage, I want to show Franklin that I do have the ability to be a good wife and mother, she thought several times when her courage began to slip as she was preparing and packing the clothes.

When dinner was over on Friday night and the children were taking their baths, Camila decided to tell them about the trip. After they cleaned up and they were in their nightshirts, she showed them pictures of her brothers and told them stories about the fun things they did as they were growing up. The children enjoyed the stories and asked her questions about her trip from Oklahoma to Colorado until they were too tired to keep their eyes open.

CHAPTER 24

George Tate was furiously pacing the floor of his boarding-house room. The loud click of his cane on the floor added to his frustration. He looked around his room with disdain. His thoughts included questions that centered around his station in life.

Why do I have to be the one to live like this? Why do I have to be the one who lives in the shadows of life? It's not supposed to be this way. I'm a good person. I'm a better person than that half-breed savage! Why is it he is always given everything on a silver platter and I have to work like a slave for the little that I get?

Even though he chose not to admit it, George's parents were different also. That was why the family hadn't lived in town when he was growing up. His father, Calvin, was half-white, and his mother, Sarah, was Black. They had been slaves on the same farm.

The owners of the farm, the Tates, fell on hard times after slavery ended, and a few years later when they could no longer afford to keep the freed slaves, they gave Calvin their last name and let him leave.

Sarah lived on the Tate farm too, all alone and with no family, so when she was told to leave or be killed, Calvin took pity on her, and they left together. They worked small jobs as they traveled, and when they made it to Alamosa, they married. Using what little money they had, they staked a claim on a small plot of land. Sarah and Calvin tried farming, and it was successful for a while—until he grew fonder of drinking than farming.

George, who looked more like his father, felt that even though he was not all-white, he was still more acceptable than a half-breed savage like Garrison LaRue and his stuck-up half-breed sister, Contessa. George had a lot of hate toward others, but he hated Garrison LaRue the most. He had hated him from the moment they met.

Garrison and Contessa's parents were also an odd pair. Their father, Thaddeus, was a freed slave, and their mother, Anna Wolf, was a full-blooded Indian. When the LaRue's bought the land that bordered the Tate farm, their ranch began to prosper almost immediately. By that time, George's father had a difficult time even making grass grow. So Mrs. Tate became the town washwoman, working for nickels and dimes just so they could eat.

George remembered his mother getting paid and having to hide the money so his father couldn't take it and run to town to drink it up, then come home drunk and beat him and his mother until he was tired or passed out.

George hated his father, but he hated the LaRues more because they were so willing to help him and his mother. George always felt it was out of pity that they offered their help.

Anna Wolf began helping Sarah with the washing, and showing her how to get away from her husband when he came home drunk.

Garrison would come over two, sometimes three days a week to help George and his mother establish and maintain the garden, as well as showing them how to care for the two pigs, five chickens, one workhorse, and milk cow that Mr. LaRue had "loaned" them.

More than a few times, George and his mother sneaked out the back door and ran across the field to the LaRue house to get away from Calvin Tate. Finally, one day, Calvin staggered up to the door of the LaRue's house, demanding to see his wife and son. He made the bad decision to strike out at Thaddeus, who proceeded to beat Calvin into a sniveling, quivering lump of drunken flesh.

Soon after that incident, Calvin Tate left Alamosa and never returned. George blamed the LaRues for his father's desertion. *If they had minded their own business,* he thought, *things would have worked out just fine. But they ruined everything, making my father look like a sluggard. Embarrassing our family and making us look like trash.*

When George's mother became worn out and sickly and wasn't able to earn enough money to pay off the last of the mortgage, Thaddeus LaRue purchased the land and told Mrs. Tate that they could stay on the property for as long as they liked. He even asked if they would consider running the property as a chicken-and-egg farm.

Almost immediately, Sarah Tate agreed. She was glad to be able to pay the LaRues back for their kindness. George was not happy about everyone knowing that those people were keeping him and his mother alive. He was not happy that he had to be beholden to a mixed-up family like theirs.

To make matters worse, Garrison began to steal George's thunder in school. So George began to tease, torment, and challenge Garrison in every way he could imagine. Watching Garrison get blamed and punished for things that he had not done gave George some satisfaction, but it was short-lived and never enough. Then, when the new teacher came and put a stop to George's shenanigans, he had to find a new way to put that uppity Black savage in his place.

Having an affair with Grace LaRue had accomplished that, but not for long. She had become too clingy just because she was carrying what she claimed to be his baby. George wasn't about to let her tie him down. Besides, she had already served her purpose to him. Although he wasn't glad when she died, George felt some relief in being freed from that woman.

Now Garrison had remarried, and his new wife was setting things back on track for him again. She was the exact opposite of Grace. She was naturally pretty; no makeup was needed. She was tall, had a full chest, a smaller waist, and nice, round hips. And now it appeared Garrison LaRue had come out on top again because she even had her own money. A lot more than he imagined she had.

George knew these things because he always made sure he waited on her when she came to the bank to deposit those thirty-dollar drafts every month, and now LaRue had deposited almost seven hundred dollars in the bank for her.

She was loyal to that mutt, and that loyalty had almost gotten George killed. George knew better than to press any issue with Garrison because he was a tall, powerfully built man with a broad chest, strong arms, and a mean, no-nonsense disposition. Now George felt he had to do something to knock LaRue down a peg again, and he had to do it soon.

With a sinister smile, he thought to himself, *This time, I won't just stop with one family member. I'm going to get them all. Then, when I leave town, I'll be a happy, satisfied man.*

CHAPTER 25

On Saturdays, the ranch hands usually rode into town. Most of the time, one would stay behind, but this weekend, all of the men would be gone. That left Camila and the children to themselves.

This was good. She was tired from all of the packing for her trip, and she was glad she didn't have to cook the large meals. Along with that, she and the children could sleep in and have their favorite Sunday-morning breakfast, fried mush cakes with mixed berry syrup and crispy bacon.

Before everyone left, Roy wanted Camila and the children to be comfortable while they were gone, and he especially didn't want Camila to have to go outside for any reason when the storm rolled in. He made sure that the ranch hands chopped extra wood for the house, and he had Jarrod get some meat from the smokehouse and put it in the cooler pantry in the kitchen along with extra eggs and butter. Then he had Wesley prepare the fireplaces and fill the storage boxes beside each fireplace.

Later that morning, when it was time to leave, Roy let the younger men go ahead while he stopped in to make sure Camila and the children would be comfortable with everyone being gone. "You know, Miz LaRue, I don't have ta go. I hate thinking 'bout you and the little ones being here all alone. Even for a little while."

Camila promptly spoke up, "Roy, you're going to the general store to get supplies for next week. You're probably also going to the saloon to sit and socialize with some friends, then you're heading back home. What could possibly happen in those few hours?"

"Well, ma'am, that's not somethin' I want to think about. So, I'm-a need you to stay close to the house. As a matter of fact," he offered, "we got a storm comin' so you may not want to leave the house. Y'all stay put, and I'll be back soon's I can."

She touched Roy's face and rubbed his scraggly beard. "Don't worry about us, we're going to be just fine. This isn't the first time we've been here alone for the weekend. Just go and have yourself a good time."

Camila got the children to settle down for bed fairly early, considering their excitement about the trip. She was glad they went down so easily because later that evening, the weather turned from sunny and bright to cold, dark, and cloudy with icy rain. The sky was beginning to rumble, lightning was flashing bright, and with each rumble and flash, Camila jumped.

It was getting late, and with each rumble, Camila became more and more fearful. She was so afraid of storms that she couldn't sleep when they rolled through at night, with the exception of the night Garrison had held her in his arms and whispered soothing words in her ear. She'd slept well that night and had been having dreams about that experience ever since.

After she cleaned the kitchen, she went back upstairs to check on the children and saw that they were undisturbed by the storm. As she went back down the steps, a bolt of lightning flashed and she thought she glimpsed someone standing in the doorway of the summer room leading into the kitchen. Before she could stifle it, a shriek escaped her lips, and she covered her mouth with both hands.

The next rumble and strike showed the figure moving toward her. She closed her eyes momentarily, but they flew open again when she felt a hand on her elbow. When she focused, she was looking into the cold, empty stare of a man who was not supposed to be in her house.

She pulled her arm away and quickly moved back, then turned and ran to the foot of the staircase. The man was close behind her. She whirled around to face him and backed up until she was against the front door.

"Who are you?" she demanded. "Why are you in my house? What do you want?"

"Hello, Mrs. LaRue. Don't be afraid. It's me, George Tate, the deacon from church and your friendly bank teller. Mildred Horn's friend, don't you remember?"

"What do you want? What are you doing in my house?" she asked again.

"I just want to talk to you. I tried to get to you a while ago at your weekend house, but you latched the doors and closed the drapes after he left. So I had to wait, and tonight seemed the perfect time."

"That was you walking back and forth in front of the house that night?"

George smiled snidely and looked Camila up and down.

She cringed inside but squared her shoulders, steadied her voice, and warned him, "You need to go. If my husband finds out you've come here, there's no telling what he'll do to you."

In the back of her mind, Camila was trying to figure out how to get the man out of her house. She was afraid to open the front door and run because she didn't want him to go upstairs and hurt the children.

George stepped closer until he was standing directly in front of her, breaching her personal space. "Oh come, now, Mrs. LaRue, is this how you treat a guest? I just came to spend some time with you. I know you are all alone here, and I thought you might be feeling lonely. And maybe even inclined to be a little friendly, too."

"Mr. Tate, you need to leave. If you leave now, I won't tell my husband that you were even here."

He smiled. "Your husband. Ha! That was a civil marriage. It's not a real marriage until the preacher has you repeat your vows. So, you see, you're not really married. A little birdie told me that you don't even have a ring. At least his first wife had a ring. Therefore it won't really be adultery with you and me. It would just be a man and a woman having a good time together."

He leaned in and tried to kiss her, and Camila raised her hands to his chest to push him away. "Get out of my house, Mr. Tate," she said in a steady voice. "I am not about to do anything that disgusting with you."

She turned to her right and tried to get to the steps or even run into the dining room, but George Tate swung his cane and struck her on the upper arm. She let out a shrill cry and grabbed her arm. He moved in front of her and put his arm against the wall to block her way. When she looked at him, he was still smiling, and there was a lecherous gleam in his eyes.

George leaned forward and rested his body on hers, pressing her to the doorframe. "Well, well, well," he smirked, "here I am in your house, and no one else is home except those two mixed-up brats of that half-breed Garrison LaRue. And if anyone were to come in right now, it would be hard to convince them that there was nothing going on between you and me."

He pressed himself closer to Camila, pinning her against the wall even more. He leaned his head forward and tried to kiss her again, but she turned her face away and his mouth landed on her hairline just beside her ear.

Feeling Camila's body tremble, George Tate's mouth formed a sinister sneer as he continued, "If you don't want me to claim that we are lovers, you are going to do what I tell you. After I get my fill of you, I'm going to go back to town, and on Monday morning, you are going to ride into town and pay me $100. And you are going to keep paying me that amount every month for a year."

Even though his body was still pressing her to the wall and she was finding it hard to breathe, Camila raised her hands, pushed his shoulders, and managed to say, "I will do no such thing!"

With his cane hooked over his arm, he reached out snatched one of her wrists, twisted it, then with his other hand grabbed Camila by her throat. Adding pressure to his hold on her throat, he banged her head against the doorframe and snarled, "Yes, you will! Now I'm not going anywhere until I get what I came for. And if you scream and wake up those annoying little creatures, I'll kill them. So play nice and we'll both have some fun."

Releasing her neck but continuing to hold her wrist, he dragged her across the wall and slammed her body against the front door. He reached out to grab Camila again, but using strength she didn't know she had, she pushed him and turned to run into the parlor.

He caught her nightgown and ripped it from her shoulder, tearing it down her back to her rear end. Then he hit her with his cane, this time knocking her to the floor.

Camila fell, and when she rolled over, he was standing over her, straddling her, trying to open his trousers with one hand, holding the cane over his head with his other hand. He was going to hit her again, but before he could bring the cane down, she kicked him in the groin.

George dropped his cane and fell to his knees. He tried desperately to fall on top of Camila so he could pin her to the floor, but she swung her free arm and struck him on the side of the face, hitting his ear as she rolled away from him.

She tried to scramble to her feet, but George had retained a little of his wits. He grabbed her ankle and pulled her back toward him. As she was being pulled back, her hand touched his cane, and as he tried to roll over on top of her, Camila raised her knee and caught him under the chin.

Groaning and grunting, he grabbed that leg and held it down as he crawled on the floor and pinned her down with his body weight. "You are quite a spitfire, aren't you? I knew it wouldn't be easy with a woman your size, but I'm still stronger than you. I'm going to win anyway, so you may as well stop fighting and let the fun begin. You never know, you might enjoy it, even more than you enjoy that half-breed savage."

"There's no way you could do anything better than my husband," Camila hissed. "He's a real man. He doesn't have to force me to do anything with him. You repulse me. Get off of me!"

"If those brats hear you and come down here," George growled, "I'm going to let them watch, and then I'm going to kill them! Stop fighting and relax, let's enjoy ourselves."

Camila's heart seemed to freeze. George Tate had a frightening look on his face. She thought about the children upstairs, and tears began to sting the back of her eyes.

"Nooo!" she moaned.

He grabbed the front of her torn nightgown and tried to pull it completely off her body. Taking advantage of his leaning to the side and rolling half off of her, she managed to hit him in the neck with her elbow and got to her feet.

With much thought of how he had hurt her, scratching and bruising her arms, her chest, and her shoulder, as well as choking her and hurting her head, she tightened her hold on his cane, quickly lifted it, and struck him twice before he could react. She was so angry and afraid that she continued to swing at him with the cane.

She had given him five good blows when someone grabbed it from her. "Stop! Camila, stop!"

Camila spun around, screaming, tears flowing down her face, and collapsed into her husband's arms.

Garrison held her against his chest. "It's okay, baby. I'm here. I'm here." He swallowed hard, trying to settle his temper. She was sobbing and trying to burrow deeper into his embrace. Her body was racked with sobs.

Wesley, Jarrod, Roy, and Garrison had come into the house during the struggle. Now, as Garrison held her up with one arm and tried to take off his shirt to cover her with the other, Wesley and Jarrod reached down and pulled George Tate to his feet.

He began struggling and trying to get away from the men. "No! Wait, it's not my fault. It was her. She invited me here! She's been coming on to me, and then when I took her up on her invitation, she started acting like she wanted to back down. She's been nothing but a flirt. She's nothing but a shameless hussy. She's a vixen! She just tried to kill me!"

Camila looked at the man and tried to pull away from her husband. She wanted to scratch his eyes out. "He's a liar. A disgusting lying beast," she sobbed into Garrison's shoulder.

Garrison pulled her closer. "It's okay, baby, it's okay. No one in this room believes him."

Without warning, Roy moved in, grabbed George Tate by the collar, and punched him in the jaw., knocking him to the floor. The other men stood back and allowed Roy to get in a few more blows before Garrison spoke up.

"That's enough, Roy. Wes, you and Jarrod cuff him and take him outside. I'll be there directly."

CHAPTER 26

Garrison wrapped his shirt tighter around Camila's trembling body, lifted her, carried her to her room, and placed her on the bed.

He stepped back and said, "I'm going up to check on the children." When he returned, Camila was still sitting on the bed, trembling. "Roy is going to stay here with you while I get Tate back to town and lock him up," Garrison said, wrapping a quilt around her.

She grabbed his hand and managed to croak, "Please. Don't. Don't . . . leave me."

Just then, Roy spoke from the kitchen. "Let me and the boys take him back, Boss. She needs you right now. I checked on the children too, and it seems they slept through the whole thing. And I stoked the fire in the stove to warm the water in case Miz LaRue wants to take a bath."

When Garrison walked into the kitchen Roy looked at him, and it was easy to see the unsettled rage in the younger man's eyes.

"Maybe it is better that you guys take him back," Garrison said, "because if I do, he definitely won't get there alive. Tell Hank Anderson to lock him in the back cell, please. And make sure you use the shackles. I don't want him to even think about getting away. Oh, while you're in town, let Doc Lands know what happened and ask him to come see my wife."

Going back into the housekeeper's quarters, his attention turned back to Camila. Garrison forced a smile and put his hands on his hips.

"You are a tough little lady, aren't you? If we hadn't come when we did, you probably would have killed that man."

She looked at him and whispered, "He came in while I was upstairs taking care of the children. He scared me. I didn't know what he wanted. I had to protect my babies, he threatened to kill them if I screamed and woke them." She shuddered and started to cry. "He was lying. I never did what he said. I never did. He said that if I didn't want him to claim we were lovers, then I had to pay him."

Garrison felt his heart skip a beat. He was trying to keep his anger under control. "I know. But you shouldn't dwell on what he said. No one will ever believe anything he says. You need to change your clothes. Do you have another sleeping gown?"

She nodded and pointed across the room. Garrison left her sitting on the bed and went to the chifforobe. He took out one of her night shirts.

"Put this on. I'm going to go check on the children. I'll be right back. Will you be okay?"

Camila didn't answer him, and when he looked back at her, he saw something so heart-wrenching that his legs almost buckled. Camila was curled into a ball with the blanket over her head, sobbing. "I hate him. He's such a liar. I feel so dirty."

"Listen to me," Garrison said. "You didn't do anything wrong. Wait here for me. I'll get the warm water, and you can take a bath."

Garrison went into the kitchen and checked the water Roy had set on the stove. He stoked the fire a little more, then he went upstairs and checked on his children again.

He was angry. So angry that he paced the floor from the front of the house to the back door. He could see in his mind's eye what George Tate had intended to do to Camila. But that weasel didn't bank on Miss Camila Rose Barnes being so strong-willed and physically tough.

Standing in the hall near the front door, Garrison lamented, "I should have let her kill him. I should have killed him myself a long time ago."

When the water was finally warm, Garrison took the two buckets into the housekeepers' quarters and emptied them into the bathtub. After

Camila was in the tub, he left the door slightly ajar and returned to the kitchen.

He put the tea kettle on the stove, and when the water was hot, he took the china tea set from the cabinet, filled the tea ball with dried orange peel and tea leaves, put two spoons of honey in the teapot, slowly poured the hot water over the tea ball, and put the top on the pot to let the leaves steep.

He stayed close enough to hear her if she needed some help. When the tea was brewed, he prepared a tea tray and carried it into her parlor. When she was dressed and had come out of the bathroom, he escorted her to the settee and poured her a cup.

Camila offered him a weak smile. "Oh, look what you did, thank you." She sipped the tea. "This is good," she said, and he noticed she was still trembling.

Sitting in the stuffed armchair, Garrison said, "You don't have to be afraid anymore. He's never going to get the chance to do that to you or anyone else again."

Camila flashed him another weak smile. When she finished her tea, Garrison took the cup from her, escorted her from the parlor to the bedroom, and when she climbed into her bed, he sat down beside her. Slowly, Garrison lifted her onto his lap and took her in his arms, wiped her tears with his shirttail, and held her until she fell asleep.

He gently laid her back on her pillows, kissed her forehead, and stood to leave. Refusing to follow his body, his heart and mind told him to go back and comfort her, to do something with her that he would later regret.

In the morning, Roy returned to LaRue Crossing with Contessa Anderson, and together they stayed with Camila and the children while Garrison went to town.

CHAPTER 27

When he rode into town, there was only one thing on Garrison's mind, and that was that he wanted to kill George Tate. And if Judge Anderson had not been in the sheriff's office along with Jarrod, Wesley, Todd, and Hank, he would have.

The only reason he wouldn't kill Tate was because the judge had already signed a transfer order, and Hank had already sent a telegram to the territorial marshal, who wired back to say he was on his way and asked that they keep the prisoner shackled until he arrived.

Sheriff LaRue snatched the keys from the hook, opened the security door, and walked determinedly into the jail toward the holding cells.

Hank Anderson fell in step beside him. "You need to think twice about what you are about to do," he warned. When Garrison didn't slow his steps or even acknowledge him, Hank grabbed his brother-in-law's arm.

Garrison stopped and looked down at the hand on his arm. "Back up, Hank. This don't concern you."

"I am *not* going to back up, Sheriff. I'm going to do everything in my power to stop you from making a very bad mistake."

"This is not a mistake, Hank. It's something I should have done a long time ago. That man is a snake. He has slithered in and out of my life long enough, and now I'm going to put an end to him and his devious ways."

George Tate heard the two men's words before he heard their footsteps. As he began to understand what they were saying, he pressed himself closer to the wall of the cell. His mouth was suddenly too dry to swallow. He held his breath, and his heart was beating so loudly that he thought the other prisoners could hear it.

Hank stepped closer to his brother-in-law. "Why don't you let the law do what it's supposed to do, Sheriff?"

"Because the law would be too kind to that varmint. I want him to suffer, and I want to be the one to make him feel the pain, more pain than he's ever felt before."

"Yeah? And what about the pain that your actions would put on those who love you? Your parents, your sister, your children, *and* your wife. What about them, Garrison?"

"What do you mean, what about them? That snake slithered into my house, threatened my children, and he put his slimy hands on my wife. He *touched* my wife, Hank. He *hurt* my wife! He tried to blackmail her. He tried to *rape* her. He. Hurt. Her."

"Brother, I can only imagine what you are feeling, and I don't blame you for it, but your family needs you. Let the law handle it. If you go to prison, who's going to take care of them?"

"Hank, get the hell out of my way!" Garrison nearly screamed.

"No, Garrison. I'm going to do everything I can to keep you from doing what you want to do to him, no matter how much he deserves it!"

Snatching his arm away from the hold that Hank Anderson had on him and slamming his brother-in-law against the wall hard enough to cause him to see shards of light dancing before his eyes, Garrison went to the cell where George Tate was shackled and chained to the wall.

"Tate," he said, "I want to kill you, slowly and painfully." He paused and glanced back at Hank. "But this man has just saved your life." Then he turned back to look at the prisoner. "And I promise you that if I ever see you again, I'm going to kill you with my bare hands. I should have let my wife beat you to death with your own cane!"

Garrison stepped close to the cell and slammed his hand against the bars. George jumped, rattling the chains that had him shackled to the wall.

"Don't think of this as a threat," Garrison added, "because it's not a threat. It's a promise!" He stood looking at Tate for a few moments and then slowly walked away. He stopped before his brother-in-law. "Thanks, Hank. I hope I didn't hurt you. I'm not mad at you."

Hank rubbed his chest. "Well, I'm real glad you're not mad at me. But I did have to stop and catch my breath. You had me seeing stars."

Garrison returned to the office and sat behind his desk, not looking at or speaking to his deputies or the judge. When he had finally calmed down enough to realize they had done the right thing and that Hank had spoken words that were very true, Garrison left them in the office and rode back to the ranch.

As he rode into the front yard, Dr. Lands was turning his carriage around heading for town. The doctor told Garrison that Camila was "going to be fine in a few weeks when the bruises and scratches begin to go away."

He also told Garrison that he was concerned about the bruises on her neck, but especially the large bruise on her back, so he had left some ointment that needed to be applied every night.

"I suggest that you don't put a lot of pressure on her for a while," Dr. Lands added. "Maybe hold off on the marital relations. Just remember that she won't heal as quickly mentally as she heals physically. These things take time. I'll stop by in a couple of days. If you need me before then, you can bring her into my office."

After Dr. Lands had gone, Garrison sat looking at the front door of his house. He wanted to go in, but not right away. He wanted to see Camila, but he was reluctant because he wasn't ready to see her bruised and scratched.

He quickly pulled up on the reins, slapped his horse's rump, and galloped away from the house. When he reached the place where his first wife was buried, he dismounted and walked to the grave site.

Standing over the marker with the horse's reins in his hand, Garrison spoke aloud, "Grace, I'm beginning to feel your hold on me slipping away. Finally, the feelings of guilt and the pain of what you did to me and the children are no longer on my mind all day, every day. It's been a struggle for me to forgive and forget the situations and actions that led to your death. I hated you for so long that it began to take over my life. Then I realized that my hateful, unforgiving feelings were not fair to little Garrison and Ella Grace. They deserve all of my love and attention, not what is left over because of my time spent hating you."

Stooping down, he continued. "I don't know if I have completely forgiven you yet, but I think I'm on my way to it. Sometimes, I would find myself wishing I had told you more often how much I loved you, and I'm sorry if my love and what I had to offer you was never enough, but somehow, I've managed to let that go. There's possibly someone else in my life now, and I don't know what's going to happen between us, but the children love her already, and that's a good enough beginning for me. Goodbye, Grace. Rest in peace."

On the ride back to the ranch, Garrison found himself for the first time in four years thinking about something other than his former wife's betrayal and demise. His mind was filled with new, more pleasant images, and they all included Camila Rose Barnes.

CHAPTER 28

After he put his horse in the barn and brushed and fed him, Garrison washed his hands and face. Then he went into the house through the summer room and saw Camila, Tessa, and the children sitting at the kitchen table. Little Garrison and Ella Grace were doing their lessons, and the two women were having tea. When the children saw their father, they dropped their pencils.

Little GJ ran to him. "Daddy, Daddy! Momma Camila fell down, she got hurt!" Taking his father's hand and pulling him toward Camila, GJ said, "Come look at her."

Ella Grace climbed out of her chair and stood beside Camila, touching Camila's leg. "Kiss her and make her all better, Daddy."

Garrison scooped them up and hugged them close, then he looked at his sister. "Contessa, I want to talk to Camila. Do you mind sitting with the children in the front parlor?"

Contessa stood slowly and smiled. "Of course I don't mind," she said, then took each child by the hand. "Come on, little ones, your daddy and Momma Camila have some grown-up talking to do. Besides that, I think it's nap time for you two anyway."

Camila's eyes were puffy, and she looked small and frightened. Garrison felt a strong urge to take her in his arms and hold her until the hurt went away. He could see the ugly bruises and scratches on her face, arms, and neck very clearly.

"George Tate is on his way to the territorial jail in Irving, the next town over. The judge and the deputies don't think he'll be safe in this town, and they are right, because I want to kill him." He took her hand and helped her to her feet, but she flinched. Stepping back, he asked her, "How are you feeling?"

Camila shook her head. "I don't know," she said, her voice hoarse from George Tate choking her.

Hooking his thumbs into the side pockets of his Levi's, Garrison sighed deeply "I'm sorry this happened to you. I feel responsible for what he did."

With wide eyes, Camila croaked, "How is what he did your fault?"

After guiding her back down onto the chair, Garrison sat down across the table from Camila. "George Tate and I went to school together," he said. "He was always trying to get me into trouble. He would steal things and blame it on me. He would destroy the other students' slates and blame it on me until the new teacher, Mrs. Aires, caught him one day and he was spanked in front of the class and told not to come back to school until after the next planting season.

"He was angry, too, because schooling came a little easier to me than him. Up to that point, we always seemed to be competing for some prize or another, and most of the time, I would win. By the time he was allowed back in school, I was a grade ahead of him, and he never was able to catch up to me. So I thought the competition was over. But as we got older, George became so jealous that he would even try to outdo me getting jobs and making friends. Especially with the girls."

Camila looked at him with vacant eyes but offered a small smile, so he continued.

"By the time Grace and I got married, I had forgotten about George and his foolishness, but he hadn't let it go. In the meantime, he had become a bank teller and a deacon in the church, and he used those positions to seduce women, including Grace. During church on Sundays, while I was working, he focused his intentions on my wife. He knew she wanted to live in town and not on the ranch. He knew she wanted to be a society woman instead of a ranchers' wife. He turned her against me. They had an affair, and at the time of her death, she was carrying his baby.

"While he was healing, he told the preacher that he felt like he had paid for his sins, and he promised to live right from then on. The preacher felt that George deserved forgiveness and another chance. I was bitter, and I accused the preacher and the church members of siding with Tate. I believed he felt no remorse for what he did to me and my children. That's why I stopped going to church.

"Tate began to subtly taunt me and seemed to build a support group among the women, turning them against me. He told them Grace was afraid of me because I was mean, and that I would beat her and forced her to have our children. He convinced the members of the Ladies' Mission Society that he and Grace were leaving town because he was rescuing her from me."

Garrison slid his chair closer to Camila so that their knees were touching, and when she didn't flinch, he reached out to slide his hand into her lap to touch her trembling hands. When Camila didn't shy away, he continued.

"But Mrs. Aires was not swayed. She doesn't like George Tate. She says he reminds her of a weasel, always trying to sneak into the henhouse. So when she heard that he was being reinstated as deacon, she didn't like it at all. She knew George Tate to be a fake. Mrs. Aires told me that she overheard him telling Mildred Horn that because of what happened, and his surviving it, he felt that he had finally won the battle against me."

Camila pushed her chair away from the table and stood in front of Garrison. He looked up, then slowly rose to face her. When he stood, she placed her hands on his chest. She could feel his chest rising and falling. Looking up into his face, she could see his pain, distress, and grief.

"Garrison," she said, "I don't think you should take on any responsibility for what that man did. He is the author of his own actions."

"You don't understand. I think I set you up. When you gave me those bank drafts, I took them to Mr. Aires and asked him to put them in your account in your name only to do with what you wanted. Because he sees things between him and me as a competition, I think that when George found out about it, he started believing that I had won again. He told Mildred Horn that no matter what happened in my life, I always seemed to land on my feet. He was angry because now I have another wife, and this time, she's not a woman who can be easily influenced. George was upset because you are a woman who thinks for herself, and it disturbed him that you did not fall for his charms when he approached you in Miss Kit's restaurant. He especially hated the way you ignored him every month when you went to the bank to make your deposit."

Garrison stepped away from Camila. He had to; she was rubbing her hands across his chest and shoulders, and they felt too good, as though they were ministering to his wounded spirit. They were soft and gentle and made him think about how much better they would feel if he didn't have his shirt on.

He cleared his throat and continued. "Yesterday afternoon, George saw the guys come into town, and when he saw me at Miss Kit's arresting a drunken cowboy, he knew you were here alone with the children. So he went to Mildred and told her that this was his last chance to get rid of me for good.

"His plan was to come out here and get you to sign over your account to him and . . . force himself on you. He told Mildred that he knew he could make you do anything he wanted if he promised to kill the children if you told anyone what happened. Then after that, he was going to claim that you and he had been involved in an affair and that you had given him your dowry so that he could take you away."

Camila could see that Garrison was agitated. He was pacing the floor, and as he spoke, his hands clenched and unclenched. She watched him as he continued.

"Mildred realized that Tate was talking like a man who had lost his mind, so she told Roy, and Roy found me and told me. That's how we caught him here."

Looking at Camila remorsefully, Garrison said, "I was on my way here anyway because of the storm, and I didn't want you to be here alone. I know how you feel about storms. Unfortunately, he got here first."

Camila slid her hands around Garrison's waist and lay her head on his chest. "I'm so glad you came."

Inhaling deeply Garrison said, "I've been thinking, and in light of what has happened, I want to ask if we could consider postponing the trip. After all, it would be very difficult for you to travel with the children in your condition."

Camila leaned back and looked into Garrison's eyes, and in her damaged, husky voice, she whispered, "I think that's a good suggestion."

Gently, he slid his arms around her waist and pulled her closer. He kissed her forehead. They stood like that for several minutes until Garrison felt her body tremble, and when he looked at her face, he could see that she was tired and in pain.

Slowly, he released his hold. Then he lifted her in his arms, carried her into the parlor, and sat on the settee with Camila resting on his lap. They sat there until Contessa knocked lightly on the door and opened it. When she saw them together, she began to back out of the room, but Garrison whispered, "She's asleep. Wait until I put her in her bed."

When Garrison stepped into the kitchen, Tessa was smiling. "You're in love with her, aren't you?"

He put his arm around her shoulders. "I don't know about all of that, big sister, but when I'm around her, I forget the pain that's constantly in my gut. I don't have that heavy feeling in my chest, and I don't hate the world so much. But to say that I'm in love with her is a stretch. I can say that it makes me happy to think about her and what she's done for the children, and maybe even me, since she's been here."

"Garrison, you need to stop fighting yourself. What happened with Grace was unfortunate, but it was not your fault. Those two people did what they did because they wanted to. You need to let go of the past and live for now. Stop denying yourself the love Camila has to offer you."

"She doesn't love me," he offered sadly.

Contessa pressed her lips together, shook her head from side to side, and softly sucked her teeth. "Really? Have you asked her?" she challenged. Waving her hand, she continued, "Just look around you. Look at your house! Do you think that a woman would do all of this if she didn't have strong feelings for you and your children? Garrison, she's treating this place like it's her home. Which is a lot more than Grace ever did. Wake up, little brother!"

Garrison smoothed his hand over his hair. "I don't know about all of that, Tessa. She is the housekeeper, after all. And housekeepers take care of the house."

Contessa shook her head. "I'm going home to my husband. I love him, and I know he loves me because we aren't afraid to tell each other about our feelings. Goodbye, Garrison. There's a pot of beef stew and a pot of white bean soup on the stove, and fresh bread on the sideboard. It should last you all for a couple of days."

It was late afternoon when Roy helped Contessa into the carriage to accompany her back to town, leaving her younger brother standing in the yard waving and thinking about falling in love with Camila Rose Barnes.

CHAPTER 29

It had been two weeks since the incident, and after experiencing one more storm, Camila finally agreed that the weather was too unpredictable for traveling and had to admit as much to Garrison. Besides, there was no way she could go home with the bruises and scratches on her face and body. It would be impossible to convince her brothers that it hadn't been Garrison who hurt her.

In the two weeks since the attack, she had not slept through the night once. She kept seeing George Tate's face over her and feeling his hands on her body, her arms, and her legs. She was having difficulty keeping herself from falling apart, especially in front of the children.

Every evening after taking her bath, Camila knocked lightly on the door of Garrison's office. Then he followed her back to her parlor, where he applied the doctor's ointment to the large, ugly bruise that covered her upper back from shoulder to shoulder and from her neck down to her waist.

The first night he had to do it was very difficult. He was nervous about seeing and touching her naked back. When he came into the parlor, Camila was standing in the middle of the room looking like a lost lamb. She handed him the tin, turned around, dropped her robe from her shoulders, and closed her eyes.

Garrison took the tin and opened it. When he looked up and saw her uncovered back, he drew in a deep breath. The color of her skin ranged from red to green to blue to yellow to purple. The bruise was ugly, and he immediately wanted to do more than rub ointment on her back.

Camila looked over her shoulder, holding the front of her wrap tightly. "Garrison?" she asked. "Are you alright?"

When he slowly nodded his head and forced a tight-lipped, "Yes, I'm fine," Camila turned back around softly said, "Well, it's okay. I'm ready."

His first touch made her gasp, shiver, and pull slightly away. "I'm sorry, Camila, I know it hurts, but I'm trying to be gentle."

She didn't know how to tell him that it wasn't just the pain that had caused her to shudder. It was his touch; it caused bursts of heat to suddenly suffuse throughout her body. His calloused fingers ministered so gently to her bruises that she had to steel herself so that her legs would support her.

When he finished, Garrison carefully slid the wrap up over her shoulders, and when she turned with her hands tightly grasping the front of the robe to her chest to thank him, he handed her the ointment and exited the parlor quickly.

After the fourth night, they both settled down and seemed to have lost some of their tension and anxiety, so much so that they talked about the events of their day with one another. It appeared they had formed a companionable bond.

When Garrison asked Camila each morning how she'd slept, she told him she was sleeping better. But he knew she was having a difficult time because every night, he could hear her as she walked the floor of her bedroom, and a few of those nights when he would walk down the steps to offer comfort to her, he could hear her crying as he stood outside her parlor door.

Garrison was having trouble sleeping through the night himself; he wanted to go into Camila's room and comfort her, but he dared not. He wasn't sure he could control himself. He was afraid he would end up doing more than offering "comfort" to that woman.

CHAPTER 30

Wednesday, three weeks after the incident, dawned cold and bright. As Garrison headed to the kitchen to make the morning coffee, a smile touched his lips. Camila was already preparing the coffee, and Garrison could also smell cinnamon rolls.

He stood in the hall just outside of the kitchen, watching and listening as she hummed softly. When she looked up, her smile caused a reaction in his body that took him by surprise. But rather than succumb to the beckoning of his desires, he spoke to Camina in a very formal tone.

"Good morning, Miss Barnes. I can tell you're feeling better. It's good to see you up and resuming some of your duties."

Looking up to see Garrison standing in the doorway had caused Camila's heart to leap in her chest. Under his stare, her body grew warm and tingled all over. She leaned her hip against the worktable. "Good morning, Mr. LaRue. Yes, I am feeling better. Thank you."

Before he could think about it, Garrison went to Camila, took her by her shoulders, pulled her to him, and kissed her slowly, being careful not to put any pressure on her back. When she put her arms around his waist, he pulled her closer and deepened the kiss. What would have or could have or should have happened next, he didn't know, because he heard footsteps. Someone was walking across the back porch.

It was Roy. Garrison quickly broke contact and stepped away from the woman that made him want to do more than kiss her in the middle of the kitchen and gently touch her back every night.

He looked at her and whispered an apology. "I have to go. I'm sorry," he said and squeezed her shoulders. Then, before he left, he offered a reminder to Camila. "Don't forget that my parents are bringing the children back on Saturday afternoon."

Garrison left the house and stormed past Roy, who was looking at the two young people with a wide grin on his face. Roy and Camila stood on the back porch and watched Garrison ride toward town.

"Okay, Miss LaRue," Roy said, "he's gone. Shouldn't we get started now?"

Camila turned to him. "Yes, let's get started. I'll wash the windows, scrub down the walls, and polish the floors so we can be sure to get everything done before he gets back on Monday morning."

Looking at her with his arms folded, Roy said, "Listen, little lady, you ain't in no condition to do any'a that. Just tell us what needs ta be done, and me and Todd is gonna do it."

In the weeks before she was attacked, Camila had been ordering supplies and gathering materials for making over the upstairs bedrooms and redressing the upstairs hall. Now that she was feeling better, she wanted to get involved in this project to help get her back to feeling whole and useful again. She worked with Roy and Todd on the upstairs hall for the rest of the week. In short time, the two water rooms and the three bedrooms were transformed.

On Wednesday afternoon, the two men washed windows and painted the walls in all the rooms, the hallway, and the staircase.

On Thursday morning, the men hung a two-lamp chandelier in the upstairs hall, hung the new drapes at the windows, laid down the almost wall-to-wall rug, and set the benches with the cushions that Camila had embroidered under the windows.

On Thursday afternoon, Little Ella's room was dressed with new drapes and curtains that Camila had made, a new dresser, a new bed with a nice new mattress covered with pink bedsheets, a pink blanket, and a fluffy pink hand-tied quilt also made by Camila. Then the floor was covered with a pink fringed rug.

On Friday morning, Little Garrison's room was also dressed with drapes and curtains that Camila had made, a new dresser, a new bed with a new mattress that was covered with blue bedsheets and a heavy home-made blue quilt, and his floor was covered with a blue rug.

Friday afternoon, Roy and Todd laid the large gray fringed rug on the floor in their boss's bedroom and spent an hour fussing as they put to-gether a large Victorian four-poster bed. When they finished and had set-tled the mattress on the bed frame, they moved the dresser and the chif-forobe back into the room. The final duty for the two men was to return the oversized leather chair back to its place by the window.

Looking things over, Camila smiled and said, "Thank you, gentlemen. You should go. You probably want to head out to town before it gets too late."

Roy said, "Well, Miz LaRue, young Todd here kin go ta town if he wants ta, but if ya needs anything, I'll be in the bunkhouse. I'm a little tired. I think I'll rest up this weekend."

Todd looked at Camila and then looked at the older man and smiled. "Actually, Miz LaRue, I don't much feel like that ride into town, so I'm going to be in the bunkhouse too." Todd tipped his hat. "Night, ma'am."

"Alright, gentlemen," Camila said, "don't forget to fill your plates and take them with you. Good night."

Roy and Too were staying because Garrison had given orders that at least one man would spend the weekend at the ranch from now on. The incident with George Tate had scared him more than he was willing to admit to anyone.

After the two men left the house, Camila spent the rest of the afternoon and evening completing the enhancements to Garrison's room. She cov-ered the nightstand and the chest of drawers with the scarves she had cro-cheted, then she covered the mattress with freshly ironed new sheets and a fresh blanket.

Finally, she laid a heavy new hand-tied quilt she had just finished on the bed, put the pillows in their pillow coverings, fluffed them, and left the room, closing the door behind her.

Early Saturday morning, Camila made some sachets for the newly up-graded bedrooms and water rooms. In Ella Grace's room, she put lilac sachets; in little GJ's room, she put crushed pine cone sachets; and in their father's room, she put cinnamon and crushed pine needle sachets. The water rooms were each fitted with crushed sage and dried apple peel sachets.

While all the work was being done, Camila was glad the children had spent the week at their grandparents' house. The changes were going to be a huge surprise for them, and she was excited about making things brighter and more personal for her children and her husband.

Late that Saturday afternoon, when Anna Wolf and Thaddeus returned with the children, Anna looked at her daughter-in-law lovingly. "So young one," she said, "how are you?"

Camila nodded her head, and her eyes filled with tears. The older woman pulled Camila into her arms, hugged her, and wiped tears from her own eyes.

When they released their hold on one another, Anna looked around. "This place looks different. What else have you done? Why don't you give us a tour?"

Smiling brightly, Camila walked everyone up to the second floor and showed the children their rooms. Their grandparents watched with pleasure and contentment as Ella Grace moved about her room, touching everything and smiling. They watched with amusement as Little Garrison yelled, jumped up and down, ran across the room, and hopped onto his bed with a big smile.

Seeing the children's joy made Camila's heart happy. "I'm so glad to see their smiling faces," she said to the older LaRues. "I know they could use a little more happiness in their lives right now."

The adults left the children in their newly decorated rooms laughing, smiling, and playing. They went down to the parlor after Camila showed them all of the changes that had been made to the first floor and sat down.

Smiling, Thad LaRue said, "You've done some amazing things around here, Miss Camila Rose, I hope my son appreciates all your hard work. And I hope that he appreciates you, too."

"Yes," Camila said, "I believe that he does like the changes, even though he hasn't seen the upstairs yet. But I'm sure he'll like those changes as well."

Anna Wolf looked at Camila and smiled proudly. "That's a good girl."

"Excuse me, Mrs. LaRue?" Camila asked.

"I said that's a good girl. And what I mean is that a good wife should stand up for her husband, just like you are doing. I know my son, and I know that he doesn't accept change very well, but here you are, being supportive of him and not letting even me, his mother, speak negatively about him. I like that. I also like you. I think you are good for our son and our precious grandchildren."

Camila shrugged. "I'm just doing my job. This is what housekeepers do. Besides, I like doing things like this. It makes people happy, and I like making people happy."

Anna Wolf and Thaddeus stayed for just a little while longer before they left to go into town to their weekend house so they could go to church in the morning. As they were leaving, the last thing Camila's father-in-law said to her was, "Be sure you put the bar across the door. I'm going to stand here until I hear you do it." Then he kissed her and pulled the door closed. When he heard the bar slide through the brackets, he said, "Good night."

That night, after feeding the children, getting them ready for bed, and cleaning the kitchen, Camila realized her entire body was hurting from the activities of the past week, so she took a warm bath. After, she climbed into bed and sat in bed with the lamp on high, reading until she was sleepy.

Just before she fell asleep, she whispered, "I hope you like all that was done for you, Garrison."

CHAPTER 31

On Sunday morning, Roy returned to the big house, and after looking again at all the work that had been done, he insisted Camila not do anything but sit in the summer room, read her scriptures, and relax.

Knowing that her present aches and pains were the result of her recent activities, Camila agreed with Roy and decided that taking his advice was a good idea. So Camila and the children spent most of their day in the summer room. Roy and Todd joined them for a simple meal of rolled biscuits stuffed with eggs, potatoes, and bacon. For dessert, there was apple pie and milk.

In town, Garrison was out of sorts the entire weekend. There was more on his mind than keeping the law in the Alamosa township. He was impatient with the deputies, but they knew he wasn't upset with them. They knew it was because he was concerned about what was happening at the ranch.

Before leaving, Garrison had tried to convince Camila she should go to town with him and stay at the weekend house, but when she explained that she was more comfortable at the ranch, he stopped insisting and made sure that at least one of the guys was at the ranch at all times.

Not so surprising to Garrison, Roy volunteered to stay. However, what was more surprising to him was the fact that Todd also volunteered to stay. Even though he was surprised, he was grateful to the two men.

On Friday night, after the businesses in town shut down, Garrison sat at his desk to supposedly complete his reports. But what ended up happening was that he spent the majority of his time thinking about Camila Rose Barnes. He thought about how he felt every time he was near her. He remembered the feel of her lying against his chest for the first time as he comforted her during the storm, and again on the night after George Tate's attack.

He remembered the feel of her skin under his hand when he applied the ointment to her bruised back. He thought about how much he enjoyed kissing her and about how much he wanted to do it again.

Garrison let his mind focus on answering the questions his sister had asked him. Why was he holding onto the past? Why wouldn't he let himself feel again? The remainder of his weekend was filled with answering those questions.

Finally, the weekend was over, and Garrison was glad to be riding home on a clear, crisp early Monday morning. He was tired and still a little cranky, but when he swung open the door to the summer room and saw the object of his thoughts standing between the summer room and the kitchen, he smiled in spite of himself.

The children saw him and ran over to hug him.

"Daddy, Daddy!" they said at the same time.

"Daddy," GJ said, "Momma Camila has a surprise for you."

Ella Grace put her hands on her tiny hips. "GJ, I wanted to tell Daddy about the surprise!"

Seeing his daughter so distressed made Garrison laugh, and he scooped her up into his arms and said, "Well, Miss Ella, why don't you show me the surprise?"

When Camila turned, she looked into the face of a man who was tired but happy. "Welcome home, Sheriff," she said. "You look worn out." Then, looking at GJ and Ella Grace, she said, "Hey, I think we should let your daddy discover his surprise for himself. You two can go out and play now. Your daddy is tired and needs some sleep."

After the children were helped into their coats, they joyfully ran out into the side yard headed to their favorite places to play. Little Garrison ran to the biggest tree in the yard and climbed the ladder to the treehouse his father had built for him. Ella Grace ran to another big tree where a swing had been hung from a low-hanging branch.

Garrison and Camila stood together, watching the children through the windows. She looked at him and saw the familiar gleam in his eye and smile on his face he always had when he looked at his children.

For just a quick moment, she wished she could see a look like that on his face for her. After mentally shaking herself, Camila said, "Why don't you go on up to your room and get some sleep? After your nap, I'll have our noonday meal ready."

Garrison looked at her suspiciously. "What are you up to, woman? Did you paint something?" he asked, sniffing the air. "It smells like fresh paint in here." As he left the kitchen and started up the steps, he called back, "Oh, you painted the staircase wall and put down stair pads! Looks nice."

Camila said nothing because she knew he was in for an even bigger surprise when he reached his bedroom.

At the top of the staircase, Garrison stood with his hands resting on his hips. "Looks like she's been busy," he said to himself. He liked the rug covering most of the hall floor, and he noticed that it matched the treads on each step. He even liked the embroidered cushions that covered the benches under the windows.

Shaking his head in surprise, Garrison looked into each of his children's rooms. He touched the walls, the curtains, the rugs, and the quilts. He was very pleased with what he saw.

Finally, he went to his bedroom door, reached out, turned the knob, and stepped inside. "Well, what do we have here?" he asked.

The first things he noticed were the set of gray curtains at the windows and the matching long rugs that were positioned by each side of the bed. When he looked at the bed, he was pleasantly surprised to see the large hand-tied quilt that was laid over the new mattress resting atop the new four-poster bed frame.

Taking a deep breath, he inhaled the scent of cinnamon and pine needles, and smiled broadly when he declared, "That woman is something else."

After his nap, he returned to the kitchen and found Camila there.

"Thank you for all of your hard work over the weekend," he said.

"You are very welcome," she said, "but I had a lot of help. The guys worked very hard and did all of the heavy work, so be sure to thank them, too."

"Okay, I can do that. But I don't plan to thank them like I thank you."

Garrison strode across the room to stand in front of Camila, then leaned forward and claimed her mouth.

CHAPTER 32

It was the beginning of October again—Camila's second October at LaRue Crossing. The Christmas season was getting closer, and she hadn't yet finished making her gifts. Her plan was to make socks, nightshirts, robes, and nightcaps for everyone. It was her intention that the LaRue household would celebrate a very merry Christmas this year.

The second week of October, she had the men set up her sewing machine in the newly decorated sitting room, and every day after the children did their lessons and were napping, she would work on her gifts. By the end of the month, she was almost finished with her projects.

The first week of November in Alamosa found everyone's attention consumed by planning and setting up the town's harvest celebration, the time of year that marked the end of the harvest season. Because the harvest celebration was a week-long community activity, Camila and the children stayed at the weekend house while she prepared the cakes and pies she had been assigned to bake for each night of the celebration activities. The house was filled with the delicious aromas from early morning until late afternoon.

When Garrison came into the house that Thursday night, he went directly to the kitchen and greeted Camila with a heated look. "Good evening. It smells good in here."

She turned to him with a welcoming expression. "Good evening. Come over and have a seat," she said as she presented him with a warm slice of apple pie.

While they sat at the table and Garrison ate, he asked, "Miss Barnes, would you go to the Harvest Dance with me?"

Camila slowly lifted her eyes to his. "I'm already going to the dance."

Garrison's eyes locked on hers. "Really? With who?" he said, and Camila thought she heard a little annoyance in his voice.

"The children said they wanted to go, so I told them I would take them," she quickly explained.

Without a word, Garrison stood, walked through the small house, and stepped into the bedroom. Camila's mind immediately went to the fact that she hadn't asked him if it was alright to take the children to the harvest celebration. She thought he was angry with her because of her oversight.

She stood and lifted his plate from the table. As she scraped the dish and washed it, she had to swipe a few tears from her cheeks.

"Why do I keep doing these things?" she asked herself in a whisper. "How can I keep forgetting that he doesn't trust me with the welfare of his children?"

Just then, Garrison's voice softly spoke into the room. "Camila?"

With a small gasp, she raised her head and squared her shoulders. He had never called her by her given name before. "Yes?" she answered, afraid to turn around.

"Look at me, please?" he asked in that soft, manly voice that sent tingles down her spine.

She finished rinsing the dish and reached for the towel to dry it. "Mr. LaRue," she said, "I'm sorry I didn't ask you for your permission to take the children to the harvest celebration, but they were so excited about everything. I'm so sorry."

When he didn't reply, Camila knew he was angry, and she knew she couldn't avoid his anger. Placing the dish on the drying board, she turned and faced Garrison.

To her amazement, he was smiling and holding a box in his hand. "Miss Barnes," he said, stepped farther into the room. "Camila, would you allow me the pleasure of escorting you to the Harvest Dance?"

"You're not angry with me?" she asked.

"No," he answered, then stepped closer to her. His smoldering voice touched every inch of her tingling body. "May I be your escort to the dance?"

"Yes, Mr. LaRue. I would be honored to have you escort me to the Harvest Dance."

Garrison closed the gap between them. "Good. Because I would hate for this beautiful dress to remain in this box instead of on your body."

Camila looked at the box then raised her eyes to his handsome face. "You . . . bought me a dress?"

"I had Mrs. Aires make it for you," he replied. "I hope you like it."

He offered her the box, and she readily accepted it. Putting it on the table, she touched the ribbon.

"Thank you," she said.

With a quick chuckle, Garrison said, "Don't thank me until you see it."

Camila reluctantly looked away from his sparkling bright eyes and removed the ribbon. When she lifted the box lid, she saw the lace-covered top to a dress. Lifting the garment, she realized she was holding a beautiful emerald-green dress.

"This is so beautiful," she said, holding it against her chest.

"You like it?" Garrison asked.

"I love it. It's my favorite color. How did you know?"

"You told Contessa that emerald green was your favorite color," Garrison said.

Camila laid the dress across the box and turned to him. "Thank you, Garrison."

"You're welcome, Camila," he said and kissed the soft supple lips of Camila Rose LaRue.

The Harvest Dance was one of the biggest gatherings of the year. It was a family affair, so to accommodate the children and the town's older citizens, it started and ended early.

On Saturday afternoon, Camila and the children dressed in their festive clothes and walked to the town hall in the town square. When they entered the large building, the musicians were already playing, the food tables were loaded, and people were enjoying themselves.

Camila took little Garrison and Ella Grace to the rooms where the children were having their own chaperoned party, and when she returned to the main hall, she noticed she was one of only a few women who were unescorted. So she went to the dessert table to see if Garrison and the deputies had delivered all of the cakes and pies she had baked. When she was satisfied, she went to the other side of the room and stood against the wall, watching everyone on the dance floor have a good time.

Earlier that day when Garrison and the deputies had come to pick up the cakes and pies, Garrison told Camila he would meet her at the dance. He apologized and promised to make it up to her. Even though she was disappointed, Camila was glad she was at least going to see him during the celebration.

As she watched the people dance, she clapped her hands and tapped her feet to the music. Then she felt a slight shift and heard a voice behind her say, "Dance with me."

When Camila turned, she saw Sheriff Garrison LaRue holding out his hand. "It would be my pleasure, Sheriff. Thank you for asking," she said, taking his hand and following him to the dance floor.

That was the beginning of an afternoon of fun and revelations. Garrison let his guard down a little, and Camila relaxed and enjoyed the feel of him.

Their enjoyment of each other didn't go unnoticed. Mildred Horn was standing behind the dessert table, watching the couple as they danced closer and slower with each passing song until they stopped dancing and went outside into the garden behind the town hall.

CHAPTER 33

After they left the dance floor, Garrison touched Camila's shoulder and said, "Wait here for me. I'll be right back." Then he went to the pegs where the coats were hung, picked up his jacket and her cape, and returned. He wrapped her cape around her and whispered in her ear, "Let's walk."

Stepping outside through the doors of the barnlike building, Garrison and Camila Rose strolled to the center of the town square and stood looking up at the beautiful sight of the sun shining weakly over the mountaintops.

Garrison stepped behind Camila and wrapped his arms around her. A soft lavender scent drifted up and seemed to engulf him. It made him feel so comfortable and natural that he moved closer, giving her the unspoken command to lay her head back against his solid chest.

They had been standing there for several minutes when Camila heard Garrison exhale and felt his arms tighten around her. At the same time, he felt her body relax and almost melt into his.

"This is my favorite time of the day," he subtly observed as he began to sway to the distant sounds of music.

"Mine too," she whispered intimately. "When you're working in town, I sometimes step out onto the front porch and watch the sunset. It gives me a sense of peace."

They stood this way for the next few minutes, and when the glow of the sun finally lost its luster, their solitude was interrupted.

"Oh, well, this is quite a surprise." Mildred Horn was standing at the head of the garden path with her hands resting on her hips. "I truly hate to disturb this . . . oh-so-tender moment . . . but, *Miss* Barnes, we are ready to serve the desserts now."

Startled, Camila tried to step away, but Garrison rested his hands firmly on her waist, turned her around to face him, and said, "I have to go now, but you did a nice job with the desserts. They look delicious, and so do you."

"Thank you, Mr. LaRue," Camila said warmly, "but you know I do remember making five dried apple pies, but only three made it to the table. Do you want to tell me what happened to the other pies?"

Garrison offered her a shameful look. "I had to use them as a reward. The pies are in my office. I gave them to the deputies so they would cover for me while I came to dance with you." Then, kissing Camila on the forehead, he turned and left.

Mildred sucked her tongue against her teeth, spun on her heels, and walked quickly back into the town hall frowning. As she walked through the door, she saw Mildred talking to the other committee members, and as she neared the table, the ladies leveled her with scathing, judgmental looks. Ignoring them, Camila stepped to the table, filled a cup with water, dipped the knife in the water, and began slicing the cakes. She did the same with the pies.

Nudging Mildred with her elbow and nodding toward Camila, one of the ladies asked in a hushed tone, "What is she doing?"

Still feeling anger over what she'd seen outside, Mildred took up the charge to challenge Camila. Looking at her rival scornfully in an attention-grabbing voice, Mildred said, "Stop! What are you doing that for? Are you trying to ruin the desserts?"

"It keeps the cakes from making too many crumbs," Camila answered calmly. "And it keeps the pies from breaking apart so easily."

"I've never heard of anything like that before," Mildred huffed.

"Well, now you've seen it," Camila said as she wiped the knives with a cloth then laid them down and began serving the people.

Back in his office, Garrison thought back on the memory of Camila's body resting against his, and a smile lifted the corners of his mouth.

During the second week of November, Camila started making wreaths from the small branches of the fragrant pine trees for the doors of the house and the bunkhouse.

"This is going to be a Christmas that everyone will remember for a very long time," she said to herself.

Roy had informed her that in the last several years, the holidays had not been celebrated in a very festive way if they were celebrated at all, and Camila herself remembered how last year's Christmas was not very merry. It was because of this that she was determined the holiday season would be special for everyone. For the next two weeks, she worked diligently to finish making gifts and decorate the house.

One week after the Thanksgiving celebration, Todd and Wesley cut down a pine tree that was not too tall but was very full. They set the tree in a bucket packed tight with rocks and sand, filled it with water, and stood it in the main parlor. Camila and the children strung popcorn and watched with delight as Jarrod, Todd, and Wesley wrapped the strings of popcorn around the tree.

Camila produced a delicate angel for the top of the tree and several large red and green silky balls for the highest limbs. The lower branches were decorated with pine cones and ornaments that the children had drawn, colored, and cut out. By the time they were finished, the tree was beautiful and filled with decorations.

Seeing the house so joyfully decorated and the space under the tree crowded with wrapped packages big and small gave Garrison a feeling of contentment he had not felt in a long time—so much so that he ordered gifts for not only the children but even for the ranch hands.

He wanted something special for Camila, so he had Mrs. Aires make her something he knew she needed, and he also had his brother-in-law order something special for her. The box that had been delivered the last week of November to Camila was not the only delivery that was destined for the LaRue ranch house.

The children were so excited that they could hardly stay away from the parlor, especially on the Monday when their father came into the house with a large box that everyone correctly presumed was filled with all kinds of things Camila had ordered to make the holiday fun.

"Hank said that this finally arrived and thought you would probably want it right away," Garrison said to Camila as he set the box on the kitchen table.

She lowered her gaze to the box. "Well, good, it's finally gotten here."

GJ jumped up from his place at the table. "Momma Camila, is it a present? Who's it for? Me or Ella?"

Laughing, Camila said to the children, "Well, let's go to the parlor so we can open it and find out."

Because he also wanted to know what was in the box, Garrison picked it up. "Okay, then, let's go."

He motioned for Camila to guide the way and watched as his children joyfully followed behind her. Ella Grace and her brother were bouncing with excitement. Garrison couldn't believe how happy they were.

He thought back on the last few Christmases in this house and how sad and empty they had been. *Camila Barnes has made a difference in the atmosphere in this place*, he thought. *She's managed to change it from a house filled with darkness to a home filled with light, joy, hope, and laughter for my children.*

With growing respect, Garrison regarded the woman walking ahead of him as he carried the box and appreciated her even more. Then he lowered the box to the floor, stood back, and watched his family. Camila pulled the components of the nativity scene from the box one piece at a time, and everyone listened as she explained the importance of each piece to the children.

As he watched, a thought crossed through Garrison's mind. *Grace never did anything like this.*

Camila lifted each child as they took turns setting up the nativity scene on the mantle.

"What do you think, guys?" she said. "Does that look good to you?"

When they each nodded their heads, she turned back to the box and said, "Well, let's see if there is anything else in here." She reached into the box again and took out several candy canes, handing one to each child, telling them that it was a symbol of love that represented Jesus and his love for his children. Then she helped them hang their candy canes on just the right branches.

Camila was on her knees hugging the children, and when she looked up and her eyes met Garrison's, he offered her a half smile then turned, walked into his den, and closed the door.

He stood on the other side of the closed door for a few minutes, confused by the surge of emotions that had overtaken him in the parlor. He didn't understand why he was feeling what he was. His thoughts about Grace never doing those things with their children made him experience a degree of sadness for himself as well as his children.

His attitude grew even more pensive as he heard Camila joyfully leading the children in singing Christmas carols.

CHAPTER 34

The atmosphere in the house was charged with excitement. Almost everyone was happy and joyful. Garrison made it a point to stay as far away from Camila Rose Barnes as he could. He had purchased some gifts for her, but now he was having second thoughts. *I let myself get drawn into the Christmas spirit by that woman and her "joy to the world" attitude, so now I have to stay away from her.*

Camila noticed the change in Garrison's attitude. It seemed that she was back to not being able to do anything right enough for him. He complained about the decorations throughout the house, the number of gifts under the tree, the food, and anything else he could think of to keep her from forcing more of her holiday happiness on him.

Two weeks before Christmas, he entered the kitchen with a scowl on his face and asked, "What are you planning to serve for Christmas dinner?" When Camila told him he said, "That's quite a bit of food. Why do we need so much for just one day?" Then he quickly added, "Are you sure you can prepare all of that properly?"

Not wanting to be drawn into an unnecessary discussion or argument, Camila replied, "If I find that things are getting to be too much, I'll ask for help."

"Who?" Garrison asked. "Who are you going to get?" When she didn't offer an answer, he took her arm and turned her to face him. "Just don't mess up the celebration with your high and mighty uppity ideas and plans."

Then he spun around and walked out of the kitchen.

Watching him leave, Camila asked herself, *What was that all about? Is he losing his mind?* She put her hands on her hips and shook her head. *Maybe he's just tired of me. Maybe he's ready for me to leave.*

On Monday, the week before Christmas, the excitement level at LaRue Crossing moved a little higher when Garrison's parents arrived to spend the holiday.

Camila was in the kitchen preparing the noonday meal when she heard the front door open and Garrison call out, "Miss Barnes!" Then she heard a softer voice, but she couldn't distinguish what was said.

Immediately, she thought, *He's met someone and brought her here to see his house and tell me that it's time for me to go.*

Taking a deep breath to calm herself, Camila lay her hand on her chest, trying to slow her heartbeat. Then she said, "I'll be right there, Mr. LaRue. Just one moment, please."

She stirred the pot of stew, removed the loaves of bread from the oven, and quickly melted butter over the tops. When she turned to leave the room, she looked up to see her in-laws.

"Good afternoon," Camila said brightly. "Please, let's go to the parlor."

"Thad," Anna said, "you go to the parlor. I want to spend some time with Camila."

Thaddeus gave his daughter-in-law a hug and left the room.

Looking at her mother-in-law, Camila smiled at the older woman. She remembered the first time she met her mother-in-law and recalled that she thought Anna Wolf LaRue was a kind woman whose soft eyes and gentle smile always put her at ease. Camila liked Anna's straight, long, dark hair that now had a few scattered strands of gray. Camila admired how Anna seemed to be ageless. And now, as they were standing in the kitchen together, Camila took notice once again that her face was a female version of Garrison.

In a melodic voice, Anna proclaimed, "Hello, my dear. There's no reason for you to stop what you are doing. Since I'm here, maybe I can help you with something."

Camila had no time to thank Mrs. LaRue before the children's voices could be heard as they ran down the steps and into the kitchen to grab their grandmother by the hands, demanding her attention and dragging her from the kitchen back to the parlor to see the decorations and all of the gifts piled under the tree.

Camila turned to check the stewed chickens again, and as she was doing that, Garrison entered the kitchen. "My parents used to come down every year, and they would usually spend the week before Christmas here, and the week after in town with my sister."

"Where do they sleep?" Camila asked.

"In the rooms where you are," Garrison replied matter-of-factly.

"Well," Camila said, "I think we have a problem, don't you?"

"No, Miss Barnes, I don't think there is a problem. This year, I'm letting my parents take my room and I'll be sleeping down here with you."

Before she could register what he'd just said, Garrison turned, and as he was exiting, he threw back, "We'll talk about it before we turn in tonight, Sweetheart."

On his way out, Garrison almost collided with Thaddeus, who had returned to the kitchen. "Hey there, son," he said, "I decided to come back here and say a more formal hello to my favorite daughter-in-law."

"Well, I thought she would at least come to the parlor to greet her guests," Garrison said, sending Camila a look of disapproval.

Thaddeus breathed in the scents in the kitchen and asked, "What are you cooking that smells so delicious?" but before she could answer, Garrison directed his father back into the parlor.

Looking back over his shoulder, he said, "You need to come up front with us."

"Not if you want our meal to be edible," Camila said with a frown.

After the meal was served, Garrison had Roy give his parents a tour of the ranch so that they could see the new calves and folds that had come since their last visit. Meanwhile, he took their baggage up to his room, and when he returned, he had his arms filled with his clothes.

Camila was left to clean up and think about sharing a bedroom with

Garrison. She also thought about the fact that with two more people in the house, she would have to do some fast work to get the last of her gifts made for her in-laws.

CHAPTER 35

Garrison was angry. "Calm down, woman!" he said. "I'm not happy about this arrangement either. But what did you expect me to do?"

"I expected you to tell your parents the truth," Camila snapped. "We are not husband and wife. You are the boss, and I am the housekeeper, babysitter, and cook. That's what I expected you to tell them. Besides that, there is another room up there. It's about time you put a bed in there and made it a guest room."

"Well, I didn't, so just settle down so I can get some sleep. Besides, we are married, and just because it was performed by Judge Anderson doesn't mean we aren't legally married."

Camila pulled back the covers, and after Garrison got into bed on his side, she rolled up the extra quilt and put it down the middle of the bed to keep them from bumping into each other as they slept.

The few days before Christmas Day were filled with lots of LaRue family fun. The children were excited about having their grandparents with them, and so they were awake earlier than usual, filled with lots of energy. Because of all the excitement, they stayed up later than their scheduled bedtime.

While everyone was having fun, those days were very busy for Camila. She had to, of course, prepare larger meals and do extra chores to keep the house in order. But then there was the added task of making the extra gifts for Thaddeus and Anna Wolf. However, the most taxing thing for Camila was the fact she was sharing a bed with Garrison, which had her lying awake most of the night with thoughts and images of them together. During those times, it took all of her self-control not to act on her thoughts, especially on those mornings when she would awaken and discover she had somehow become encased in Garrison's strong arms.

On Christmas morning, everyone awoke early, exchanged gifts, watched the children open their gifts, and enjoyed a special breakfast that consisted of sliced oranges, glazed pecans, pancakes with chopped bacon in the batter, and hot milk flavored with cocoa powder, orange peel, and sugar.

Roy, Jarrod, Todd, and Wesley were surprised and pleased with their gifts, and after breakfast, they left to do their chores and to rest until dinner.

Camila served dinner in the formal dining room; the fully stuffed turkey was plump, moist, and golden brown. The ham was coated with a sweet, crisp mustard glaze. The cornbread dressing was full of spicy sausage. The mashed potatoes were loaded with butter. The winter greens were nice and tender.

Even though by the end of the meal everyone was stuffed, they still had slices of butter pound cake drizzled with an orange-flavored glaze.

Garrison let the children play with their new toys while their grandparents watched them and he helped Camila clean the kitchen. The tasks were completed in companionable silence.

Just as the last dish was being put away, Garrison finally spoke. "I guess you noticed that I didn't give you a gift," he said, and when she nodded her head, he added, "I wanted to wait and give them to you privately."

Surprised, Camila looked up and replied, "Well, I didn't give you all of your gifts either. I wanted to wait until we were alone also."

"Let me get the children settled in bed and check on my parents. I'll be right back," Garrison said. "Meet me in the parlor."

Camila's gifts to Garrison included not only the slippers, nightshirt, robe, and nightcap that she had given him earlier in the day, but she now presented him with three new Stetson hats—one black, one brown, and the other a light gray. Each hat had his name burned into the band, and there was also a scarf and a pair of leather gloves for each hat.

He was very pleased to receive all of his gifts. He tried on the hats and the gloves and said, "These are the best gifts that I've received in quite a while. Thank you, Miss Barnes." Then he flashed her one of his rare smiles.

Garrison's gifts to Camila included a red wool cape with fur around the hood and matching leather fur-lined gloves. Along with those, he presented her with a black cameo lapel watch and a pair of pearl earrings for her pierced ears. She was pleasantly surprised to receive gifts from him. "Thank you for these beautiful, thoughtful gifts as well, Mr. LaRue."

As she gathered her gifts and turned to leave the parlor, Garrison said, "Camila . . . before you leave, can we talk?"

She set her gifts back down and looked into his face. "Of course," she said.

Garrison looked as if there were something weighing heavy on his mind, and Camila immediately thought something was wrong. But as the activities of the day ran quickly through her mind, she couldn't think of anything that he would have a complaint about for today. As a matter of fact, she couldn't think of anything he could complain about at all.

Garrison took Camila's hands in his. He breathed in deeply, giving himself a full experience of her lavender scent. Not wanting to prolong the situation, he smiled and said, "Marry me, Miss Barnes. I want to make you my wife in the biblical way."

"Why?" Camila asked. "I'm not the kind of woman that a man would want to marry."

"Listen, woman," Garrison teasingly replied, "I should be the one who decides that."

Camila took a deep breath then said seriously, "I don't know how to be a wife. Why me? I believe that there's at least one woman in town who would be more than glad to be your wife."

"Well, then, you would be wrong," Garrison said. "I don't trust any of those busybody women in town. Besides that, I believe that, as the man, I get to choose the woman I want as my wife, and I choose you. So, will you be my wife?"

"Yes," Camila said, smiling. "How could I deny you when you are so sure that I'm the one you want to marry?"

CHAPTER 36

Garrison had a surprise for Camila, so he left for town early on the Wednesday morning after the new year. There were several things he had to put into place before Camila and the children arrived. His sister, his mother, and Mrs. Aires helped him with most of his plans, so by the next morning, everything had been put into place.

Thursday after the noonday meal, Roy escorted Camila and the children to town. When they arrived, Jarrod met them at the entrance to the town and said, "Miz LaRue, I'm suppose ta take the buggy to the stable and let you know that the boss asked me ta have you and little Miz Ella go to Mrs. Aires' dress shop and pick up a couple o' packages for him. He said he was gonna meet you at the house in a bit."

Roy looked at her with a silly smile on his face and said, "Well, then, Miz LaRue, I guess I'm jus' gonna take this young'un with me to see his grandfather and his daddy in his office." Roy touched Little Garrison on the shoulder and said, "Come on, li'l man, let's go."

Camila took Ella's hand. "Well, Miss Ella Grace, I guess that leaves us girls to ourselves." Inside the dressmaker's shop, Camila greeted her friend. "Good afternoon, Mrs. Aires. I was asked to pick up some packages for Mr. LaRue."

Mrs. Aires was beaming. "Certainly, dear," she said and handed Camila two packages. One was rather long and deep, while the other was smaller and shallow. Before she left the shop, Mrs. Aires gave Camila a big hug.

Looking a bit perplexed by the affection, Camila turned her attention to getting to the weekend house. When she got there, she opened the door and several ladies yelled "Surprise!" in unison. There was Contessa, who was very pregnant with her second child, Anna Wolf holding Contessa's first child, Mrs. Anderson, and Mrs. Johnson. Then Mrs. Aires came in behind Camila.

Camila saw the table was dressed with a linen tablecloth and napkins. There was a tea set on the table next to a three-layered cake, and beside the cake was a beautiful bridal bouquet.

Looking at the women, Camila asked, "Ladies, what's going on? What is all of this?"

Judge Anderson's wife stepped up and embraced Camila. "How are you doing?" she asked as she helped Camila remove her cape.

Next, Mrs. Johnson, the pastor's wife, stood beside Camila. "Why don't you come to the settee and open those packages?"

"You ladies are certainly acting very strange," Camila said.

She opened the smaller box first and lifted out a beautiful dress for Ella.

Holding it up to the little girl, Camila said, "Oh, Mrs. Aires, this is wonderful. Thank you so much." Then, looking into Ella's surprised eyes, Camila asked, "Do you like it?"

Ella nodded her head. "I like it, Mommy, it's pretty."

"Okay, then, let's see how it looks on you," Mrs. Anderson said as she took the dress in her hand and led Ella to the small bedroom.

When Camila opened the bigger package, she found a wedding dress and veil inside. There was a note inside that read: *Come to the church. You are the one that I want to be my wife . . . in the biblical way.*

Gently lifting the dress from the box, Camila was surprised; it was a Victorian-style gown with a form-fitted bodice, cut low to show the top curve of her breast. The low-cut bodice of the dress was covered with a high-neck blouse with long satin sleeves that were cuffed at the wrists with lace, while the ruffled skirt starting at the waist flowed gently down to the floor into a short train. The waist was enhanced with a satin ribbon tied in a large bow with the tails falling from the back of the waist to the train.

The ladies curled her hair and let the curls fall down her back and around her shoulders then applied a light rouge to her cheeks and lips. Then Contessa directed her to dab a little of her lavender body oil behind her ears, across her collarbone, and at her wrists.

When they were finished, Camila was fitted with her veil and led to the mirror. Looking at her reflection, Camila gasped, "Oh, how risqué!" But she loved how she looked in the dress all made up.

She couldn't help getting teary, but Contessa stepped behind her and said, "No, you don't! You can't cry until after you've taken your vows."

Ella Grace was led out of the room in a dress made much like Camila's, only without the veil and the train. The little girl with her newly curled hair smiled. "Mommy, we look pretty."

Garrison, along with his father, Judge Anderson, Hank, Mr. Johnson, Little Garrison, Mr. Aires, Roy, Wesley, Todd, and Jarrod were all in the church all dressed up in suits and polished boots when the ladies led Ella and Camila through the doors.

As soon as they entered, the organist began playing. Contessa handed Ella a basket of lilac petals. "Okay, Ella, do just like I showed you."

Ella took the basket and walked down the aisle, throwing the petals on the floor. When she stopped in front of her father, Garrison stooped down and kissed her cheek. Then the music changed and the ladies urged Camila to walk down the aisle.

Camila squared her shoulders, held her bouquet with both hands, fixed her eyes on her husband, and slowly made her way down to the altar. Garrison was dressed in a black suit with a long jacket. His boots were polished, his hair was loose and resting on his shoulders, and his bright, genuine, beautiful smile filled his eyes with light.

Watching her walk down the aisle, Garrison became mesmerized. To him, she looked like an angel. He whispered, "She's so beautiful."

When he swayed slightly, Hank stepped up and put his hand on his brother-in-law's shoulder. "Steady, man. And yes, she is beautiful, and she's yours. You deserve this. Congratulations."

Garrison's eyes were fixed on Camila; he couldn't look away even if he wanted to. His heart was hammering so hard that he thought everyone could hear it and see it beating through his chest. He was glad Hank had put his hand on his shoulder because the very sight of Camila Rose took his breath away and made him lightheaded. He knew it was because the blood in his body had quickly rushed from his head to another part of his anatomy, and he was glad he had on a suit with a long coat.

When Camila reached him, Garrison held out his hand and guided her beside him. She looked at her incredibly handsome man and said, "Did you do all of this for me?"

Grinning broadly, he replied, "Of course. This is what people do when they get married for real."

The ceremony was scheduled to be simple and quick. Everyone in the sanctuary was pleased with what was going on. They were happy for Garrison. All except for one person. So when the pastor asked if there were any objections to the union, there was an interruption.

Mildred Horn stood from the last pew and moved down the aisle toward the couple. "Pastor Johnson," she said, "I have something to say. Sheriff LaRue is a liar and a womanizer. He promised me that he would marry me, but he imported this woman here and forced her to marry him right off the train in a civil marriage. Now he finally wants to make her decent by getting you to marry them. It's wrong, and I disagree with the whole thing. Church weddings are for women of virtue, and I don't believe that she is a virtuous woman. She's probably in the family way right now. That's probably why he's marrying her. To save her so-called reputation."

Mrs. Aires and Mrs. Anderson stood and intercepted the woman; they each grabbed Mildred Horn by the arms, turned her around, and began to escort her from the church.

"Mildred, this is not going to happen!" Mrs. Aires said. "Your time for being obnoxious is over."

Garrison's parents stood from their seats on the front pews. Mr. LaRue stepped to his son. "What is she talking about, Garrison? Have you dishonored this woman?"

The pastor then spoke up. "Hold it, ladies," he said. "Mildred Horn and

Mrs. Johnson should go to my office."

Mildred smiled and pulled her arms free of the hold the ladies had on her and walked back down the aisle, stopping momentarily to look at Camila, offer her a sinister smile, reach out, and flip the end of her veil. Then she swaggered through the door beside the pulpit that led to the pastor's study.

The pastor turned to Garrison. "You two should follow me," he said, then turned to the people in the pews and added, "This should only take a few minutes, folks, and then we'll be back."

Garrison faced his father. "Dad, I have not done anything that would discredit Miss Barnes or soil her reputation. I just thought that she deserved more than a civil ceremony marriage."

Thaddeus smiled at his son and patted him on his shoulder. "I'm proud of you, son."

CHAPTER 37

Once everyone was standing in the pastor's office, Mildred began to talk. "Pastor, I have carnal knowledge of Garrison LaRue. Right after his wife died, I went to his ranch to help him take care of his children."

She pulled a handkerchief from her sleeve and dabbed her eyes, then continued. "He enticed me to his bed and lay with me. Garrison promised that he would uphold my virtue by marrying me, then when she came to town, he married her in a civil ceremony and turned his back on me, not honoring his promise of marriage." Mildred dropped her head and took several deep breaths.

Pastor Johnson looked at the groom. "Well, Garrison, what do you have to say about this? Did you lay with her?"

Garrison quickly answered with a strong, "NO! Pastor, you know what this is all about, don't you? She's still trying to make something out of the time I caught her in my bedroom, and she's angry because I didn't want to marry her. I told her to get out of my bed, get dressed, and leave my house. Then I left the room. I had Jarrod escort her to town, and since then, I have tried to not be in her presence at any time for any reason."

Looking at Camila, Pastor Johnson asked, "Well, Camila, do you have anything you want to reveal to me?"

"Pastor Johnson," she said, "even though we've been in a civil marriage for just about two years, I've never had a wedding night. I've been taking care of the children and serving as the housekeeper for Mr. LaRue. The ranch hands, Contessa Anderson, and Dr. Lands can tell you that I have been living in the housekeeper's quarters off the kitchen. We have no carnal knowledge of one another whatsoever."

Garrison asked the preacher, "What about her? Are you willing to marry us in spite of what this woman has just accused me of?"

"Sheriff," the pastor said, "I have no reason to take her word over yours. I remember when you came to me and told me about the incident. I decided then and there that you were telling me the truth."

Mildred leaped to her feet. "Pastor Johnson, how can you do this to me? How can you take his word over mine?"

"Because, Mrs. Horn," the pastor said, "my wife and I have had several conversations about you over the last few years, and quite frankly, she doesn't like, nor does she trust you. She thinks you are a lying, backstabbing gossipmonger. Sister Johnson is a very good judge of character. And I trust my wife's judgment."

Mildred walked across the room and stood between Garrison and Camila. "I can be a good wife to you, Garrison. I know I would be better than her. I know what you like, I know what you don't like. I've known you longer than you've known her. She's not even the kind of woman who measures up to you. She's not small and delicate like a woman should be."

"Well, then, I guess you really don't know me as well as you think you do, Mildred, because this woman is exactly what I want and need as a wife," Garrison said, pushing past Mildred and taking Camila's hand. "She has restored me. She's given me a reason to live again. This woman has been a blessing to me and my children. Since she's been in our house, my children have joy and laughter in their lives again, and I have a peace that hasn't been in my life in a long while."

Mrs. Johnson turned to Mildred and said, "Sister Horn, you can't win this battle. I'm convinced that this is a union that's been set in place and sanctioned by God."

Mildred glared at Pastor Johnson and his wife. "I thought you were on my side. She's an outsider, a city girl! She doesn't belong here with folk like us." She dabbed at her eyes once more. "She doesn't love you, Garrison, she only came here and married you to get your money." Then, before she left the pastor's study, she pointed at Camila. "As far as I'm concerned, this is not over. I'm not going to let you get away with this."

"Give it up, Mildred," Mrs. Johnson said as she followed Mildred out. "You never had a chance anyway."

Mildred squared her shoulders and huffed, "Well, I have never!" Then she stormed down the hall and left the building by the side exit. She didn't even bother to close the door.

After the dramatic exit, the pastor turned to the couple and asked, "Do you still want to get married in this church today?"

The bride, the groom, the pastor, and his wife all returned to the sanctuary and the ceremony continued. When Garrison was instructed to place the ring on Camila's finger, her eyes began to sting again with unshed tears. The ring was a wide gold band with an inlaid cross that was filled with small diamonds.

When Garrison slid the ring on her finger and said, "With this ring, I make you my wife," Camila lost the battle with her tears.

Lifting the veil, Garrison cupped her face in his hands and used his thumbs to brush away the tears.

"Don't cry, Mrs. LaRue, this is supposed to be a happy occasion," he whispered, then he soundly kissed her.

Clearing his throat, Pastor Johnson whispered, "That comes after the ceremony is over."

Smiling, Garrison stepped back as the pastor finished the ceremony. After he received his ring, Garrison waited until he was instructed, and then he kissed his bride again, much to the pleasure of the guests.

After the kiss, Mrs. Aires laid out a broom and they jumped over it, walked down the aisle, and everyone followed them to their weekend house.

For the next hour, there was a reception for the bride and groom. After that, the men began leaving as quickly as they could, each using the excuse of going back to work—including Garrison.

"I have to get back to work," he told Camila. "Don't wait up for me. I'll be pretty late. I'll see you in the morning." Then he went into the bedroom to change his clothes.

Immediately after that, the ladies began preparing to leave. Contessa took the children by the hands and said to Camila, "I'll bring them to the ranch on Thursday after the noonday meal."

Camila hugged her sister-in-law. "Contessa, you don't have to do that. Leave them here. You're probably tired, and they can be quite a handful sometimes."

Contessa opened the front door and led the children out onto the front step. "Nonsense, Mrs. LaRue. You and your husband need to have some bonding time."

When the ladies heard Contessa's last comment, they laughed, and Mrs. Aires offered, "Bonding time . . . is that what they call it nowadays?"

Mrs. Johnson looked at Camila and said amusingly, "You better take a nap before that bonding time, girl. I have a feeling you are going to need all the rest you can get before that man of yours returns home."

The ladies all laughed again and left the house, waving goodbye to the newly church-married Mrs. Garrison LaRue, wishing her a long and happy union.

When Garrison opened the bedroom door, he was dressed for work. "Don't you want to spend some bonding time with me, Mrs. LaRue?"

Smiling, she looked over her shoulder at him. "Well, I don't rightly know about that. What do you have to offer that will make me want to spend some *bonding* time with you, Sheriff?"

Garrison stood behind his wife, leaned over her shoulder, wrapped his arms around her waist, and kissed the side of her neck. Then he spun her around and pulled her close. "I offer you a happy life, Mrs. LaRue."

After receiving a kiss that left her breathless, in an almost trancelike state, Camila watched her husband walk out of the weekend house and down the street toward his office.

She changed her clothes, set the house in order, then followed the ladies' suggestion and took a nap. In spite of his recommendation, Camila waited up for Garrison. By the time he was off work, she had a light meal in the warming oven and water warming for his bath.

It was plain to see from the smile that lit up his face that he was glad to find Camila sitting in the parlor. Camila stood and greeted him with a kiss. "Do you want dinner," she asked, "or do you want to take your bath first?"

Garrison gave her a sideward grin and said, "I'm going to take a bath. Even though I'm hungry, it's not a hunger for food." He laughed when he saw her eyes widen. "But before we do anything, we need to talk."

Taking her hand, he led her to the parlor. She sat on the settee, and he sat in the armchair. "It's been four years since I've wanted to be with a woman," he said, "and in all that time, I've been angry with Grace and every other woman who crossed my path. I never wanted to have another woman share my life with me. I focused my time and energy on doing my job, taking care of the ranch, and keeping my son and daughter happy. By the time that I advertised for a mail-order bride, I thought I was losing my mind. I was of the notion that the candidate would be a woman who was fat, not very attractive, and desperate enough to accept the situation. But instead, I got you."

He looked at Camila and offered her a sad smile. "You are the most beautiful woman I've ever seen. Being near you awakened feelings that I thought I had buried so deep that they would never surface again. You are smart, and you have a way of making people feel comfortable whenever you are near. And most of all, you are strong and stable and wouldn't let me bully you. Whenever I pushed you, instead of being frightened and running away, you pushed back. And to be honest," he said as he stood up and held out his hand, "I was a little afraid for you."

"Why?" she asked.

"Because no one has ever disputed me, and I was so angry at times that I wanted to snatch you and shake you until your teeth rattled. But that was then. For right now, I want to hold you and kiss you until we're both breathless."

Then he acted on his comment, gathering Camila in his arms and satisfying his desire. When they both needed air, he lifted his head and stepped away from his wife.

"What we are about to do is going to bond us together for the rest of our lives," he told her. "Are you ready?"

He held out his hand, and she took it and stepped before him. Garrison looked at her beautiful face. "What's so funny?" he asked.

"I think that right now, at this moment, I'm the happiest that I've ever been in my whole life," she said.

"Why is that?"

Camila lowered her eyes. "Because you're about to make me a woman. I'm going to be your wife in the truest sense of the word. Being married and sharing your marriage bed is the answer to a prayer for me."

Garrison lifted her chin and looked at her with a puzzled expression. "What was your prayer?"

"I didn't want to become an old woman and not have experienced a relationship with a man," she sighed. "I know that sounds silly to you, but I've always thought that having a husband would be the best gift that God could give me. I wanted to know how it felt to have someone to touch me and hold me and . . . I never thought I would be blessed enough to have a handsome husband with two beautiful children."

Garrison had no words to say. He just stepped close to his wife and held her to his chest. Camila felt as though a weight had been lifted from her heart. She had shared one of her deepest desires, and he didn't laugh at or belittle her for it. She rested her head on his chest, wrapped her arms around his waist, closed her eyes, and exhaled.

CHAPTER 38

While Garrison was taking his bath, Camila freshened up and changed into a sleeping gown with a matching wrap that Mrs. Aires had given her. When he entered the bedroom, she was sitting in the large leather chair near the window. He could smell her lavender scent as soon as he entered the room, and it drew him to her like a magnet.

She stood, looking nervous, and when he took her hands in his, he could feel the tension. He pulled her close and wrapped his arms around her.

"I'm beginning to enjoy holding you next to my heart," he said. "It feels so natural and comfortable." He lowered his head to kiss her slow and gentle. "You always smell so good. Lavender is quickly becoming my favorite scent because it reminds me of you, my Lavender Rose."

He continued, "I don't want to do anything wrong with you. I want us to enjoy each other tonight. I want your first time to be special."

"It will be special for me because it's you," Camila said. "Besides, I won't know if what you do is right or wrong. I'm going to follow you and do like my mother told me." When Garrison raised his eyebrows, she said, "Mother told me that on my wedding night when my husband takes me to the marriage bed, I was to just be still and don't make any noise and wait for you to be finished."

Garrison's laugh filled the room. "Really? That's what your mother told you, huh? Well, my dear Mrs. LaRue, you've given me quite a challenge, because I intend to make you move a lot, and I truly want to hear you tell me how you are enjoying our union."

After Garrison turned down the lamp, he took charge of the moment. When he turned back to Camila, he reached out and untied the belt to the wrap, and slid it off of her shoulders and down her arms. He tossed it over the back of the chair, then looking at her with a smoldering stare, he reached up unbuttoned the shoulder straps of her bedgown and watched as it slid down her body and pooled at her feet.

Garrison pulled in a deep breath and stood mesmerized looking at Camila's unadorned body. She was full in all the right places. Her legs were long and shapely. Her ample breasts were plump and perky, full and much larger than he had imagined. He slowly raised his hands and captured one in each hand. They were so firm that his mouth watered. His heart slammed against his chest, and another part of his body had an immediate and strong reaction that he could not control.

When her gown slid from her body Camila closed her eyes. She wanted to cover her nakedness, but before she could lift her arms, she felt her husband's hands caress her breasts. Immediately, she became breathless and her body began to tingle. All she could do was delight in the unexpected pleasure his hands were causing her to experience.

Then just as a moan slipped past her lips, she swayed forward and her legs refused to hold her up. She felt those strong, slightly calloused hands slide around her body, and she was lifted from the floor. Opening her eyes, Camila looked into her husband's handsome face, his eyes now black pools of desire.

She put her arms around his neck and lay her head on his shoulder, and inhaling deeply, she breathed in his clean, fresh scent. She enjoyed feeling his muscular arms holding her close to his broad chest, and she enjoyed the sensation of being carried to and gently laid on the marriage bed.

The room was quiet, and the only thing that could be heard was the soft intake of breath from both newlyweds. As he eased her down onto the mattress, he began ministering to her body from head to toe. Under his slow and deliberate ministrations, there wasn't a place on her soft, curvy, supple body that hadn't been caressed, touched, and gently stroked.

He enjoyed the soft moans, cries, and whimpers of pleasure that she made under the guidance of his massaging, caressing, kneading, and stroking touches. When he felt she was ready to receive the full marriage bed experience, he stood and removed the towel.

Camila caught her breath, her eyes fastened below her husband's waist. He looked at her, and when their eyes met, he said, "Don't worry, it'll fit. Maybe not all at once right away, but it will fit."

He held out his hand and guided her from the bed. He spread a towel over the sheet, and when they returned to the bed, he positioned himself over her and asked, "Do you trust me?"

He didn't continue until she looked into his eyes and whispered, "Yes."

Garrison LaRue was more experienced at making love than his wife, but he proved to be a man who was thoughtful and gentle when making love to Camila. He was patient and took his time showing her what to do, introducing her to the way things were in the marriage bed.

Kissing her, nipping her neck, and savoring her breasts one more time just before he joined their bodies intimately, Garrison said, "Open your eyes, Camila, I need to see your eyes."

After an hour of cautious lovemaking and several climactic moments of great intensity, the newlyweds lay under the sheet, breathing heavily and trying to regain a sense of mental and physical stability.

"What was that? What happened? What did you do to me?" Camila asked in a quivering, wispy voice.

Garrison kissed the hollow of her neck and rolled onto his back, pulling her with him to rest her head on his chest. "That, my Lavender Rose, is called a complete act of love. Did you enjoy it?"

"Yes," she said, covering her face with her hands. "I enjoyed it very much."

Reaching over and gently pulling her hands away from her eyes, he said, "Good. And by the way, your mother would be very disappointed in you, because you definitely did not lie still, and you were certainly not quiet.

And let me tell you that I truly enjoyed every minute of it, too."

Camila offered Garrison a smile then whispered, "It hurt. Is it going to hurt every time?"

He kissed her forehead. "I'm sorry. I tried to be as gentle as I could. It's going to hurt less and less, and you are going to enjoy it more and more each time. I promise."

When morning dawned, Camila opened her eyes, moaning as her husband's hands roamed over her body. She looked into his handsome face and heard his deep voice say, "Good morning, Mrs. LaRue."

He was dressed for work, but he knelt on the bed and kissed her.

"I filled the bathtub with warm water for you because I know you are sore. I have to go to work."

He looked at her longingly, kissed her, then forced himself to stand up.

"I'll see you tonight," he said as he left the bedroom.

When Camila heard the front door close, she stretched as much as her tender muscles would allow, threw back the cover and top sheet, then stood beside the bed, almost falling. He was right; she was sore.

She looked at the soiled towel and snatched it from the bed, glad that they had used it or she would have had to wash the sheets, and she doubted she could get her sore muscles to work that hard after her first marriage bed experience.

Once she was settled in the tub, she lay back and closed her eyes, letting the warm water soothe her achy body.

"I'm sorry, Mother dear," she said, "but I couldn't follow your instructions. What he was doing to me felt so good I had to enjoy it. And Mom . . . I want to do it again . . . the same way."

Camila smiled to herself, lathered, and gently sluiced the scented water over her body. She luxuriously immersed herself for another few minutes then got out of the tub and dressed for the day.

Later that morning, Camila was having a difficult time keeping her mind on the work before her. She realized that her mind kept returning to the experience with her husband last night. She happily admitted to herself that she could hardly wait for her husband to get home from work. She missed him and wanted to experience that closeness they had shared once again.

Around midday, Camila had guests: Mrs. Aires, Mrs. Johnson, Mrs. Anderson, Contessa, and the two little ones who were now her son and daughter. When the children saw her, they grabbed her hands.

Little Garrison said, "Hello, Momma Rose," and Ella Grace raised her hands to be lifted into Camila's arms: "Mommy, Mommy, up, please."

After the greeting, the children were sent to their room where they could play with their toys while the ladies visited with one another.

"We came to see if you survived your first night of marriage," Contessa said. "You look pretty good, except you look tired. My suggestion is that you take a nap before your husband gets home."

They all laughed as Camila invited them into the kitchen for tea. Camila noticed that the ladies were whispering and smiling at her.

"What? What is it?" she asked.

Everyone laughed and Mrs. Aires spoke up for the group. "We were gossiping about how it looks as though you had a full night with your husband last night. How do you really feel right now?"

The other women giggled behind their hands.

"What are you talking about?" Camila asked, perplexed.

Contessa stood, put her arms around Camila's shoulder, and asked, "Have you looked at yourself in the mirror today, Mrs. LaRue?"

Without waiting for Camila to answer, Contessa took her hand and led her to the mirror beside the wall near the front door.

"Look at your neck, girl."

Contessa pointed to the small bruises that dotted Camila's neck. Seeing the bruises on her neck. Camila quickly raised her fingers to lightly touch them, but because she was blushing, they seemed to stand out even more.

Mrs. Johnson stepped beside the embarrassed young woman and said, "Don't be ashamed. We've all had them. It just means that you both enjoyed yourselves last night. Just bathe them in cool water and cover them with some mud for an hour, and in a couple of days, they will fade."

Mrs. Aires smiled and added, "And while you're waiting for them to fade, you can wear high-collar dresses and blouses."

Hearing that advice, the ladies all laughed and agreed with her.

After the advice session was over, Camila realized that the four ladies had come bearing gifts. Mrs. Anderson had a casserole that she had just baked, and Mrs. Aires had another bedgown and wrap.

"Just in case the one you wore last night needs repair," she stated with a smile as Camila opened the box.

Contessa had Camila's order of lavender hair and body oils that had just arrived, and Mrs. Johnson had a copy of the official marriage decree signed by Pastor Johnson and two witnesses and sealed with the official territorial stamp.

CHAPTER 39

When Sheriff LaRue left the office to do his morning rounds, Wesley said to the others, "The sheriff seems pretty danged happy today. I haven't seen him in this good a mood in I don't know how long. Him and Mrs. LaRue must have had a good time last night. Of course, I can't much blame him. That Miss Camila is a pretty woman with a nice body. He was probably all over her last night.".

Jarrod looked at the deputy. "Shut up, Wes, show some respect and stay outta their business."

Then Todd said, "The kid's right, Wes. But I do have to say so myself, the boss is acting a little unlike himself today. They must have really had a good time. All I know is if I was her husband, I would be a happy man today myself."

The three men laughed and bumped shoulders with each other.

The deputies were right. Garrison was happy. He had, indeed, had an enjoyable time on his wedding night, and he planned on having an even better time tonight. Most of his day was spent trying not to think about Camila Rose because just the thought of her and the vision in his mind of her smooth, full, soft, brown body lying in the bed next to him made his body react in a way that was not acceptable in public.

It was after midnight when Garrison was walking down Main Street toward his weekend house.

Tonight, he thought as he was walking, *I'm going to have dinner first then take a bath, and finally, I'm going to enjoy my wife.*

Garrison stopped in mid-stride. He rested his hands on his hips just above his gun belt and repeated two words: "My wife." Then he chuckled to himself. "I'm going home to enjoy spending time with . . . my wife."

He shook his head, smiled, and quickened his steps toward the house, where Camila was waiting for him.

Walking in the front door and seeing Camila standing there waiting for him caused his heart to skip a beat. She was wearing another one of those bedgowns with a matching wrap. This one was pink. Her hair was loose, and her eyes were bright. She looked so inviting that his body's reaction was evident to her even across the room.

"Hello, Mrs. LaRue," Garrison said, "thanks for waiting up for me. I needed to see you. I missed you."

He looked so handsome that she hungered for his touch, his kiss, his body. "Hello, yourself, Mr. LaRue. I couldn't go to sleep. I wanted to see you, too. I . . ." She looked down at the floor.

He stepped up to her and placed his hands on the sides of her face. He put his thumbs on the side of her mouth and lifted her chin until she was looking into his eyes. "You what, Camila?"

"I want you to hold me and kiss me, and I . . . and I . . . want us to be close again tonight. Like we were last night."

As her face began to heat from embarrassment, Garrison's expression went from concern to surprise to amusement. He laughed, pulled her close to his chest, and in a husky, passion-filled voice, he said, "It will be my pleasure."

Kissing her forehead, he let his hands roam from her shoulders to the sides of her breasts, then to her waist, where he untied her wrap and slid it down her arms to the floor. Then he picked her up and carried her to the bedroom.

"You wait here for me," he said, leaning forward to kiss her. "I'm going to take a bath. Don't go anywhere. I'll be right back."

Exiting the water room wearing only a towel, Garrison stepped into the bedroom. Camila was still seated in the middle of the bed, waiting. Their eyes locked as he strode across the room. Tonight, he wanted to enjoy her more than he had the night before. Dropping his towel, he crawled onto the bed and reached for his marriage bed partner.

As he and Camila reached another climactic moment, Garrison leaned on his arms above her, enjoying the sated look on his wife's face. He lowered his head, kissed her, then as he was rolling to his side and pulling her with him, he heard her say, "I love you, Garrison."

Her unexpected declaration of love caught him off guard. He was not ready to hear her say those words to him because he had no intention of saying them back to her. The last person he'd said those words to had betrayed him and turned his heart to stone. He felt that if he forced himself to say them to Camila, they would be empty and insincere.

Without commenting, Garrison released his hold and pushed away from her. He quickly rolled to the edge of the bed snatched his towel. Wrapping it around his waist, he strode out of the room.

Camila was stunned as she watched him leave. After a few moments, she left the bed and slipped into her wrap. When she walked into the darkness of the parlor, she watched his skin glisten as the light from the low flames in the fireplace danced across his body.

She observed Garrison as he stood looking out the window into the darkness of the late night. To her, he looked just like a statue: hard, stiff, and cold. When she touched his back, he flinched and moved away as if she had burned him.

Backing away with her hand still in the air, she asked, "What happened? What did I do?"

"I'm not going to say that to you, because I don't . . . no, I won't have those kinds of feelings for you or any other woman ever again. I appreciate you being here in Alamosa, and I truly appreciate all that you've done for me and my children. I even enjoy having you as my bedmate. But I can't say that to you."

Looking at her with emotionless eyes, he added, "You are a good housekeeper as well as a great cook, but I'm not going to say those words to you. I told someone once that I loved her, and she took my love and threw it back in my face. When she died, I felt like such a fool. After she was buried, I vowed that I would never say that to another woman ever again." He turned his back. "You need to go back to bed. I want to be alone."

Camila stepped around Garrison so that she could look into his face, but he started to turn away again, so she stopped him by putting her hands on his chest.

"Wait, please." Camila looked up into his eyes and smiled sadly. "I never asked you to tell me that you loved me. I know that you aren't capable of loving me because you are still in love with her. I knew what was going on with you when I said yes to your proposal. I went into this with my eyes wide open. You can relax. I'm not expecting anything more from you than what you are willing to give until I don't want it anymore."

With that said, she dropped her hands and walked across the parlor into the children's bedroom. Before she closed the door, she turned, and when their eyes met, she asked, "Why did you even ask me to marry you? If it was because of the sexing, then you had every right without going through the church ceremony!"

Inside the room with her back against the closed door, Camila found herself exhaling a breath she wasn't aware she'd been holding. She felt like she had been used again, just like her family did to her back in Checotah. Only this man had used her in a way that was far more damaging.

After what they had done over the last two days, she was now damaged goods. It was almost a sure thing that she would spend the rest of her life as a divorced and tainted woman. She had given Garrison LaRue her body, she had surrendered to him the only thing that she could really truly call her own, she had given her virginity to him under what she now considered false pretenses. She felt like she was no better than a whore.

When that door closed, Garrison felt a sharp pang of regret settle in his heart. After a while, when he felt the coolness of the night settle on his bare skin, he went into the master bedroom and sat on the edge of the stuffed armchair. He sat leaning forward with his elbows resting on his thighs while his hands hung between his knees and his head hung down to his chest.

"Damn you, Grace," he said with deep anguish filling his voice. "She deserves to have someone love her. I want to love her, but I can't because of you!"

He sat for quite a while and thought about his first wife. Grace had been a beautiful woman, shorter in stature than Camila, with a petite frame that she was proud of and flaunted freely. Her skin was light and creamy, and her youthful face had slightly rounded light-brown eyes with long, thick lashes topped off with thin, naturally arched brows. Her mouth was small and soft with a slight pout. She was graceful in her movements and was very reserved sexually, at least with him anyway.

Garrison continued thinking about Grace, remembering how vain she had been. He recalled that because Grace was so shallow and self-centered, she refused to do any cooking or cleaning, so he was forced to hire someone to do the household chores.

She would also never leave their bedroom in the morning until she was completely made up and dressed in a manner she labeled properly attired. Then she would come downstairs to either sit around having the housekeeper wait on her hand and foot or go to town and spend money that she shouldn't have spent.

Garrison thought about how he had made such a fool of himself loving Grace because she wasn't willing to love anyone but herself. She didn't even show motherly love to her own children. As soon as she could ween them, she was more than happy to let someone else deal with them.

Next, he focused his thoughts on Camila Rose Barnes, a woman with a strong will. A woman who refused to let anyone take unfair advantage of her but exhibited compassion toward others like it was a natural part of her personality.

From the day she walked into his house, she worked like LaRue Crossing was her home. He recalled how Camila had determined to make his home comfortable, making sure that the needs of others were taken care of without complaint or thought of getting something for herself in return.

His mind's eye went back to the ranch house and how she had

transformed it from a house where people ate and slept to a showplace home where every room had its own personality and was meant to be enjoyed. She ushered into his house a pleasant atmosphere, one where there was genuine joy and happiness and laughter.

"This is a mess," he thought out loud. "She doesn't deserve to be unhappy. She deserves a more carefree life. She deserves contentment. But most of all, she deserves to be loved. And right now, I'm not the one who is capable of giving that to her."

Garrison slowly rose from the chair and walked over to the bed. When he lay down, his nose was immediately engulfed in Camila's scent. He pulled the pillow closer and lay his head on it while Camila's voice kept looping through his mind: "I never asked you to tell me you love me. I know that you can't love me. Why did you ask me to marry you?"

His heart was heavy. *I have to admit that she stirs feelings in me,* he thought, *but I think they are more sexual than anything. But I'm not going to say that it's love. I refuse to put myself through something like that ever again.*

Before sleep claimed him, Garrison's mind kept showing him the beautiful vision of his new wife enjoying their marriage bed. He saw her trusting eyes as they bore into his just as their bodies joined, bonding them as close to one another as two people could get.

Camila awoke the next morning feeling a little groggy, but she was not going to let lack of sleep stall her day. After her morning regimen, she went to the kitchen and filled the large pots with water for the laundry. While she was waiting for the pots to boil, she studied her scripture and then prepared breakfast for Garrison.

The smell of his breakfast being prepared dragged Garrison from his restless sleep, and soon he came into the kitchen to find breakfast sitting on the table, but Camila was not there.

When he finished eating, he washed his dishes hoping that she would return to the kitchen, but when he looked out of the window, she was in the side yard wringing the laundry and hanging it on the lines.

He looked longingly and sadly at her. She was more than he deserved in a wife. After a few minutes, he realized that she was not coming back in and had no intention of doing so until she was sure that he was gone.

"She would rather stay out in the cold than be in here with me," he said aloud.

He would have gone out to speak to her if he didn't have to go to work to relieve his deputies, but he promised himself that they would talk when he returned tonight. He strapped on his guns, set his hat on his head, shrugged into his jacket, and left the house.

As she was hanging the sheets, Camila heard the front door close, signaling to her that her husband was going to work. She closed her eyes and said, "I pray that you will be safe today. I love you, and I know that you could love me, too, if you let go of the past."

CHAPTER 40

By 10:00 that morning, Camila had completed washing all the clothes, the house had been dusted, and all of the floors had been swept. During that time, she was thinking about the situation that she'd found herself in since letting her feelings for Garrison slip out. She decided that she wanted to go back to her home now more than ever.

"When the spring comes, I'm going back to Oklahoma. There's nothing here for me. If I'm going to be unhappy and unloved, I may as well be back there in my own house."

Camila bathed and dressed in a day gown, combed her hair, and pinned it up so that it fit under the hood of her cape. Then she left the house and slowly walked to the general store.

"Oh, great, Camila, I'm so glad to see you," Hank said as he stepped to her and took her hand. "Contessa is in labor. She needs you. Go on upstairs. She's in the big bedroom in the back. All the kids are with my parents, and the doctor is on his way."

When she got to the room, Camila took off her cape and immediately began to help her sister-in-law. "Come on, Tessa, let's get you undressed and I'll help you bathe, then we'll get you in the bed."

Contessa smiled weakly. "Cammie, what are you doing here? Oh, never mind. I'm truly glad to see you. Hank is so nervous that I'm afraid to have any birthing pains around him. He falls apart on me. You would think that since this is our second baby, he wouldn't be so nervous. Thank God you're here."

Camila reached out to hug her sister-in-law, and at that moment Contessa was charged with a labor pain. Holding onto Camila, she closed her eyes, leaned on her shoulder, and waited for the pain to ease.

"That was harder than the last one," she said, taking a breath and wiping the tears from her eyes.

Four hours later, Camila was looking at her new nephew. Henry Joseph Anderson III was nestled in his mother's arms having his first meal with his father looking on proudly.

Dr. Lands commented, "You did a great job, Mrs. LaRue, thanks for your help. And I'm sure Mildred, my nurse, would like to thank you, too, since she couldn't be here to help."

A while ago, Dr. Lands realized he needed a nurse to help him. When he began asking the town officials if they knew of anyone who could help him, word got around to Mildred Horn. She informed the doctor that after her husband died, she had pursued some light training, and he asked her to help him. This made Mildred rather happy because it was a way of finding out people's business without having to snoop around to get it.

The doctor checked Contessa's heartbeat and pulse rate, examined the baby again, cleaned and packed away his instruments, then picked up his hat, his coat, and his satchel. As he was leaving, he said, "Congratulations again, Mr. and Mrs. Anderson. You've got another healthy baby. Good day to you all."

Returning to the weekend house, Camila took in the laundry and threw the sheets over the back of the kitchen chairs to take off the chill while she stood by the stove to fold the other items that had been washed. Because she had cleaned the house and it was still early, she thought it was best that she should take the children and go back to LaRue Crossing.

Half an hour later, she had the sheets folded and put away. She then packed the rest of the clothes, left the house, went over to the corral, and asked Old Sam to prepare the carriage. Then she walked to the senior Andersons' house to get her children.

Camila thought about how nice it would have been if things had turned out differently. She thought about being married to someone who loved her and how perfect it would have been if she had children of her own with him.

Well, she thought to herself, *since that's not the case, I'm going to enjoy my two little ones while I can. At least until spring comes in full bloom and I go back home. I hate to leave them, but I have to do what I have to do. They will be just fine, and anyway, by the time they get another two or three years older, they won't even remember me.*

Old Sam delivered the carriage and helped Camila load the trunk in the wagon. When the children were in place and covered with blankets, she headed out of town toward LaRue Crossing. To keep the children from getting too cranky and bored with the trip, Camila told short stories and sang songs with them, and before they knew it, they were home.

When they arrived, Roy was just leaving, so he turned his horse around and helped them to unload. Then he curried the horse and stored the carriage.

Returning to the house, Roy rubbed his hands together. "Alrighty, now, young lady, how 'bout I gets us some heat started in this place while you gets our dinner started, then later have us a nice, quiet night."

"Roy you were on your way to town. You go ahead, we'll be just fine."

"Oh, no, you don't think that I'm goin' to leave y'all here by yur lonesome, do ya?"

"Roy, it's going to be just fine. There are locks on the doors now, and I have my pistol. No need for you to worry."

"Oh, I ain't worried, little lady. How 'bout we have some of your good-tastin' tater pancakes for dinner?"

CHAPTER 41

Hank walked into the sheriff's office, passing out cigars. "Have one on me, fellas. It's a boy."

Everyone stood patting him on the back, congratulating him, shaking his hand, and accepting their cigars.

Answering the questions that were being thrown at him, Hank gave everyone the vitals. "His name is Henry III. He was born at 1:31 this afternoon. He weighs seven and one-half pounds, and he's nineteen inches long. His aunt, Camila, helped in his delivery, and mother and son are doing well. Right now, they are both asleep."

Garrison looked at Hank and quickly blew the cigar smoke into the air. "Camila helped her deliver? That's nice. How did that happen?"

"Well, Uncle Garrison," Hank said, "when you see your wife again, why don't you ask her that very question?"

Instead of answering his brother-in-law, Garrison thought to himself, *I'll ask her if she's speaking to me.*

Later that evening, after visiting his sister and his new nephew, Garrison stepped quickly down the walkway toward the weekend house, but as he got close, he noticed the house was dark. When he walked in, he found the house was dark because no one was there. She was gone.

Anger seized him, and he stood in the parlor with his arms folded across his chest. "So she wants to act like that, does she? Well, I'm not chasing after her. I'm going to stay here and go home when I get good and damned ready. I'm not going to let that woman play cat-and-mouse games with me."

When Monday morning rolled around, Garrison sent a message to Camila by way of Todd. "Miz LaRue, the boss said that he has some extra work to do in town so he won't be home this week. He said that you should take care of his children and keep them safe."

It was a long week that followed. Camila cooked the meals, cleaned the clothes, dusted the house, and tended the children. But she missed him. She chastised herself throughout the week for letting her true feelings about him slip out the last time they were together.

For Garrison, it was a lonely week. He missed Camila, but he wasn't going to let her believe that her leaving disturbed him at all. *I'm not going to let her control me with her feelings.* All the while, he was sleeping in the bed at the weekend house with his head resting on her pillow; the one that had been infused with her fragrance.

Not wanting him to believe that she was upset, Camila drove the carriage to town on Sunday morning. She took the children to church and returned home that afternoon after a visit with Contessa and her daughter, Anna, as well as the newest edition to the Anderson family, little Hank.

Garrison saw them ride into town and watched them leave later that afternoon. As a matter of fact, both times, their eyes met—but neither acknowledged the other.

Inhaling, he whispered to himself, "This is a mess. Lord, how am I going to fix this? What do I need to do to make things right?"

On the following Monday afternoon, Wesley delivered another message to Camila from Garrison. "Missus, the boss says that he'll be home tomorrow. He says you should take care of his children and keep them safe."

Forcing a smile, she said, "Thank you, Wes, for delivering the message." Then, to herself, she said, "What does he think I'm going to do, kick them outdoors and let them starve? He is such a dunce!"

As he was riding down the road to the entrance of LaRue Crossing, Garrison saw two little bundled-up figures standing on the front porch jumping up and down, waving their arms, and he could faintly hear their screams and shouts.

He nudged his horse into a trot, and when he got to the front porch, he dismounted and said, "Hey, you two. What are you doing out here like this?"

Little Garrison spoke first. "Daddy, Aunt Tessa and Uncle Hank say we gots a new mommy, but me and Ella don't want a new mommy, we want Momma Camila."

Ella said, "Yes, Daddy, we want her. She love us, she say so."

Garrison sat on the steps and pulled Ella onto his knee. "Listen, you two, Momma Camila is your new mommy. We got married three weeks ago, remember?" When they both nodded their heads, Garrison said, "She's not going anywhere. She has to stay here with us because you love her, don't you?"

Again, they nodded their heads.

"Well," Garrison continued, "when you love someone and they love you, that means they can never leave you. They have to stay until you're all grown up and don't need them anymore."

Camila was standing in the hall, looking out through a narrow opening of the door and listening to the conversation. When she heard what he said to the children, she gasped then covered her mouth and ran to her room.

Later that night, after putting the children to bed, Camila went into the kitchen and saw Garrison sitting at the table, waiting for her. "We need to talk," he said, and when she leaned against the worktable and folded her arms across her chest, he continued. "We can't let a misunderstanding get in the way of our relationship."

"We don't have a misunderstanding or a relationship. I'm your housekeeper. I'm the cook, and I'm the babysitter. Nothing more and nothing less."

"There is more to it, Camila, and you know it," Garrison responded gruffly.

"Oh, yes, you are absolutely right. There is something more. As of three weeks ago, I became your concubine, your bedwarmer, your bedmate. Well, just let me know when the feeling hits you again, and I'll drop my nightgown and let you have your way with me. And this time, you can rest assured that I'll follow my mother's advice!"

"Stop making it sound ugly. There's nothing wrong with us sharing ourselves with one another. I enjoy you, and I know you enjoyed what we did. I miss you in my bed."

"If you miss me so much, why did you stay away from your own home? We don't have to see each other while you're here. This house is big enough for us to not bump into each other."

She turned and went into the housekeeper's quarters and directly to her bedroom and lay on the bed. After a few minutes, she heard him say, "Why are you in here? Our bedroom is upstairs."

"*Your* bedroom is upstairs. *My* bedroom is down here, and this is where I'm staying. You're probably tired, so why don't you just go on up to *your* bedroom and get some rest? It's been a while since you slept in *your* own bed."

Garrison crossed the room in two steps and sat on the bed beside Camila, quickly engulfing her in his arms. Then he leaned back on the bed with her beside him and rested his head on the pillow.

"You left me," he said to her. "You took my children and you left town. Why?"

"There was no reason for me to stay. Our time together was over, and the house was in order, so after Contessa delivered, I decided to come back to this house." Her lips trembled as she offered her logical explanation.

"*Home*," he corrected her. "You decided to come back *home*." Camila tried to pull away from him, but he drew her back. "This is about what we talked about the last night we were together, isn't it?"

Camila sighed. "Listen, Mr. LaRue, I think we made a mistake. You are a man who is set in his ways. You've made up your mind about how you want to live your life and who you do or don't want to spend it with. I know that it's useless for me to expect you to do something you don't want to do. So . . ."

He didn't let her finish. "You asked me why I asked you to marry me. Well, I've thought about it, and Camila, I need you! I need your help!"

She sat up and turned to look at him, but he put his hands behind his head and stared at the ceiling.

Feeling her eyes on him, Garrison decided to present his thoughts to her honestly. "I want to change. But I can't do it by myself. I want to be with you. But old memories keep getting in my way. I want to change. I want to try to be what you need me to be. I don't want to be by myself. Not anymore."

He stretched out his arm as she lay beside him.

"I'm tired of being alone," he said. "I'm tired of pretending that not having a wife doesn't bother me, because it does. I want someone who will be loyal to me. Someone who will let me be enough for them. Someone who is mine and mine alone."

Camila turned her head to look at her husband. When their eyes met, he rested his head on her chest. She put her arms around him.

"Garrison, I love you." When she felt his body tense, she quickly added, "You don't have to tell me that you love me. I'm not asking you to tell me you love me. Just let me love you, and maybe by doing that, you can get back to the place where you can start loving again."

Even though their bedroom was upstairs, they spent the night downstairs in each other's arms.

CHAPTER 42

A month later, Camila found herself standing in the main parlor looking out of the window, watching her husband ride into town. The weather had been bad all week. There were high winds and lots of snow, and at least two feet of snow in the yard. When Garrison saw a break in the clouds and saw the sun was shining weakly, he decided to go to town while it wasn't snowing so he would be there in case another storm came, making the roads impossible to navigate. He informed Camila of his plans very nonchalantly then turned and walked out of the house. No hug. No kiss. No "take care of yourself." Nothing.

Since that night in the housekeeper's quarters, the relationship between them had gone through some highs and lows. He was amorous when he returned from his weekends in town. He was moody a day, sometimes two days, before he was to return to work. Camila worked hard to keep the atmosphere in the house positive, but his mood swings were wearing her down.

This marriage thing is really hard, she thought to herself. *It can't be good when sometimes you would rather the person you are married to be away from you more than they are near you.*

She looked up at the dark, cloudy sky and said, "Lord, please help me to continue to hold my peace. I'm feeling that there's no reason for me to stay with Garrison LaRue. He's cold and uncaring most of the time. I'm so lonely, there's nothing and no one here for me. I may as well be back in

Oklahoma in my own house for all the love and attention I get around here."

I'm sorry it has come to this, she thought, but I need to start thinking more about myself. I need to start protecting myself from any more heartache. I need to stop taking care of everybody else and start taking care of myself. Mom used to always tell me, 'If you don't take care of and think of yourself first, you can rest assured that nobody else will think of you, either.'

Stepping away from the window, she continued her thoughts, repeating a promise to herself she had made earlier: *As soon as spring sets in fully, I'm going to leave. What kind of life is this, anyway? Wasting my time loving someone who refuses to love me back. I'm tired of being a fool. When I leave, there will be only two regrets. The first is that I'll be leaving behind my two little ones. The other is that I have nothing to show for having been married. I wanted a baby, but since my monthly hasn't stopped, I guess it's not meant to be.*

Camila was dusting the parlor and the dining room as those negative thoughts kept making themselves at home in her mind, causing her to be sad.

Garrison knew that she was unhappy, but he believed there was nothing he could do about it. He certainly wasn't going to compromise himself and tell her that he loved her just to make her happy. Even if he did love her, he couldn't make himself say it. He had to protect himself from more shame and humiliation.

Instead of going directly to town, Garrison rode to the waterfall. He was sitting on a rock by the frozen falls, talking to God. "I love her so much it hurts. When we are apart, I can't stop thinking about her. I don't want to live the rest of my life without her, but I just can't bring myself to tell her that I love her. What's wrong with me?"

He looked up. "Lord, I need your help. I don't want her to leave me. I need her. I can't be alone again."

Putting his hands to his face, he broke down. After a few more minutes of praying and contemplation, Garrison mounted his horse and rode to town.

For the next two months, Garrison and Camila behaved like a loving married couple around others, but when they were home, they acted more like intimate strangers.

By keeping herself busy and doing unnecessary projects when Garrison was in town, Camila managed to make herself tired enough to fall asleep as soon as she lay down so that she wouldn't have to think about him in bed before falling asleep. She never refused him when he wanted to have relations, but it was one-sided. He had stopped considering her needs and only satisfied himself most of the time.

One morning, Camila awoke in pain. As she tried to get out of bed, she had a cramp that doubled her over. Her monthly had started, but this month it was different. She was cramping, and her body was weak.

Garrison felt her weight shift from the bed, and when he opened his eyes, he saw her holding onto the bedpost, leaning forward and holding her abdomen with her other hand.

"What's wrong with you?" he asked.

She slowly raised herself up to her full height and looked at him. "Nothing, you can go back to sleep. I'm fine, thank you."

Giving her a doubtful look, he turned over and immediately went back to sleep.

CHAPTER 43

By the next morning, Camila was not feeling too much better, so when she drove the children to town to get their once-a-year examinations, she asked if Dr. Lands would see her also.

He listened to her complaint, and after a few questions and a quick noninvasive examination, he said, "You've had a miscarriage." When she looked at him confusedly, the doctor explained, "Your body has rejected a baby. I'm sorry."

After she dried her tear-streaked face, Camila asked, "Why is this happening? What's wrong with me?"

"Mrs. LaRue," the doctor said, "there's nothing wrong with you, it's just that your body was not able to accept a baby at this time."

Taking a deep breath, Camila asked, "So now what do I do?"

Dr. Lands regarded her sympathetically. "Go home and tell your husband. He'll probably agree with me that you work too hard, that you need to get more rest. Take a day off once a week and stay in bed, or take a nap during the day. Give yourself about two to three months. Then you two should try again."

Before she left the office, Dr. Lands gave Camila a sack that contained a heavy thick glass bottle with a cork stopper on its side and a jar with a thick, cloudy liquid in it. He instructed her to "fill this bottle with hot water, wrap it in a towel, and hold it on your abdomen when you go to bed. This afternoon before you go to bed, take three drops of this in a half-glass of water. It will help you to stop hurting."

Then he placed something that looked like a canteen with a hose and a tube and a tin of white powder into the sack.

"Mix a teaspoon of this powder with four cups of lukewarm water in this, and do an internal cleansing. Do it once a week for the next four weeks, and then come back to see me. Stay off your feet as much as possible. And, Mrs. LaRue, you and your husband are to have no relations until you come back to see me. I mean that. Your body needs to heal."

As the nurse to Dr. Lands, Mildred Horn was privileged to everyone's business. Now she knew Camila Barnes' business, and she knew just how she was going to use it against her.

This could be just the thing I need to get rid of her, Mildred thought to herself, grinning wickedly. *I told you that it wasn't over at that sad excuse of a wedding, now watch what's going to happen.* Then she laughed out loud.

Anxious to put her plan in place, Mildred watched as Camila and the children climbed into their carriage and headed out of town. Almost immediately, she snatched a sack and filled it with several items then quickly left the doctor's office.

CHAPTER 44

Mildred Bright grew up on what most people called the right side of the tracks. Her parents worked hard to keep the family living better than they could afford. Afton and Lilith Bright gave all appearances of being members in good standing of the upper-middle social class of Pottsville. But they were living beyond their means.

Lilith's family owned a small portion of several of the coal mines outside of the town, and this contributed considerably to the Brights' income, but it wasn't enough to sustain the lifestyle they were living.

Afton was the owner and operator of Bright's Hauling and Freight. His company owned the wagons that transported the coal and ore to the trainyards and loaded them into freight cars to be shipped across the country. It was a dirty job, but with his four employees, Afton earned enough to keep the family in the house his wife, Lilith, had inherited, keep Mildred in the best clothes, get her private tutoring, and send her to a well-known finishing school.

The only person in town who knew about the Brights' financial affairs was Philip Horn, the president of Pottsville Bank and Trust. He helped Afton Bright get the loans to expand his company, and so when Philip Horn came to the Brights with his proposition, they thought about it before they consented.

After church one Sunday afternoon in the year of Mildred's sixteenth birthday, Philip Horn approached the family and said, "Good afternoon,

Mr. and Mrs. Bright," and with a slight bow, he offered, "Good afternoon, Miss Mildred." Then he said, "Afton, do you mind if we have a quick chat?"

When they were out of earshot of everyone, Philip said, "Afton, you applied for another loan, and while there are no problems with your getting it, I think I have a way to guarantee that you never have to take out another loan again."

Seeing the interest on Afton Bright's face, Philip Horn continued. "I would like to have your daughter's hand in marriage."

"What? Mildred? Why? Mr. Horn, you are thirty-five years old and Mildred is sixteen. You are a widower, and she's never been married. Why don't you want an experienced woman for your second wife?"

"Well, as you know, Afton, I don't have any heirs, and a young woman like Mildred could surely provide me with one or two sons, I'm sure." Philip stepped close to Afton Bright and said, "I'm prepared to give you $20,000 for her hand, and for each year that we are married, I'll give you $5,000. That would have you set for life, don't you think?"

Within less than three months, Mildred and Philip Horn were married. The wedding was very lavish, and it was paid for by the groom.

For six months, Philip showed off his new bride by hosting holiday dinner parties, as well as presenting an extravagant Christmas dance. Mildred was the perfect hostess; she used her finishing school training very well.

Her parents were now accepted as full members of the highest social level in not just the city but the state, as well.

Mildred and Philip slept in separate rooms. And for several months, he did not demand that Mildred fulfill her wifely duties. Instead, he insisted that after dinner every evening they sit in the parlor and discuss issues of various topics. For the most part, Mildred enjoyed their evenings together, but for the majority of the time, it was a dull experience.

On Sunday mornings, Philip would wait at the front door for Mildred as she descended the winding staircase. Some of the time, she would be dressed in a new outfit that he had purchased for her. And she would smile with great appreciation as they were driven to church in his beautifully adorned carriage.

Mildred was living well, and she enjoyed the manner in which her husband respected her. She was being treated like a lady not only by him but by the servants, as well as the townspeople.

The first Christmas of her marriage was a very pleasant one for Mildred. She had used her holiday allowance to order gifts for her parents, the servants, and especially her husband.

The day's celebration was perfect. Mildred conferred with the servants, and so the house was decorated very well inside and out. She and Miss Bertha, the cook, agreed on a menu, and the meal was delicious.

Philip was very pleased, and so when the guests had all gone home and the couple was sitting in the parlor, he said, "You've done very well, my dear. This holiday season has been a joy. Thank you for making it special."

Mildred smiled and accepted his praise. Little did she know that her perfect world was about to become flawed.

On New Year's Eve, after dinner and the fireworks celebration, Philip knocked on the door that joined their bedrooms, and when Mildred opened it, Philip took her by the arms and led her to the bed.

"After tonight," he said, "the next time I knock on this door and you open it, you should be undressed and waiting to perform your wifely duties. Take off your clothes."

She could smell the liquor on him. His words were slurred, and he could hardly stand up. She went to her vanity table to remove her jewelry, and as she was removing her dinner gown, Philip stumbled over to her. "Hurry up, you're taking too long. When I give you an order, I expect that you will do it right away."

Mildred was confused and afraid; her husband was behaving strangely. He spun her around and unfastened the hooks on the back of her gown.

"Philip," she said, "what's the matter? Why are you being so mean? Have I done something to displease you?"

"I don't want to hear any whining from you. It's time for you to perform your duty as a wife. Get on the bed!"

The rest of the evening was very unpleasant for Mildred. She was introduced to the marriage bed in a very unloving, insensitive, and painful way. The next morning, her body was very sore from the unexpected mauling and intimate invasion. Her arms, legs, back, and chest hurt from the numerous bruises she had received.

When she opened her eyes, her husband was standing over the bed with trembling lips. "I'm sorry. I thought that I had been cured of that. I didn't mean to do this to you. It's just that I become someone else when I drink. I'm going to try my best not to do that ever again. You can't tell anyone, or we will be ruined."

Unfortunately for Mildred, it did happen again. Over the next ten years, she learned to fear the holidays because her husband's uncontrollable drinking would come to the forefront, and the results were always the same: forced, unpleasant sexual experiences that always left her bruised and feeling violated.

Mildred learned to live with that one problem because the rest of her married life was so good. Philip was a good provider, and she never wanted for anything. She was treated with respect wherever she went, and she had plenty of money to spend.

Although she realized that the money was somewhat of a bribe, she accepted it, and over the years she gained experience in how to read her husband's moods and learned how to escape his drunken wraths . . . most of the time.

She became so good at reading his moods that she could sometimes talk him out of violating her, but she found that he would replace that with verbal assaults and complaints about everyone's financial woes. She even found out how she had literally been sold into marriage by her parents and that they were being paid for every year she remained married to him.

When Philip Horn was found dead in his bed on January 2nd of the eleventh year of their marriage, Mildred served as the deeply grieving widow. And when the will was read, she became a very wealthy woman.

After informing them that she knew about how they sold her to Phillip Horn and were being paid every year on the anniversary, Mildred stopped speaking to her parents. She returned to school to get her nurse's training certificate, turned the house into an orphanage called House of Hope, and left town.

Arriving in Alamosa, Mildred began her new life as a rich widow. She decided that she wanted to remarry and that this time, it was her turn to choose her mate.

When she first saw Garrison LaRue, she was immediately drawn to him. He was the exact opposite of her late husband. He was twenty-four years old, three years younger than her, but she didn't care. He was a hard-bodied, moral, principled gentleman. And she wanted him to make love to her like a real man.

Setting out to learn everything about Garrison LaRue, she discovered that he wasn't wealthy but was very well-to-do. She learned that he was a hard worker who earned every penny he had.

Garrison LaRue was a very handsome man. He had long, wavy black hair; smooth, reddish-brown skin; a deep, sexy voice; and dark, sometimes hard eyes. Along with all of that, his other attributes included the fact that he was tall with long, muscular limbs, a broad chest, and he filled out his Levi's very well.

She pined for him and coveted him, even though he was a married man. When he and his wife had children, Mildred became jealous. It was all she could do to remain civil to Grace LaRue.

Garrison was a loyal husband and a caring father, even though his wife had begun to stray from her commitment to him and the children. When Grace LaRue was killed in such a shameful way, Mildred felt that she could get into Garrison's good graces by making him and the children part of her mission duties. And for almost three years, she administered off and on to their needs, hoping to establish herself to the handsome, brooding widower as the next most eligible woman to become his new wife.

Even though he had several housekeepers come and go, Mildred remained steadfast on her mission. Despite all of her efforts, Garrison LaRue didn't seem to be taking the hint, and Mildred was getting tired of waiting for him to realize her intentions. One day, she decided to force his hand;

it happened to be on his once-a-month free weekend when he didn't have to serve as sheriff.

She was happy that Garrison's parents had taken the children to their ranch so that Garrison could get some much-needed rest.

After everyone had gone, Mildred, instead of going back to town, climbed the stairs to the second floor and waited in his bed for him to come home. Surprised to see the woman was still in his house, and even more surprised that she was in his bed completely undressed, Garrison was so taken aback that it took him a few moments to react. When he did, he quickly grabbed Mildred's clothes, threw them at her, and ordered her to get dressed. His final order to her was to never, ever come back to his house again.

Irate, Garrison rode to his parents' house, told them what had just transpired, spent the night there, and returned to LaRue Crossing the next day with his children.

Even though things didn't go as Mildred Horn had wanted, she still had hope. So she decided to use another tactic. She began sending lunch to him when he was working in town. She had no idea he wasn't the one eating the food. And she made it a point to sit with him and the children in church until he stopped coming to services.

In spite of all that he was doing to avoid her, Mildred made up her mind that he was her choice, and she set out to entice the grieving, shamed widower.

But a year later, just as she was about to make her final, boldest move, a mail-order bride showed up in the form of Camila Rose Barnes. But Mildred was not deterred. On the contrary, she was even more determined to have Garrison LaRue as her husband, by hook or by crook. And even his rejection of her advances and his mail-ordered bride were not going to hinder her, because since becoming a rich widow, Mildred always got what she wanted . . . and she wanted Garrison LaRue!

Even though Camila Rose Barnes was still in the picture after almost two years, it didn't matter to Mildred how long she had to wait. She was going to get the man she wanted.

CHAPTER 45

Looking down at his new nephew, Garrison thought about his stagnated marriage. *If we had a baby, she wouldn't be able to leave me. Babies need a mother and a father to turn out right.* Gently, he gave the baby back to its mother.

Questioning himself about the thoughts that rolled through his head, Garrison was just leaving the general store when he looked up and caught a glimpse of Camila and the children in the carriage leaving town.

"What are they doing here?" he asked himself.

Stepping out of the doctor's office, Mildred saw just the person she was looking for. "Sheriff," she called out. "Oh, Sheriff. Sheriff LaRue . . ." When she caught up to Garrison, she held up a sack. "Your wife left this at the office. She's going to need them if she doesn't want to get *in the family way*." She whispered those last words, leaning close and cupping her hand around her mouth.

"What?" Garrison asked. "What is it?"

"Why, it's some of those sponges like the girls at Miss Annie's House of Comfort get every month when they come for their checkups like you insist they do. It keeps them from getting, you know . . . pregnant."

"What did she say to the doctor to make him give her these things?" Garrison asked.

Schooling her face to keep it from giving her away, Mildred began presenting the lies that she hoped would cause a divide between Garrison and that mail-ordered bride of his.

"She said you both had agreed that having two children was enough and that neither one of you wants a baby anyway." With great joy, she continued. "Then she told Dr. Lands that she herself didn't want a baby because it would destroy her figure. So here you go. She was told not to have relations with you unless she was using one of these."

Barely containing her smile, Mildred handed Garrison the bag then happily returned to the doctor's office.

Angry to the point that he wanted to hit something, Garrison snatched the bag from Mildred Horn and stormed back to his office. "Wesley," he said when he got there, "I'm going home for a while. You guys hold down the fort 'til I get back."

By the time he arrived at the ranch, Camila had gotten the children down for their naps and was in the bedroom changing her clothes. Trying to be calm and control his anger, Garrison stepped into the room and stood watching Camila button her house gown. Then she picked up a jar of liquid and put several drops into a glass of water and drank it.

After swallowing the bitter elixir, Camila turned to leave the room, and when she saw Garrison, her face brightened. "Hello, what are you doing here?"

"This is my house, can't I come home if I want to?"

She saw that his eyes were dark and stormy, and a muscle in his jaw was jumping. "Garrison? What's wrong? Why are you so angry?"

He grunted, "I saw you leaving town. And was wondering why you were there. But then I found out why." He held up the sack. "You forgot this at the doctors' office."

She looked at the sack. "No, I didn't. I have my sack right here." She pointed to the bed. "But I am glad you're here. We need to talk."

"About what? About you telling Dr. Lands that you don't want to have any babies, especially my babies? About you asking for these sponges like the whores who use them to keep from getting pregnant? Why didn't you tell me that you felt that way? I would never have touched you, ever!" He folded his arms across his chest and gave her a scornful look. "I guess it's my turn to ask *you* this question: Why did you marry me?"

Before she could say anything, he stepped close to her and looked into her eyes.

"If you don't want to be here, you can go. As a matter of fact, I don't want you here, so get out. Don't worry about packing. I'll do it for you."

Reaching out to slam the bedroom door, he began pacing the floor.

"I thought you were different, but you're not. You're just as bad as she was. No, you're worse, because you're a phony, a gold-digger, and a liar!"

As he was pacing the room, his hands were clenching and unclenching with every word he spoke.

"You walk around this place pretending to be kind and loving when all the while, you're scheming and calculating all kinds of deception. What other secrets am I going to find out about you? Wait, before you answer that, let me say this. I'm through. Through with you and this whole situation."

Camila felt herself getting angry but remained calm so that she could understand what he was talking about. "I told you, that is not my sack. My sack is on the bed. Almost everything that Dr. Lands gave me is still in it. Why are you attacking me? Why are you accusing me of these things before you even know the truth?"

"So you admit it. You did go to the doctor's office. I'm not accusing you of anything, I'm trying to get you to tell the truth." He stormed over to the bed, grabbed the sack, and snatched it open. After looking inside, he looked at her, puzzled.

Camila turned her back so that he couldn't see her tears, but she was too late. "I went to see Dr. Lands because I've been sick. I was hurting, and my monthly was different. After he examined me, he said I had a miscarriage." She covered her mouth so that she wouldn't sob. "He said that my body had rejected a baby."

Garrison felt like all of the air in his body was gone. "What?" he managed to whisper.

Camila's voice was full of sadness and despair. "He told me to come home and talk to you about it. He told me that he couldn't tell me exactly why it happened, but he thinks that I was probably working too hard and that my body was just too tired to hold a baby right now."

Wiping her face with her hands, she turned back to face Garrison. She squared her shoulders and lifted her chin.

"I'm supposed to stay in bed one day out of the week for a while. Then, after that, he wants me to take a nap during the day. We are supposed to wait about four months and try again to have a baby. But I didn't tell him that we won't be having any babies. I didn't tell him that babies were born out of love and that you don't love me, so I probably won't be having any babies ever!"

Slowly moving across the room to the big leather chair, Camila asked, "I don't know anything about that sack. Who gave it to you?"

"Mildred Horn," Garrison told her reluctantly.

Leaning against the back of the chair, Camila asked, "You actually believed what she told you? You let her convince you that I wanted something like that? Instead of asking me why I was in town, you listened to her and came here to berate and humiliate me."

When he didn't answer her, she pursed her lips and continued.

"So I'll tell you what I'm going to do . . ." She swayed a little, and she was slightly slurring her words. "I am going to pack my clothes myself and go to town for the night. Then I'll get on the train in the morning."

When she stepped away from the chair, she felt faint, and before Garrison could react, Camila crumpled to the floor. He saw her falling but couldn't get to her in time. He lifted her from the floor and took her to the bed. "Are you okay? Do I need to get the doctor?"

"You need to get your hands off of me. As soon as I feel better, I'm leaving. I'm going back home. There's nothing here for me. There never was. I was only fooling myself. Get away from me."

Hearing Camila say those words made Garrison's heart pound. When he set her on the bed, he released his hold on her and stepped back. "I'm going to get you some tea. Stay there. I'll be right back."

"No. Don't get me anything. Just let me rest for a while, then I'll be leaving." By the time she said that, he was already out of the room and down the hall to the steps. And by the time he returned with the tea, she was sound asleep.

Garrison set the tray on the table by the window, removed his gun belt, and hung it on the post in the chifforobe. Then he climbed into bed behind her, pulled her into his embrace, inhaled her lavender scent, kissed the back of her neck, rubbed her abdomen, and thought about how beautiful she would have looked with her body swollen, carrying his child.

He whispered, "I'm sorry, Lavender Rose. I do love you. Don't leave me. I want you to stay with me forever, and I want you to have babies with me. More than anything."

CHAPTER 46

It was late the next morning when Camila awoke to bright sunshine flowing through the windows. The first thing she noticed was that she wasn't dressed like she was when she'd gone to sleep. Her dress, slip, camisole, shoes, and stockings were gone, and she was dressed in a bedgown and her hair was loose. She turned over and saw Garrison was gone.

Lying in bed reviewing the events of the previous day brought back a deep sorrow for her loss. Refusing to get up, Camila let the tears fall.

"Why, Lord?" she moaned.

Through her moments of despair, reality began to set in. Camila was hearing the children talking. She could smell food cooking then heard footsteps running up the stairs.

When the door opened, the children came in. Ella ran to the bed and climbed up. "Mommy, Daddy say you sick and so we needs to be nice to you."

Little Garrison stood at the foot of the bed and said, "I hope you get better soon. Daddy's food don't taste like yours."

Camila lifted her free arm, beckoning to her son. When he stepped to the bedside, she hugged him and said, "I'm going to be just fine in a little while." Then she chuckled. "What did your daddy cook for you?"

From the doorway, she heard their father say, "Oatmeal. I cooked oatmeal, and it wasn't that bad." He looked at his children and his wife and smiled at the beautiful picture they made. "Say goodbye, you two. Go help Mr. Roy clean the kitchen."

After the sound of Ella and GJ's running feet faded, Garrison turned his attention to his wife. When their gazes met, she saw sadness in his bloodshot, red-rimmed eyes.

"Are you hungry?" he asked. "Roy made you some soup. He says that sick people need soup."

After setting the tray on the bedside table, Garrison sat at the end of the bed, facing Camila. He touched her foot and began rubbing her ankle and leg. When she tried to move her foot away, he tightened his grip. He could see she didn't even want to look at him, much less have him touch her.

As he sat watching her, he had a silent conversation with himself. He knew she had not been really happy for a while. It had been over six months since she'd told him that she loved him, and his stupid response had been to tell her that he'd loved once in his life and was never going to give anyone that kind of power over him ever again.

He knew that she deserved to have someone love her and to hear that person declare their love for her as well. He knew this was the time he should let her know how he truly felt.

His thoughts went back to the conversation he'd had with his sister the day before seeing Camila and the children leaving the doctor's office. He was standing in Contessa's parlor, holding his nephew and watching his niece as she played on the floor. He raised his eyes and mutely looked at his sister, who was giving him a piece of her mind about his relationship with Camila.

"Garrison, you treat her like she's a necessary evil. Like you think she's going to do to you what Grace did, and let me tell you, I don't like it, not one bit. Open your eyes, brother, that woman is a jewel, and you'd better realize what you have before you lose her!"

Finally, Contessa pointed her finger at him and said, "Garrison LaRue, stop making things difficult. You need to do the right thing and stop buck-farting around. I know you love her. Hank knows you love her. *You* even know that you love her, so just stop this stupid man-pride thing and tell her!"

Speaking up for himself, Garrison said, "Look, Tessa, I know I've made a mess of everything, and I want to do something about it, but I just don't know how to fix it." His eyes grew pleading. "With everything that's been happening, she wouldn't believe me now if I told her how I feel about her."

"Well, you'll never know if you don't try, will you?"

Now, seated at the foot of the bed before Camila, Garrison cleared his throat and waited until she looked at him to speak. "I'm sorry. I acted like a fool. I said some terrible things that I didn't mean. I called you names that I should never have said because they aren't true, and I knew it when I said them. I'm so very sorry. Do you think you could ever forgive me?"

Camila looked dispirited. Her eyes were sad and dull like they had lost their light. Her face was drawn, and her lips were trembling.

What have I done? Garrison thought. *Will she ever forgive me?*

Camila was trying to control her emotions. She couldn't speak for fear of losing her battle with the tears clogging her throat, so she shrugged her shoulders.

"While you were sleeping yesterday, I went back to town and talked to Dr. Lands about what Mildred did," Garrison told her. "He's going to fire her if she doesn't give you a written apology and then make a confession in church when you get better."

Camila looked surprised. "Why did you do that?" Her voice was flat, and she wouldn't look at him.

"Because you called my bluff and said that you were going to leave, and at that moment, I felt empty, alone, and afraid. Having you here makes me feel like my life is manageable. Your being near me takes away the loneliness and the fear of being a father with no wife to help raise my children."

Garrison moved to the top of the bed and took Camila's hands in his.

"We need you, Miss Lavender Rose," he said. "I need you."

Camila's hands tensed, and she tried to pull them away.

Garrison leaned forward and kissed her lightly. "I'm not too late, am I?

Please tell me that I haven't destroyed your love for us." When she didn't answer him, he rested his head on her shoulder. "I'm so sorry. I'm going to make this up to you, I promise. Don't leave, please. We need you." He slowly wrapped his arms around her.

As much as she tried to remain indifferent and unemotional, Camila found herself giving comfort to the man she loved. When his body trembled and she felt his tears on her neck, she raised her arms and held him tight.

CHAPTER 47

The winter was long and cold. The weather had been bad for weeks. And it seemed that spring would never arrive. But then the weather broke, and spring slowly began to show itself.

The last week of March marked the fourth anniversary of the civil marriage and two years of the church marriage between Camila Rose Barnes and Garrison LaRue.

The onset of spring was beautiful. The trees were budding, the animals were losing their winter coats, the sky was showing more of its blue hues, and the warmth of the sun was growing stronger and stronger. The ice and snow were melting more and more each day, leaving the grasses looking lush and green.

Garrison and Camila spent the winter building their relationship, and the emergence of spring had the couple looking like they were healing from their marital woes. For a while, he was more cordial to her and began acting like a man who was falling in love.

He smiled at her, teased her, and made love to her every chance he could. But he never said those three words that would prove to her that she was no longer a replacement wife.

Even though Garrison couldn't bring himself to tell her that he loved her—mainly because he was determined to never let another woman have that kind of control over him again—it seemed that calculated attentive application of what she assumed was unspoken love was making her blossom.

Camila's actions showed Garrison that there was no doubt in her mind he loved her, but he could tell she was still a little broken inside. There were times when he knew that she was thinking about what their baby would have looked like, and how he or she would be growing and behaving, because she would from time to time grow quiet and withdrawn. Sometimes she would stand by the tree in the side yard with her arms folded around her body, softly humming lullabies.

Garrison knew Camila was not as happy as she could have been. He felt that she was emotionally shattered, and he knew it was because of losing the baby and not being able to conceive another one over the last few months. However, he was determined to see her through. He longed to see her smile genuinely again. He made up his mind to do everything in his power to make her whole again.

The warmer weather seemed to serve as a balm to Camila. She was smiling more and wanted to show her husband that she appreciated his attentions. On several occasions, she would do something special just for him, and that included taking lunch to him in town.

This particular Saturday, intending to go to town to meet Garrison to celebrate their anniversary, Camila asked Anna and Thad to sit with the children for the rest of the weekend. That afternoon, she drove the carriage to town with a picnic basket full of sandwiches, fried chicken, potato salad, lemonade, and thick slices of butter pound cake under the seat. But instead of staying for a while, Camila returned home rather quickly and didn't offer a reason to anyone for her speedy return.

On Monday morning when he arrived home, Camila was sitting in the summer room when Garrison returned.

"Hello, welcome home," she said. "I'm surprised to see you today."

Sending her a smile, he took off his gun belt and put it in the box on the high shelf. Then he hung his hat and jacket on the peg and finally pulled his boots off and set them in the mud box. Leaning on the arms of her rocking chair, he kissed her. "Hello yourself. I'm glad to see you. How are you feeling?"

She looked cautiously at him. "Garrison, can we talk?"

"Of course. Where are the children?"

"They're in the barn with Roy and Todd." Then, without giving Garrison a chance to speak, she said, "I want to go home."

Garrison's legs felt weak. He sat in the rocking chair opposite Camila so he wouldn't fall to his knees and took a deep breath. "Okay. When do you want to leave, and how long are you all going to be gone?"

Camila was staring at the floor. "I want to leave on Thursday. I'm not taking the children, because I'm not sure when or even if I'm coming back."

Garrison tried not to explode. His chest was tight, and his ears were ringing. Taking another deep breath, he tried to calm himself. Then he realized that she was still talking.

". . . said that they would take the children whenever you are on duty." She took a deep breath herself. Then she rose, crossed the floor, and stood between Garrison's knees, placed her hands on his shoulders. "This doesn't mean that I don't still love you. Because I do. I will love you for the rest of my life. I just need to get away. I don't feel like myself. I don't feel like I'm loved, and I want to feel loved. I *need* to feel loved."

When he reached out to take her hands, Camila stepped back. "I need to leave. I need to go back home. This situation is not working for me anymore. I want more, I need more, I deserve more. I want to be in a marriage that's real, one that gives love as well as takes love. I want to be sure that my husband is mine. I'm tired of being the replacement wife, doing all the work, giving all of myself, and getting less than that in return."

Feeling slow anger building up within him, Garrison stood up. "Where is all of this coming from? Why are you all of a sudden so tired of everything? You knew the situation when you agreed to be my wife. I didn't hold anything back. I explained everything to you, and you stayed. So why do you want to leave now, Camila? It's been more than four years. How can you even think of doing this to me and my children after all this time?"

He paced the room, then came back to stand in front of her. "You're doing this to get back at me for not falling under your spell, for not telling you that I love you! You want to make me into some soft-spoken, hen-pecked, moon-eyed, half-man running around behind you like some little puppy dog. Well, if that's what you want, you can forget it, because that's never going to happen. Not now, not ever!"

"You are so wrong," Camila said. "But there's no point in arguing with you." She turned aside. "Excuse me," she said and went into the kitchen to check her pot of chicken vegetable soup.

Garrison watched her move around the kitchen seasoning the soup, taking the bread from the oven, and buttering the tops of the loaves. When she returned to the summer room, he threw at her, "You're not telling me the whole truth, are you, Camila? What else is going on? If you have a point to make, you need to tell me the whole truth about why you want to leave."

She rested her hands on her hips and said, "The truth, huh? You want the truth? Why? Is it because you are such a truthful person yourself? Well here's the truth. I went into town Saturday. I was going to surprise you with an anniversary lunch, and when I was near the house, I saw you and the woman that you were with, leaving the house. I didn't want to start a scene, so I turned around and came home."

With his heart pounding, Garrison looked at Camila with hard and stormy eyes. "Are you following me? Are you checking on me? I'm a grown man. I don't need you checking on me. You are not my mother!"

"Who is she, Garrison?"

"None of your business."

"Really? So how does it feel to be the unfaithful one? The one that's doing the cheating instead of being cheated on? You are nothing but a cheat and a liar! Are you enjoying yourself? Is she worth it?"

"Unfaithful . . ." he said. "Cheat . . . don't you dare call me that. You have no right. What I do when we are apart is none of your business!"

"And what about this? Is this also none of my business?" Camila reached over to the table beside the chair where she had been sitting and picked up an envelope. Holding it in her hand, she shook it at him. "You do recognize this, don't you?"

"What are you doing with that?"

"Is this letter of divorce the reason you've been so moody lately?"

He snatched the letter from her and shook it in her face. "This letter is four years old! I had it drawn up right after our marriage at the courthouse. How did you get this?"

Camila couldn't believe him. "Does she know about the children? Is she ready to become their mother? Is she ready to be the cook and house-keeper, or is she too pretty for that?"

"She's their aunt. Her name is Mercy Peterson. She's Grace's sister. Mercy came to town to see the children, and I let her stay at the weekend house for the night. Yesterday morning, I took her to Miss Kit's for break-fast. She'll be back there this evening, and I told her she could stay as long as she wanted to."

Camila raised her hand and poked Garrison in his chest with her finger. "Now who's lying, Garrison? I don't believe you. I don't believe one word you've said!"

She saw the veins in his neck standing out. His jaw was clamped tight, and his lips were pressed into a thin line. But she didn't turn away from his intense gaze. She met him straight on with a malevolent stare of her own.

She knew from experience that he was hiding something, and she knew beyond a shadow of a doubt that he was certainly not going to tell her the truth. She also knew that he had just shut down and that he wouldn't be speaking to her for a while. And that suited her just fine. She didn't want to speak to him anymore either.

Garrison didn't want to keep a secret from Camila, but it was necessary this time. It was true that the woman at the weekend house was Mercy Peterson, his first wife's sister, but she was not in town to see the children. She was under protective custody after seeing her boss, Jake Johnson, get murdered behind the saloon where she worked in Springville.

One week earlier, a U.S. marshal delivered Mercy Peterson to Alamosa for Garrison to take charge of until the man who shot the saloon owner could be found and she could testify against him in court. Garrison was told not to tell anyone why she was in town for any reason.

Thinking about it now, he figured it must have been when he'd escorted

Mercy Peterson from her jail cell to the weekend house to take a bath and change her clothes when Camila saw them walking through town.

Garrison wanted very badly to tell his wife everything, but he didn't want to put Mercy in any more danger, and he certainly didn't want his wife, the woman that he possibly loved, to become part of the mess that Mercy had brought to town.

CHAPTER 48

For the rest of the day, the atmosphere in the house was tense. While the ranch hands were having dinner, it was obvious to them that Garrison and Camila were not speaking to each other. As a matter of fact, the only conversation presented at the dinner table came from the children and the ranch hands.

Immediately after dinner, Garrison went to his office and closed the door with a certain amount of emphasis while Camila cleared the table and scraped the dishes with her own certain amount of emphasis.

In the office, instead of going over the ledgers, Garrison paced the floor. He was angry with Camila for wanting to leave. He wondered why she couldn't make herself satisfied with the situation between them just the way it was for a little while longer.

After a couple of more hours of fuming, pacing, and talking to himself, he thought, *If she's so unhappy here, then she does, indeed, need to be gone. She should go back to her lonely spinster life in her lonely spinster house doing whatever lonely spinsters do!*

Finally, after the house was quiet and he could no longer hear the children, he left his office and went into the kitchen, but Camila wasn't there. He climbed the stairs and found her in their bedroom packing her clothes.

"Okay, so you're packing," he said. "Good. I've been thinking, and I feel that it's best that you leave. If you are that unhappy, then I agree that you should go back to Oklahoma, and then we both can get back to living the life we want without having to answer to anyone but ourselves."

He stood looking at her with his arms folded across his chest, but she wouldn't make eye contact with him. Instead, she continued folding and packing her clothes. He turned on his heels and stormed back to the den.

Even though it was late when she finished packing, Camila took her carpetbags down to the summer room and piled them by the back door. As she was returning to the bedroom, she knocked on the office door, and when Garrison snatched it open, she asked, "Would you mind bringing my trunks down, please?"

Without a word, he came out of his office, went up the steps, and brought down the trunks one at a time. When he had set them in the summer room, he went to the parlor where Camila was sitting. He took hold of her arms and lifted her to her feet.

"I'm not bedding that woman," he told her. "I haven't bedded anyone but you since we've been married. But as far as we are concerned, I think we need a break from each other."

Still holding her hand, Garrison led her to the housekeeper's quarters, where they joined together like a loving married couple. He was very passionate and acted like he couldn't get enough of her. Much later, as she lay sleeping beside him, Garrison let his true feelings surface.

He finally admitted to himself that he was going to miss having Camila around. He admitted that he was going to miss the soothing sound of her, the gentle touch of her, the pleasing sight of her, the flowery smell of her, and most of all, the sweet taste of her.

He knew that it would be hard, but she had to go. She had gotten through his defenses, and it was getting harder and harder to keep his feelings to himself. There had been several times when he'd almost slipped and told her that he loved her. But he definitely wasn't going to do it now because he didn't like being pressured into doing anything. And he was convinced that this was just what her going home was all about.

Camila awoke just before dawn and realized that Garrison was not in the bed beside her. She took a thorough sponge bath and dressed in her traveling suit. She hadn't worn this outfit in the four years she had been in

Alamosa, and it was now too big.

Stepping into the kitchen, she saw Garrison was pouring himself a cup of coffee. When he looked up, she could see a look of resignation on his face.

"Good morning," she ventured.

"Good morning? You really want to wish me a good morning?" he snarled.

She saw that her luggage was no longer in the summer room. Garrison told her that he had already been to the barn, hitched the horses, and loaded the luggage into the wagon.

"Yes," Camila said, "I do want to wish you a good morning. As a matter of fact, I want to wish you a good rest of your life. Just because we couldn't make it as a married couple doesn't mean that I hate you. I want you to be happy, and I hope that you find someone who loves your children and makes you happy also."

Just as Camila and Garrison were leaving the house, Roy came across the yard, and without greeting, he asked them, "Are ya sure ya want ta do this?" Then he turned to Camila. "Is there somethin' that can be done that'll make ya stay? I hates to see ya leave like this, Miz LaRue. Hell, I hates ta see ya leave at all!"

Instead of answering his questions, Camila hugged the older man as fiercely as he hugged her. When she stepped back, she reached up and rubbed his scruffy beard. "My time here has come to an end, but I will always remember you, my friend."

Roy turned to his boss. "What's wrong wit' you? Do ya really want her ta go? Don't you know this here woman is the best thing that ever done happened ta this place and most 'specially ta you?"

Garrison looked at Roy as he spoke to Camila in a deadpan voice. "If you want to get that early train, we need to go now."

Driving into town, Garrison was distant. He didn't speak to Camila at all, he didn't look at her, and he didn't touch her. When they arrived at the station, he went to buy her ticket while she went to the telegraph office to send Sherman a telegram informing him that she was going to be home on the Saturday-morning train.

While handing Camila her ticket, Garrison said, "Thank you for all that you did for me and my family. Have a good life." He tipped his hat and walked away just as the train was pulling into the station.

Camila stood still, almost like she were in a trance, trying to digest what Garrison had just said to her. He was so detached.

After walking several feet away, he turned and came back to where she was standing. "Listen, I'll let you get settled before I send the letter of divorce. Don't worry. I'll take care of everything. All you'll have to do is sign the letter and send it back."

Camila stepped close to him, and looking up into his face, she replied, "Don't bother. I've already signed it. All you have to do is sign it yourself and have the lawyer send me a copy."

Instead of commenting, and without warning, he reached out and pulled Camila forward for a quick kiss that brushed her lips. "Goodbye, Miss Barnes."

Camila sat on the train, looking down at her hands folded in her lap, listening to the sound of the wheels on the tracks taking her far away from people that she had accepted as her family.

She refused to look out of the windows, afraid she would see the lonely vision of Alamosa fading into the distance as she moved farther and farther away from a place she had begun to consider her home. But as it turned out, she was wrong.

She didn't want anything to make her change her mind about going back to Oklahoma. It was a tough decision, but she had to do it because she was wasting her time living with and loving a man whose heart wasn't free to love her.

As the train rolled down the tracks, Camila thought about the life she was leaving behind. She was already missing the children; they were so sweet and innocent and didn't deserve to be hurt like this, but their grandparents were more than willing to take over caring for them.

Besides, she rationalized, *they won't remember me for too long. One day, I'll just be another faded memory.*

Camila let her thoughts drift back on the more than four years she had spent away from Checotah. She thought about her first day in Alamosa, the civil marriage ceremony, later meeting and getting to know the ranch hands, meeting her in-laws, becoming friends with Roy, helping Contessa deliver her second baby, and meeting GJ and Ella Grace. Those two innocent faces with the big, expecting eyes would remain part of what she loved most about Alamosa, Colorado.

She recalled the kindness of the women in town, especially Mrs. Aires and Mrs. Johnson, along with the jealousy-driven pranks of Mildred Horn that most of the time made her smile at how silly that woman was thinking Garrison would ever be interested in her.

Almost immediately, the memories of the love of her life began to flood her mind. She remembered the injured look in his eyes, the stoop to his shoulders, and the sadness in his voice that was there when they first met, and she smiled sadly to herself as she remembered seeing that look there again when she'd had the miscarriage.

She recalled how those things began to go away gradually and were replaced by a sparkling twinkle in his eyes, a strong, deep voice, squared shoulders, and a straight back. Garrison was a warm, passionate man when he let down his guard, but that wasn't very often, and that refusal to be totally free of his demons was what had her on this train with a broken heart.

Dabbing her tears and smiling weakly to herself, Camila made up her mind that she was at the beginning of another new chapter in her life and that she had to make herself believe this was a good decision. And even if it wasn't, she was going to make the best of the situation.

After all, she thought, *I have to live by the decisions that I make until they don't work for me anymore. Then I'll make some new ones.*

CHAPTER 49

When the train finally pulled into the Checotah depot, Camila was more than ready to disembark, collect her luggage, and get to her house. When she stepped onto the platform, she knew that in no time at all her arrival would be all over town because Belinda Kirkland, a girl she had gone to school with, was standing in the doorway of the ticket office.

"Yoo-hoo, Camila Rose! Camila Rose Barnes? Is that you? I heard you were happily married and living in Colorado. What in the world are you doing back here?"

"Hello, Belinda," Camila said. "It's nice to see you. It's been a while. I thought you would have moved away by now yourself."

Before the conversation could get more personal, Sherman stepped up beside Camila. "It's about time you got back here, little sister. We've missed you. Welcome home."

Grabbing her, he kissed her cheeks and folded her into a bear hug, picking her up and spinning her around.

Then, pointing to someone standing behind them, Sherman said, "I want you to meet my family." Looking at a pretty, petite woman standing a few feet away, Camila's brother said, "That lady is Athena, my wife. That pretty little one standing behind her momma's skirts is your niece, Amanda. And in Athena's arms is our son, Manny, Jr. Athena, this is Camila Rose, my sister."

The ladies hugged, then Camila stepped back to look at her nephew. As she folded the blanket back, she felt a small twinge of regret in her chest as she looked at the beautiful, innocent little baby boy. When she stooped down to greet her niece, a tear slid down Camila's cheek.

Sherman lifted Amanda into his arms and led them to the wagon. "You all wait here while I collect Camila's luggage. Then we'll be off."

While they were waiting, Camila and Athena talked and got acquainted with one another. After fifteen minutes, Sherman and several other men returned and loaded the trunks and carpetbags onto the bed of the wagon, and they were off.

"Cam, it's good to see you. We enjoyed getting your letters, so you can imagine the surprise when we received the telegram. Let me say that I'm so very sorry things turned out like they did. But I am glad that you came back home. I love you, baby sis."

Camila dropped her head. "I had to come here, Manny, I have nowhere else to go."

Athena patted Camila's hands. "We wouldn't expect you to go anywhere else. This is your home, and this is where you should be."

Three miles outside of town, Camila looked up and saw her house come into view. It looked like it could use a fresh coat of paint, and the flower beds needed weeding.

Sherman guided the wagon into the front yard and around to the carriage house, where he stopped the horses and jumped out to help the women and children down and begin unloading. The ladies walked around the veranda to the front of the house, and as they walked past the parlor windows, Franklin snatched the front door open and stepped out of the house with his arms folded across his belly.

"So, here you are. It certainly didn't take the cowboy too long to get sick and tired of you. I do have to admit, however, that he put up with you much longer than I ever imagined." Franklin looked at Camila and let his distaste for her show on his face. "Well, since you're here, you may as well come in. But let me warn you, don't start anything with my family in here, or you'll be out on your ear."

"Well, Franklin," Camila said, "from the looks of you, life has not been easy on you. However, let me say this. You must have forgotten that this is my house, and I will behave the way I choose to, and you have nothing to say about it. Let me also remind you that *if* anyone will be out on their ears, it will be you. I don't have a problem putting you out of here if you decide you're going to act a fool. So watch what you say *and* do around me in *this* house, brother!"

Camila looked him up and down and continued, "By the way, big brother, I don't like the way this house looks. It could use some paint, and the flower beds are long neglected. Looks like instead of worrying about me and what I *might* do, you need to make this place look more presentable. Why don't you try painting this house, or even getting down on those knees and pulling some weeds instead of lifting that fork so much?"

With that said, Camila turned to her new sister-in-law and winked. Then she took her niece by the hand and walked into the house with her head held high, leaving Franklin with an expression of utter dismay on his face.

The two ladies walked into the parlor and saw Franklin's wife, Willa, standing there with two cute little girls. Walking over quickly to hug Camila, Willa smiled and whispered, "Don't pay too much attention to him, Camila, he's not happy unless he has something to complain about. Welcome home, I'm glad to see you."

Camila was introduced to her other two nieces, who were five and three years old, before they were sent with their cousin to the hallway to play. For the next half hour, the ladies sat in the parlor drinking tea and eating finger sandwiches.

Not being one to waste words, Willa Gilmore-Barnes asked without hesitation, "Why did you come back, Camila? What happened? How long are you going to stay?"

Looking at Willa, Camila offered a sad smile. "Well, just so there will be no misunderstanding, all I'm going to say is that Garrison LaRue and I have decided to divorce."

After a few moments of uncomfortable silence, Camila presented her sister-in-law with a weary look. "You know, Willa, I really would like to stay and talk, but I've been on that train all of four days and I'm tired. I want to take a bath and sleep lying down for a while. Let's talk tomorrow morning."

When she stepped into her bedroom after her bath, Camila saw a woman unpacking her clothes and putting them in the drawers of the dresser and hanging them on the hanger bar of the chifforobe. "Well, hello there, little miss," the woman said. "My name is Mrs. Deannie Mae Wills. I'm the housekeeper. I'm just about through, so come on in, get into that there bed, and get you some rest."

"Thank you, Mrs. Wills, but you don't have to do that. I'll get to them after I take my nap."

Mrs. Wills looked at Camila. "You just hush up, little girl. Like I said, I'm almost finished. You just climb yourself into that bed and close your eyes."

Gladly following instructions, Camila went to the bed and folded back the covers. After she lay down and pulled the covers up to her chin, it didn't take more than two minutes before she was asleep.

Just as she was finishing the unpacking, Mrs. Wills found two frames of pictures. One was of the children, and the other was of Garrison and the children. Looking at them, Deannie Mae Wills shook her head.

"Lord," she said, "put this family back together again, please."

She put the pictures on the bedside table where Camila could easily see them and left the room.

CHAPTER 50

During her first night home, even though it was the first night in four days that she'd been able to sleep in a bed, Camila slept fitfully. She was bone tired but kept waking up and reaching out to the other side of the bed. She wanted to feel her husband's body lying next to her. Each time she whispered his name and touched the empty space, she shed tears.

Finally, around midnight, Camila threw back the covers and got out of bed. She paced the floor for a while then pulled back the drapes and stared out into the darkness.

At the very same time that Camila was pacing the floor in her bedroom, Garrison LaRue was riding his horse to the waterfalls where he dismounted and sat on the rock listening to the water splashing over the rise, looking up at the starry sky. He was trying to formulate a plan to get Camila to come back to Alamosa. He hadn't had a full night's sleep since she boarded the train. His temper was short, and people kept their distance from him.

"I don't know when or how it happened, but I love that woman, and I miss her. It seems like since she's been gone, I can't breathe. I need her to be here with me. I don't feel complete without her."

When he realized what he had spoken into the night, Garrison quickly sat up, jumped to his feet, and mounted his horse. "Damn!" he declared, slapping the reins and galloping full speed back to LaRue Crossing.

After an hour of staring out the window, crying, and pacing the floor,

Camila took the picture of Garrison and the children to bed with her and was finally able to sleep. By the time she walked into the kitchen the next morning, it was after nine o'clock, and Mrs. Wills was kneading dough.

"Well, good morning, little lady. How did you sleep?" she asked Camila.

"Good morning," Camila said. "I managed to get some sleep."

Mrs. Wills looked at her knowingly. "Baby, I know you're heartsore and feeling at loose ends, but if you needs to talk at any time, just let me know. I have good listening ears, broad shoulders, and strong arms." When Camila made no comment, the older lady said, "You need to eat. Go on over to the stove and get your plate out of the warming oven."

Meanwhile, Franklin was still steaming. He left the house that morning angry. "Who is she to come back here being so uppity? How dare she show such disrespect to me? It's obvious that she didn't learn a thing about staying in her place and respecting a man! No doubt that's exactly why the cowboy sent her back here."

The rest of the day was miserable for him. He didn't want his sister to come back and mess up his life. If she couldn't stay out west with that cowboy, then he had to do something to get her away from him, and he had to keep her from taking that house away from him and his family.

Franklin earnestly believed that he deserved Camila's house. He felt that he should have gotten it and the largest amount of the inheritance in the first place.

"After all, I'm the oldest. I worked for everything that I have. All she did was take care of them until they died. That's what she was supposed to do. Besides, she'll never spend all of that money anyway, if she hasn't given most of it to that dirt farmer by now."

After the mercantile closed that evening, Franklin walked into *his* house and ordered his sister into the den.

When the housekeeper gave him his slippers and the daily paper, he demanded, "Mrs. Wills, tell my sister I said to get down here to this den right now."

Mrs. Wills turned toward the staircase. As she was climbing the stairs, she rolled her eyes and thought to herself, *Man, you must think that your sister is 'fraid of you.*

In Camila's room, Mrs. Wills said, "Little missy, your brother is demanding you come to his den, he said right away."

"Well, then, that means that you and I have time to talk, doesn't it?" Camila laughed. "So how did the day go for you?"

Mrs. Wills put her hands on her hips. "Gal, you is somethin' else. Don't keep him waiting too long. He gets nasty when he thinks he's being disrespected." Shaking her head, Mrs. Wills returned to the kitchen to finish preparing the evening meal.

Because Camila didn't come right away, Franklin was truly angry when she did finally arrive. When she opened the door to the den without knocking and stood in the doorframe with her hands folded across her chest, he was so angry that he almost couldn't breathe.

After a few moments, he started talking. "Camila, we have rules in this house. Every adult is up and ready for breakfast by seven o'clock, dinner is served promptly at noon, and supper is served no later than five o'clock. If you are not at the table, then you don't eat. Your being here is an inconvenience to me and my family, so I would appreciate you not trying to insinuate yourself into my family's business. Just because you couldn't keep your marriage together doesn't mean that you can come back here and interfere with my family's happy life."

Camila stood looking at her brother, his words cutting her to the quick. "Frank, what did I ever do to you? Why do you always treat me so cruelly? I don't ever remember you being nice to me. It was always you doing and saying mean things to me. Why?"

Giving a loud snort that made his paunchy belly jump, Franklin sneered at his sister. "Don't ask me any silly questions. I'm the man of this house, and you will do what I tell you to do or you can leave! Our mother and father spoiled you and made you think you were special."

He stood, rested his fists on the desk, and leaned forward, looking into her eyes.

"They would always say 'Don't make so much noise, you'll wake your sister. Take your sister out for some fresh air. Watch out for her, don't let anything happen to your sister.' It was always you. I *hate* you."

Camila gasped, but Franklin continued. "I tried to be so good. Tried to be perfect so that they would pay attention to me again. I took over the general store and made it a very successful mercantile. I even married the woman they wanted me to marry instead of marrying someone I'd fallen in love with. Then, when they died, you got everything. You didn't work for anything. Everything you have is because they gave it to you."

Camila couldn't believe what Franklin had just said to her. She'd never known that he felt that way. "Well, I guess that answers my question. You're jealous of me because I was born. I'm sorry you feel that way, but I can't do anything about it. So now what?"

Franklin's breathing was heavy, and his face was puffed up and turning dark. "Just follow my rules and stay away from me!" Franklin fell back into his chair and stared at her.

After a few minutes of them staring at each other, Camila turned to leave the room. Then she stopped and look back at him. "Well, now that you've had your say, I'm going to have mine. I didn't ask to be born, and I certainly didn't ask to have you as my brother. I didn't ask for this house or the money. I surely didn't ask you to sell me to that man in Colorado, and I especially don't ever remember asking you for anything. It seems that you have a problem, and you want to use me as the scapegoat. Well, let me tell you that *if* I want to, I can move back into this house and tell you to take yourself back to those three rooms in back of the store. I can even buy that store out from under you and throw your sorry self out into the street. You better stay away from me and leave me alone, or you will be the one who is out, brother!"

Franklin looked at Camila with hate-filled eyes.

Camila stared back. "What? Do you have something else you want to say?"

When he didn't answer, she gave him a smile and winked before she turned and walked away.

Willa was in the parlor when Camila walked past on her way to the front porch. Following her sister-in-law outside, Willa said, "Listen, Camila. I'm so sorry about all of that. This thing has been like a disease to him. It's been festering in him for years, and he won't let it go. I don't know what to do anymore."

Sighing sadly, Camila said, "Don't worry about it, Willa."

The women hugged one another and separated. Camila picked up her gloves and her basket and walked toward the flower and vegetable gardens.

CHAPTER 51

By the time Camila had been gone a month, life at LaRue Crossing had taken on a dull and boring routine. The ranch hands were missing Camila and spent much of their mealtimes talking about how their boss was hardly ever home as well as their boss's loss. They continually lamented that, since this second Mrs. LaRue was gone, things had turned sad and gloomy again, maybe even more so this time since Miz Camila was such an open, friendly, and compassionate person. Her absence left a void in everyone's life. Whenever that discussion came to an end, one of the men would say, "I sure hope that Mr. LaRue can figure out a way to get Miss Camila back here, and do it soon."

During that time, Garrison was preparing to return Mercy Peterson to the custody of the U.S. Marshals for the beginning of the murder trial. Marshal Benjamin Tate had finally caught up to the man who committed the crime and requested that the witness be returned to Springville.

The request was a good thing for Garrison, who had grown weary of protecting the woman. To him, Mercy was tiresome. She was a classless vixen. It was obvious to anyone and everyone that Mercy was a saloon girl in every sense of the word. Being around her made Garrison long to see his wife again. Camila was nothing like this worldly woman who made her living enticing men.

He promised himself that as soon as the trial was over, he and his children were going to get on the train and go see Camila Rose LaRue in

Checotah, Oklahoma, and pray that he could convince her to come back to Alamosa.

It took another two weeks for the trial to end. As soon as the verdict was handed down to the prisoner, Garrison rode back to Alamosa with Todd and Jarrod then went directly to LaRue Crossing, packed clothes for himself and the children, rode back to town, picked up his children from his parents at their weekend house, took them to the train station, and he and his children were on their way.

Just before they boarded the train, Garrison sent a telegram of his own to Camila's brother Sherman Barnes. Four days later, when Garrison, GJ, and Ella Grace stepped off the train, the two men met for the first time. They introduced themselves to one another and shook hands. Then, after gathering the luggage, Sherman took his sister's family to the hotel.

As they were riding to the Resting Place Hotel, Sherman chanced to speak frankly to the tall, lean, muscled man with the no-nonsense attitude who looked more native than Black. "Just so you know, Sheriff LaRue, my sister doesn't know that you were coming. I thought that if you wanted her to know, you would have sent her a telegram. Was I wrong?"

Garrison looked at the thick, muscular man who was a little more than three inches shorter than him and offered, "Mr. Barnes, I really don't mind one way or the other. I came here to talk to my wife, and her knowing or not knowing about us coming doesn't matter to me."

"Well, if you want to see her today, I think she's going to be at church, but I can't be too sure because she's been sick off and on for the last few weeks. If she doesn't make it to church, we usually have the weekly family meal at the big house after church, and that's usually around one o'clock."

"Sick? She's sick?" Garrison's heart skipped a beat. "What's wrong with her?"

"It could be a bad cold or even that she's just tired and worn down from the traveling, and if you'll excuse my saying so, she could be trying to get past a broken heart."

Garrison's chest expanded as he pulled in a deep breath. "A broken heart can make you sick. I know all about it."

Sherman recognized a deep pain in his brother-in-law's eyes but didn't offer a word. He simply nodded and turned his eyes to the road.

Garrison looked at his children and then back at Sherman. "Maybe we'll wait until tomorrow morning. I don't want to interrupt the family meal. My children are tired, and they need to get some sleep in a bed for a while. I'll come to the blacksmith shop in the morning for directions."

Garrison was anxious to see Camila, but he had to think about the children's comfort first, and it didn't hurt to put off the inevitable for one more day. He needed to decide what he was going to say to his wife to convince her to come back home.

Before he left them, Sherman offered, "I'm going to leave this carriage for you out back of the smithy in the corral just in case you change your mind. Let my stable boy know who you are, and he'll get you all fixed up."

After Garrison asked where the sheriff's office was, the two men shook hands again, and Sherman returned to his home. Garrison registered at the hotel and took his children to the room so they could get a few good hours of sleep.

GJ and Ella Grace were tired, and as soon as they did a light toilette, they both fell into the bed and let sleep totally and completely consume them. Their father was not so fortunate. He was warring with several emotions that he had never claimed to have experienced in his life.

Garrison LaRue was, for once in his life, feeling fearful, anxious, and almost helpless. By not being open and honest with Camila, he had chased her away, but now he had developed a plan he hoped would bring her back to him.

He desperately wanted his plan to unfold perfectly and achieve the results that would reunite his family again. He wanted his wife back; he wanted her to come back to Colorado to the house she worked so hard to turn into a home for him and his children. He wanted his Lavender Rose back in his bed, and he wanted to plant his seed in her and watch her body blossom.

But first, he had to let the sheriff know that he was in town and offer his help if he needed it like U.S. Marshal Tate warned Garrison to do.

Marshal Tate's exact words were, "You be sure to check in with the town's law enforcement officer as soon as you get there. If not, you could be arrested and lose your badge. Now, go get your wife, boy. And you better not come back here without her, or you'll have to answer to me! It's hard being a law enforcer, but it's even harder being a daddy without a woman by his side."

CHAPTER 52

It was close to the time for church service to begin, but as much as she wanted to go, Camila couldn't. The church hour found her in the water room, retching just like she had been every morning for the last three to four weeks. She was glad the doctor was coming by today, and she hoped that Dr. Janey Jones could give her something that would finally settle her stomach.

"I'm so tired of being sick," Camila whined to herself.

At the moment that she finished her morning toilette, Mrs. Wills was walking into the bedroom with a tea tray in her hands. "Little girl, you needs somethin' to settle that stomach," she said and placed the tray on the table by the window, filling two cups with hot tea.

Camila hummed as they sat in the cushioned straight-backed chairs. Mrs. Wills was holding her cup while Camila sat with her eyes closed, sipping the tea.

"Mmm," Camila said, "this is good. What kind of tea is this?"

"Chamomile, and it's gon' settle that funny little belly of your'n. Now, drink up and get back in bed. You look worn out."

That sounded good to Camila, but she had promised herself that she would make it to church today. "Mrs. Wills, I think I'm going to get dressed and . . . ugh . . ." Before she could finish, another wave of nausea hit her, and she jumped up and ran back to the water room.

Camila was greeted by the doctor when she was returning to the bedroom for the third bout of stomach upset.

"So, Mrs. LaRue," Dr. Jones said, "you've not able to keep anything down? How long has it been since your last monthly?"

With a furrowed brow, Camila asked, "Are you suggesting that I could be pregnant?"

"Well, yes," Dr. Jones said. "It's always the first thing I want to consider when I examine a young, married woman."

Dr. Jones examined Camila and told her that she was about two months along in her pregnancy. During the examination, Camila told the doctor about her miscarriage, and that she was afraid the same thing was going to happen again.

Dr. Jones said, "Mrs. LaRue . . . Camila, this is going to be a healthy pregnancy for you. I want you to relax and enjoy it. All you have to do is get lots of rest, drink warm milk, and eat a few soda crackers before you go to bed at night, and your morning sickness won't be so bad."

As soon as the doctor left, Camila did exactly what she and Mrs. Wills suggested, and that was to climb back into the bed, where she slept through the remaining church hour. In the afternoon, when she finally left her bedroom, it was time for Sunday supper, and she was starving.

"Well, it's about time you made your appearance. The bulk of the day is passed, and you're just getting out of bed. No wonder you're back here with your tail between your legs. That ex-husband of yours must have gotten tired of your lazy good-for-nothing ways, and I can't say that I blame him one bit."

Franklin was standing at the base of the staircase with his thumbs resting in his vest pockets, emphasizing his protruding stomach and looking at Camila in a condescending way.

Camila stopped midway down the staircase when she saw Lincoln Gilmore was standing beside Franklin, looking smug.

Franklin continued, "If you expect to be married and be a good wife to Lincoln Gilmore, you are going to have to stop being so lazy and learn what it takes to be a good wife."

"Franklin, leave me alone," Camila said. "I don't feel like hearing you run your mouth today. Let's pretend that we are strangers and ignore each other. And what do you mean if I expect to be married to Lincoln Gilmore? I'm not trying to be married to him, not now, not ever. Are you crazy?"

Franklin walked up two of the three steps that separated them and stood in front of his sister. "Listen, Camila, I'm not going to be embarrassed by you. Linc here has agreed to marry you so that the rumors about you don't get any worse. This man has agreed to help you save face. Stop being so mean and for once in your life try to be humble and very grateful."

Sherman and his family had just walked into the house, and he overheard the exchange between his sister and brother. "Frank," Sherman said, "I think it's best you leave Camila Rose alone. Can't you see she doesn't feel well? Put your jealousy aside for once and practice a little compassion. After all, she is your sister. Where is your family loyalty?"

Franklin turned, walked back down the steps, and strode over to look at his brother, intending to make a curt remark, when Sherman quickly added, "What do you think you're going to do? You don't want to say anything to me, brother, I've been waiting for an excuse to whip your behind! Say something, please!"

Franklin looked at his younger brother then turned to look Camila up and down. He snorted, "Neither one of you is worth the trouble," and walked away.

Sherman looked at Lincoln Gilmore then turned to Camila. "What's going on?" he asked, looking from one to the other.

"Ask your brother, or you can ask him," she said, pointing at Lincoln.

Before Sherman could say anything, Lincoln took Camila's hands in his. "Don't be that way. Your brother and I only want the best for you. Here, you are a disgraced woman, sent back home after being a mail-order bride. The people are saying all manner of things about you. I thought you would be more than glad that I would want to help you keep your dignity. Your brother all but promised me that you would be my bride for sure this time."

Too angry to speak, Camila snatched her hands from the smirking, money-grubbing lecherous man's cold, damp, fleshy paws, and rubbing her palms on the side of her skirt, she stormed into the dining room. "How dare you!" was all she could say to Franklin before the sound of the front-door knocker came.

Hearing her brother Manny, who was still in the hall, say her name, Camila gave Franklin a scathing look as she turned and went back to the entryway where Sherman was standing beside the opened door. Camila saw three people standing on the porch.

"Mommy!" the two little ones called as they ran to her. Ella hugged her legs while GJ hugged her waist.

Camila leaned forward and tightly hugged her children. "My babies. My babies," she whispered as she closed her teary eyes and held them close.

"I thought you were going to wait until tomorrow," Sherman said to his brother-in-law.

Garrison responded, "The children were too excited to sleep more than a couple of hours. They wanted to see their mother."

"What is going on out here? Who is making all this noise?" Franklin looked at the uninvited visitors to his home. "Who in the world are these people?" he said in a demanding voice, and when no one offered an answer, Garrison stepped through the doorway, took off his black Stetson, and offered his hand.

"Sorry about the disturbance," he said, "I'm Garrison LaRue. These are my children, Garrison Jr. and Ella Grace, and I'm here to talk to my wife. And, as you can see, these two here are more than glad to see their mother again."

Franklin tried to stretch to make himself taller. "So, you are Garrison LaRue. Well, well, well. I certainly never expected to meet you. What can I help you with, Mr. LaRue?"

"Listen, mister, you can't help me with anything. Like I said, I'm here to talk to my wife."

"Your wife? What do you mean you are here to speak to your wife? It's my understanding that my sister is no longer anyone's wife!" Franklin planted a smile on his face. "If you want to talk to my sister, then you have to come through me to do it. I'm her oldest brother, Franklin Barnes, the family patriarch."

Rather than focus his attention on Franklin, Garrison was looking at Camila. She looked tired and thin, he thought. *If she was in Colorado, she wouldn't look like that. She needs to be home with me.*

Franklin cleared his throat and stepped into Garrison's space with his thumbs in his vest pockets stretching his vest across his protruding belly. Garrison looked at the little round man standing in front of him and wanted to swat him away like a fly. Garrison shifted his eyes to the man standing too close to him.

Stabbing Franklin in the chest with his index finger, Garrison warned, "I didn't come here to talk to you, so step back before you get knocked down a peg or two."

Franklin's face fell as he took two steps back. "Now, see here, this is *my* house. How dare you come into *my* home and talk to *me* like that?"

Taking a calming breath, Garrison laughed at Franklin then looked over his head and settled his gaze on his wife's face. "Camila, can we talk, please?"

Trying to break the tension, Mrs. Wills stepped into the hallway and cleared her throat. "Excuse me, but I'm ready to serve dinner. And Mrs. Barnes wanted me to say all of you people needs to git to the table and start fillin' your plates before the food gits too cold to eat." When no one made a move, Mrs. Wills stepped to Garrison. "Good afternoon, young man. I'm Mrs. Wills, the housekeeper, and I would really like it if you had dinner with us this afternoon."

"Just one moment, Mrs. Wills. As the housekeeper, I would appreciate it if you stayed in your place," Franklin said, then stepped past the woman, looking Garrison up and down from head to foot. "You can't seriously think that I'm going to let my sister speak to you."

Ignoring him, Garrison looked at the spunky little woman and smiled politely. Nodding his head, he said, "Good afternoon, ma'am. I'm not very hungry right now, thank you. I'm here to talk to my wife, but I'm sure that my son and daughter would appreciate a good home-cooked meal."

Mrs. Wills thought to herself *I like this young man* as she took GJ and Ella by the hands. "Hey, little ones, come with me. We're about to have dinner. Are you hungry?"

When the children nodded their heads, Mrs. Wills led them into the dining room, leaving Camila, Sherman, Lincoln, and Franklin standing in the hall staring at Garrison.

"Garrison, what do you want to talk to me about?" Camila asked, her hope-filled eyes still brimming with tears.

Before Garrison could answer, Lincoln stepped up to stand behind Camila, wound his arms around her waist, and pulled her back against his body, breathing heavily on the side of her face and neck. "Look, mister, you're too late. Her brother has already given his permission for me to marry his sister. You disgraced her and sent her home. You have no more legal right to her. She's mine now."

With as much force as she could muster, Camila forced her elbow back, hitting Lincoln in the stomach. Then she stepped away from the sweaty, heavily breathing man. "I. Am. *NOT* chattel! My brother doesn't control me! I'm not his to give away as he pleases. And there's no way that you own me either!"

Looking at Lincoln with unconcealed disgust, Camila continued. "I turned down your marriage proposal years ago, Lincoln, and I haven't changed my mind. Being married doesn't mean that a woman is owned by her husband. It should mean that she is loved and respected by him."

She walked across the room and stood in front of her oldest brother. "When are you going to realize that I'm not your possession? And I know that it was you who spread those rumors about me being disgraced. It's a shame that you are so hateful. We are adults now, and all of that childishness needs to be forgotten."

Franklin looked at her and squinted his eyes. "How am I supposed to get past the fact that my own father cared for you more than he cared for me? He did more for you and gave you more than he ever gave me. I should have gotten the largest amount of inheritance. I'm the oldest, and I'm a man. You are nothing but a woman. All you're going to do is waste that money on clothes and shoes, and what you don't spend is going to be given to some man who's only with you for your money, and then when he gets tired of you, he'll rob you blind and leave you broke with a house full of brats to take care of!"

Garrison stepped forward and grabbed Franklin by the lapels, lifting him to his toes, but before he could say anything, Camila and Sherman grabbed Garrison's arms. "Let him go, brother-in-law, he's not worth it," Sherman said, trying to suppress a grin.

Camila looked at Franklin's fear-filled face. "You are a pitiful excuse of a man, and I can't stand to look at you. I should let him rip you apart." She turned to Garrison. "It's okay, let him go, please. No matter what he says and tries to do to me, he's still family, and I have to respect that, even if he doesn't."

When Franklin was released, Camila stepped between him and Garrison She pressed her lips together, flared her nostrils, and raising her fisted hands, she lunged at Franklin, making him gasp and flinch. With a gleam in her eye, she said, "Mmm-hmm. Just what I thought. All hot air."

Then, knowing that her brother was no longer a threat to her, she turned her back to him to face Garrison. "Like I asked you before, what are you doing here? What do you want to say to me?"

CHAPTER 53

Sherman was watching all of the drama unfold. He liked seeing Franklin get knocked from his self-appointed podium, and he was glad that Camila finally put Lincoln in his place, but he especially enjoyed watching his baby sister stand up for herself. With a broad smile on his face, he watched as Garrison LaRue looked at her and asked nervously, "Can we go somewhere less crowded so I can talk to you?"

Sherman recognized that look. It was one of anxiety, pain, and helplessness. He had experienced it himself when he first realized that he was in love with his beautiful wife, Athena, and didn't know if she felt the same about him. She had given him a run for his money, and as a result, he knew what Garrison was going through and wanted to spare the poor man any more agony.

So he decided to help his brother-in-law. Sherman opened the front door. "Why don't the two of you go out to the garden house and talk? We'll take care of my cute little niece and good-lookin' nephew."

Garrison gently received Camila's hand, and they stepped out onto the front porch. "Which way?" he asked.

Instead of replying, with their hands still connected, Camila led him across the porch and down the steps. She then directed them to the opposite side of the large house, and after a short time of walking hand in hand down a winding brick path, they came to an extensive garden that was fragranced by the late-spring early-summer flowers. In the very middle of the garden was a large wooden summerhouse.

It was screened in, and the entrance was guarded by a large ornate screen door. Stepping inside the cool, fragrant garden house, the couple stood holding hands. Each was afraid to speak to the other.

Then, being the man he was, and especially since he was the one on a mission, Garrison stepped toward the benches that lined the far wall and, using both hands, guided Camila to the bench seat.

"I need to talk to you, and I hope that you will give me a chance to explain myself," he said.

"So talk," Camila said. "What do you want? Why are you here?" She was trying to be tough to ward off whatever hurtful thing Garrison had to say to her.

Garrison could tell from her tone of voice that she was nervous, and as a matter of fact, so was he, but he had to make her understand some things. Slowly, he began.

"After you ran away from home, I missed you so much I didn't know what to do. My mother told me that I had lost my gift from God, and my father told me I was a fool. They both told me that I had robbed my children of their happiness. After you were gone, no matter what I did, the only peace I could find was when I prayed and finally had to face the truth. And the truth is that I love you. I love you so much it hurts."

Camila slowly raised herself from the bench, folded her arms around her waist, and turned to look out through the screened walls at the garden. She wanted to say that she hadn't run away. She wanted to remind him that he had given her no other choice but to leave.

When Camila stood, Garrison stood also. He hesitated as he watched her. He didn't want her to walk out on him, so he continued, "And for the most selfish of reasons, I wouldn't tell you how I was feeling toward you. I refused to look past my own misery to see that you really are a gift to me and the children. You walked into my house and made it a home. You gave love to my children and made them your own. Truth is that I love you so much more than I have words to say."

He sat down again, leaning forward with his forearms resting on his knees, his head and hands hanging down.

"I never slept with Mercy Peterson," Garrison said. "I was never unfaithful to you. She was in town because the U.S. Marshals brought her to Alamosa so that we could protect her. She had witnessed a murder, and the marshal wanted her safe until he caught the man who murdered her boss. That day you saw us, I had escorted her from the jail to the house so she could take a bath. Nothing happened between us, I swear to you. Mrs. Aires was there when we arrived, and she stayed the whole time Mercy was bathing. I couldn't tell you about it then because we were told to keep it quiet. Besides, I didn't want you involved in that mess."

He stood and crossed the pavilion to where Camila was standing listening but not looking at him.

"I came here to tell you it's time for you to come home," Garrison said. "You've been gone long enough."

Camila uttered four words that crushed Garrison's heart. "This is my home."

Before she could say anything more, Garrison spun her around and pulled her into a tight embrace. "No. No, it's not! Your home is with me at LaRue Crossing."

Camila tried to pull back to look at him, but he tightened his embrace. "Besides," she said, "we are not married anymore."

"We are married! I burned that letter. We are not divorced." She could feel his chest rising and falling. He was breathing deeply, and his voice sounded weak and unsure. "Camila. I need you there with me. I can't do this anymore. I need my wife with me."

Resting her head on his chest, he felt her body lose its tension and felt her arms slide around his waist, returning his fierce embrace. They stood that way until their breathing settled down and it seemed that their hearts were beating as one.

Camila leaned back and said, "Leave the children with me, and I'll be home in a few weeks. They need to get to know this side of their family. As long as they are with me, you know that I'm coming back. But when I come back, some things have to change."

"I know, and one thing is this," Garrison said, looking into her beautiful brown gold-flecked eyes. "I love you, Camila Rose, and I'll spend the rest of my life telling you." Then he lowered his head and kissed his wife with all the love he could display at the moment.

Standing on the garden path some distance from the pavilion looking at the couple as they made up, Mrs. Wills whispered, "Thank you, Lord, for answering my prayers."

A short distance behind her, Sherman Barnes whispered, "Amen," then raised his hand to put a finger on his lips to hush the older woman, who had turned to him, smiling.

CHAPTER 54

Garrison and the children stayed in Checotah for over a week. GJ and Ella Grace stayed with Camila at the big house so that they could get acquainted and play with their cousins. Garrison slept at the hotel every evening, but early every morning, he went to the house to have breakfast with his wife.

During that time, the tall, handsome, powerfully constructed man managed to capture the hearts of Willa, Athena, and especially Mrs. Wills with his helpful and charming behaviors. He would come to the house early every morning, have breakfast, and then he would take care of some of the odds and ends that needed to be done to and around the house.

Camila had to reprimand the women several times about standing on the porches looking at her husband working with his naked upper body drenched with sweat and his muscular physique glistening in the sun.

Willa said, "Why do you want to deny me the pleasure of looking at that handsome, well-put-together man? It's not like he has eyes for anybody but you. Stop being so selfish."

Mrs. Wills said, "My Henry, may he rest in peace, looked like that young man, except he was shorter. Oh, yeah, he wasn't nearly as handsome, and he sure wasn't as strong, but I sure loved that man, and he loved me. I know because he looked at me like that young man looks at you, Miss Camila."

Athena winked at her sister-in-law. "Nevertheless, it is nice to look at a man in all of his glory and appreciate him. Looking don't hurt a thing, it's when some heifer crosses the line and tries to touch that glory that becomes the problem."

Everything seemed to stand still as the women stood with large eyes and open mouths looking at Athena Barnes.

"What?" she asked. "You all know good and well that there are certain ladies that will try to get between you and your man."

After their initial shock, the ladies agreed with Athena, and they all laughed.

Two nights before Garrison was to leave, Mrs. Wills handed Camila a packed carpetbag and said, "You and your man need to spend some time together, little lady."

"Mrs. Wills, you know how mornings are for me. How can you expect me to spend one night, much less two nights, with him?"

"Because he's that there baby's father, ain't he?" When Camila nodded, Mrs. Wills continued. "And you know goodness well that he deserves to know his wife is going to have his baby."

"I wanted to wait until we get back together in Alamosa before I tell him," Camila said.

"Well, you know what's best, I guess. But don't let that man get away from you without letting him show you how much he loves you. And don't worry about the little ones. I'll take care of them."

The couple spent their first night at the Resting Place Hotel in wedded bliss. For almost two months, Garrison had yearned to see how she looked, felt, and sounded in the throes of passion again, and he had to talk to himself so that he wouldn't rush things and ruin the night for them both.

Camila was so glad to be back in his arms being the subject of his gentle, patient, and complete lovemaking that she had to remind herself they were in a hotel and didn't want to let all the guests know how much she was enjoying her husband.

As a matter of fact, Camila was so sated with her husband's expressions of his love for her that her body forgot to be sick in the mornings, especially since he didn't give her a chance to get out of bed until noon on his last day in town.

For Sheriff Garrison LaRue, it wasn't easy for him to have to leave his family in Checotah, but he had to get back home. These were busy days for a frontier town like Alamosa. Every day, the cattle drives were beginning and ending in and around the town, and the drovers as well as the negative element that followed them around needed to be kept in line.

Late that afternoon, Camila and Garrison went to the train station, and while they were waiting, he said, "I'm glad I said goodbye to the children last night, because it's hard to say it here." He put his arm around Camila's waist and pulled her to his side. "How long do I have to wait before you come back?"

Camila said, "As soon as I can. Probably no more than two weeks. I need time to pack and go to the lawyer so I can give each brother one-third ownership of the house and property and take care of some other business. Then we'll be home, and you'll never be rid of me again."

With one final kiss and a whispered, "I love you, my Lavender Rose," he boarded the train. This time, it was she who stood watching as the train disappeared into the distance.

After standing on the platform until the train was long gone, Camila felt engulfed in a pair of strong arms. She turned and lay her head on Manny's shoulder.

Wiping her tears, he smiled at his sister and said, "Look at you, in love with your husband." Then he added, "Let's get you back to the house and get everything packed up so you can go home."

Camila lifted her head and looked into her brother's eyes.

He smiled and said, "Yes, I said so you can go home. Don't look at me like that. You and I both know that Oklahoma is no longer your home. You don't belong here anymore. Your heart is with that man who just left on that train, and you also know that you love those two little ones like they are your own."

With a tearful smile, she replied, "It is time for me to go. You're right, this place is no longer my home." She kissed her brother's cheek. "I love you, Manny, and I hope you bring your family to visit us, because I probably won't be coming back here again any time soon."

CHAPTER 55

One week after Garrison's arrival in Alamosa, the town was full every night of cattle drovers who had just been paid as well as trail bums who followed the herds trying to steal a few cows and sell them as their own. They all were looking to have a lot of fun. It was a time when the town was in an uproar because, as expected, the men were rowdy, and some had to be detained until they sobered and paid for any damages they caused.

Sheriff LaRue and his undersheriff, Hank Anderson, as well as their four deputies, were kept busy stopping fights and keeping the rambunctious cattle drovers in line.

On Thursday night after all of the guns had finally been collected and labeled, several men had been jailed, the saloon was closed and the bordello locked down for the night, the streets quieted and most people were in their beds.

Garrison gave his final orders for the night. "Hank, you go home so you can keep an eye on the store. Be sure to keep Tessa and the children safe. Roy, you guard the prisoners. Todd, Jarrod, and Wesley, you guys get some sleep. I'll be back as soon as I make the rounds."

As soon as the sheriff left, Roy told Wesley, "Follow him. If he gets mad, tell him I sent ya to keep an eye on him. Now watch his back and don't ferget ta use that there whistle if ya have some problems."

Wesley thought he was being careful so the sheriff couldn't tell he was following him, but right after he checked the front doors to the bank, Garrison stepped into the side street that led to the back door, and when his deputy walked up, Garrison snatched him.

"Why are you following me, Wes?"

"Hey, Boss. Roy told me to watch your back. He's nervous about the late-arriving drovers coming into town tonight and he didn't want you out here alone."

"Well, let's get these rounds finished so we can get back to the jailhouse and get some rest ourselves," Garrison ordered.

At just that moment, two men stepped out of the shadows in the alley. Garrison and Wesley heard their footsteps, and when the two lawmen turned, they were both hit with wooden planks. The sheriff was hit on the side, while the deputy was struck on the forearm.

The largest man said, "Sheriff, my cellmate at the prison, George Tate, promised me a lot of money if I killed you."

He began swinging the wooden plank again. This time, Garrison spun away from the board and returned a few blows of his own, rendering his attacker unconscious. He quickly turned to see if his deputy was faring well with his attacker.

Wesley, as well, had gained the upper hand on his attacker and was beating the man with the very plank that had just been used on him.

After the two assailants had been cuffed, Wesley blew the whistle just before several shots rang out from across the street. By the time help arrived, the sheriff and his deputy were lying on the ground near the handcuffed men, who were still unconscious.

The sheriff and his deputy had both been injured. Garrison was shot in the thigh and lower chest, while Wesley was shot in the shoulder, however, he had managed to blow the whistle again while Garrison held on to consciousness long enough to shoot the two other men dead-center in the chests as they walked across the street to finish the job.

Things began to fade to black when Garrison heard Roy's voice say, "We're here, Boss. We got you. Hang on, you're going to be okay."

Roy wasn't sure, but he thought he heard the sheriff mumble two words that sounded like, "Lavender Rose."

The train ride this time was more comfortable, and Camila was happier because she knew that when she returned to Alamosa, her husband would be able to see her rounding belly. She thought about how happy and excited she was to get back to the town she now called home.

As the train finally pulled into the station on Tuesday morning, Camila saw a crowd of people standing on the loading platform: the ranch hands Roy, Todd, and Jarrod, along with Mr. and Mrs. LaRue and Mrs. Aires.

Almost immediately, the ticket master boarded the train, and while Camila was gathering the children and their carpetbags, he pointed to her and told another man, "Right there, that's her."

The man standing bedside the ticket master spoke. "Mrs. LaRue?"

When Camila looked at the man, she saw that he was wearing a badge. With a pounding heart and a dry throat, she answered, "Yes."

The man slowly reached out to take her elbow as he asked, "Ma'am would you follow me, please?"

Moving away from the man and gathering the children to her side, Camila inquired, "Who are you?"

The man pointed to the badge on his vest. "I'm the territorial marshal. My name is Jeremiah Thomas. Would you come with me, please?"

Camila felt a chill roll down her spine. "What's the problem? Where's my husband?"

Marshal Thomas patiently replied, "Miz LaRue, if you'll come with me, I'll answer all of your questions. Please, ma'am."

With the children in tow, Camila stepped off the train and saw that her trunks were already sitting on the platform. Todd and Jarrod were standing by the baggage.

"Miz LaRue," Todd said, "we sure are glad you're finally back. Wesley and the boss have been shot."

Her knees suddenly became weak, and as she felt herself falling, the marshal grabbed her. After she collected herself, Camila asked "Is he? Are they? Alive?"

Marshal Thomas looked at Todd disgustedly and answered, "Both men are alive. But your husband is in bad shape, Miz LaRue. We got to get going, ma'am."

"Where is he?" she asked, and Marshal Thomas quietly replied, "He's at the doc's place."

To Camila, it seemed that everyone around her was rushing around, but she felt like she was moving in slow motion. She could hear that the children were crying, she could hear several voices call her name, she could also feel someone touch her elbows, but she couldn't make herself react to everything in real time because through all of that, she was trying to stay as calm as she could.

Trying to stay in control as she prompted herself to remain in control, she thought, *If I walk slow and don't expect the worst, I'll get to see Garrison. I know that if I can touch him, he will be just fine.* She repeated over and over to herself in her mind.

Todd collected the luggage while Mrs. Aires wrapped her arms around the younger woman and whispered, "Trust in the Lord with all your heart."

Camila was slowly released from Mrs. Aires' hold as she looked up to see her in-laws standing near the ticket office door.

Anna Wolf smiled sadly as Thaddeus LaRue ushered his wife across the platform to stand in front of Camila and the children. Before she had the opportunity to speak, her father-in-law took hold of his frightened grandchildren while her mother-in-law reached out and captured Camila's hands.

"So, Camila Rose, you came back. We're so glad you did."

"How did everyone know that I was on that train?" Camila asked quietly.

Roy said, "We sent you a telegram the night after it happened, and your brother Sherman sent one back letting us know that you had already left Checotah."

After handing the children to the ranch hands, Thaddeus stepped forward and said, "Garrison is waiting for you. Let's get going."

"How is he? Is he going to be alright? How badly was he hurt?" she asked.

Hearing the desperation in her voice, her father-in-law took Camila by the elbow and guided her down the platform to a carriage. After helping the women and children in, he got in and drove them to Dr. Lands' place.

"He's asleep," Thaddeus told her. "The doctor thought it was best to help Garrison handle the pain. We've been in town since Thursday afternoon, and we've only seen him awake twice since everything happened."

CHAPTER 56

Just as they stepped through the door of the small hospital, Camila could see that in the waiting area sat the rest of the ranch hands and several other townspeople. When they saw her, most of the people jumped up from their chairs and all began talking words of comfort and welcoming her back home.

Both of the children grabbed her and pressed their bodies close to her. "Mommy!" Ella Grace cried, holding on so tight that Camila could hardly keep her balance, while GJ remained quiet, standing on Camila's side, sliding his arms around her waist with his head on her side.

Camila hugged the children to her. "I want you to go with Mrs. Johnson. She's going to get you something to eat, and she's going to help you pray for Daddy. Okay? I'll see you soon. Don't worry, Daddy's going to be just fine."

"I want to see my father!" little GJ exclaimed.

She looked at the boy that she thought of as her son and said, "Listen, GJ, I need you to do what I've asked you to do for right now, and a little later, I'm going to let you see your daddy. I have to see him first to make sure things are alright."

While the children were being taken away, Camila stood in the middle of the floor in a daze. Ella pulled free from Mrs. Johnson and ran back to her new mother. "Mommy, you have to go see Daddy. Mrs. Johnson said he doesn't feel so good right now. You have to kiss him and make him all better."

Camila gave her daughter a half smile and said, "I'm going to do my best, Miss Ella, okay?"

Looking straight ahead, Camila let her mind go blank. She was trying to steel herself for what she would see when she was on the other side of the door to the room that Garrison was in.

"Alright, Camila," Dr. Lands said softly, "let's go in. Try not to overreact when you see him. Just remember that he's much better now than he was when he first got here."

When the doctor opened the door, Camila couldn't make her feet move. She saw her husband lying still, lightly covered with a sheet. His upper body was wrapped in thick bandages, his leg was resting on several pillows, and he looked ashen.

After a few minutes, when the doctor had completed his quick examination, Camila slowly crossed the room and stood beside the bed. With silent tears and trembling hands, she prayed for her husband. She asked for God's mercy to be over him, and she prayed for a complete healing for him. Then she sat in the chair in front of the window and determined not to leave Garrison's bedside until he opened his eyes again.

Several hours later, when the LaRues were shown into the room, they saw that Contessa had joined Camilla and was sitting beside the bed, rocking her youngest child and staring at her brother with a sad, distant look on her face.

When she heard the door to the room open, Contessa stood and turned toward them. She hugged her parents and started talking. "I was just thinking about Garrison when he was a little boy. You remember, Momma and Daddy, how he was always doing those daring things, always getting those scrapes, bumps, and bruises, but that never stopped him, and I know that this won't stop him either." Then, looking at Camila, she said, "You keep on loving him and being strong for him until he gets better."

After hugging and kissing her sister-in-law, Contessa stepped to the door, but before she touched the knob, the door was pushed open and Pastor Johnson stepped into the room. "I'm here to pray with you and the family," he said softly, looking around at the sad faces of Sheriff LaRue's family members.

The last person to enter the room was Dr. Lands, and he stood while the pastor and family prayed. Thad and Anna stepped to the bed and looked at their son. Anna touched her son's face, and his father lay his hand on his son's shoulder.

They both thought back to the time when Garrison was elected sheriff, and how they each dreaded the day that someone would come and tell them about something like this.

Camila began to pray with the pastor as tears rolled down her cheeks. She was afraid that Garrison was not going to wake up again. When the pastor finished and left the room, Camila sat on the side of the bed, lifting Garrison's hand to her mouth for a gentle kiss.

She pressed his hand to her chest and whispered to him, "You can't leave me."

Dr. Lands approached Camila. "Mrs. LaRue, the sheriff is going to be fine. It's just going to take him a while to heal. He has two gunshot wounds and some broken ribs. He was in a lot of pain, so I gave him some medicine that will help him continue to sleep comfortably with less pain. You know how stubborn he is, and he wouldn't settle down. He doesn't want to hear that he has to be still to heal."

After Dr. Lands finished his check on Garrison's condition, he patted Camila's shoulder and whispered to her, "In your condition, you need to take care of yourself."

When she looked at him with a questioning gaze, Dr. Lands raised his hand to her shoulder and said, "Your doctor in Checotah was concerned about you. I received a telegram asking me to follow you through your waiting time." He patted her shoulder then left the room.

Camila returned her gaze to her husband's bedside. She raised her hand, and with her fingers traced the planes of his face across his forehead, down his gently throbbing temple, to his prominent cheekbones, his strong jaw-line, and his soft, well-shaped lips. She smoothed his hair from his fore-head, kissed her finger, and pressed it to his lips.

Then, leaning close to his ear Camila, continued her one-sided conversation. "I love you. I don't want us to have to live without you. Come back. Come back to us, come back to me, please."

She couldn't say any more, her silent sobbing and trembling consumed all of her energy.

Taking her by the shoulders and helping her stand, Anna Wolf asked, "Are you pregnant?"

Camila nodded her head. Thad took her other hand in his, looking at his daughter-in-law with a gleam in his eyes, and asked, "Does Garrison know?"

When she shook her head, the older couple embraced their daughter-in-law until, not being able to stand anymore, Camila sat on the bed, returning her gaze to her handsome husband's face.

Because she had to keep a connection with him, she returned her hand to his face and head, brushed his hair from his forehead, delicately cupped his face with her hands, leaned forward, and kissed his forehead, his eyes, his cheeks, and finally, his lips.

"Don't leave me. You have to be here to help me raise our baby," she whispered, raising his big hand to rest it on her belly.

CHAPTER 57

When the door opened again, Mildred Horn stepped into the room carrying a glass of water and a medicine bottle. "It's time for you to leave. He doesn't even know that you are here anyway."

"I'm not going anywhere. Just give him his medicine and then you get out," Camila said with a strong edge to her voice.

Mildred looked at Camila and then across the room at Garrison's parents, who she hadn't realized were also in the room. From their expressions, she knew that she was pushing her luck, so she placed the tray on the table. "Dr. Lands will be here to administer the medicine."

Looking at Thaddeus and Anna Wolf, Camila insisted that her in-laws go to the weekend house and get some rest. "If anything changes," she promised them, "I'll have someone come to let you know."

They hugged and kissed her and reluctantly left Camila with her husband.

Throughout the night, Camila would doze then awaken to touch his face and squeeze his hand, then sit back down in the chair beside the bed and take another short nap. He would move and had reactions to her touch, but he didn't open his eyes.

Just as the sun was rising, Camila felt a hand on her head and heard her husband's raspy voice whisper, "Lavender Rose." When she lifted her head and looked into the weary eyes of Garrison LaRue, he said, "It really is you. I thought I was dreaming."

"No, I'm not a dream. I'm right here beside you, where I belong."

Smiling weakly, Garrison took Camila's hand and held it tight. "I wanted to believe that you were really here. And my heart kept telling me that I was right as soon as you came into the room, because I could smell you. I could feel you. I could hear you. The only thing I couldn't do was see you. All I could see was darkness, and I wanted to see you."

His eyes were intense as he scanned her face then reached up to touch her cheek and let it slide down to her neck, shoulder, and elbow. Finally, he took her hand in his and squeezed it lightly.

Camila sat beside the bed looking at her husband. Her heart was hurting for him. He had just been through an arduous ordeal. She wanted to soothe him, to ease some of his pain, but he wouldn't let her speak.

Adding pressure to her hand and guiding her from the chair to the side of the bed, Garrison continued, "But here you are, I can see you. I can feel you. I can smell you. And what I want to do more than anything, my Lavender Rose, is to kiss you and hold you next to my heart." He pulled her close and guided her head to his chest.

They were so focused on each other that neither realized Mildred was standing in the doorway. It was her intention to get Camila out of Garrison's room so that she could be there when he woke up. She wanted to be sure that her face would be the first one he saw when he regained consciousness.

She looked at them sadly and whispered to herself, "He loves her." She quietly backed out of the room, gently closing the door while dabbing at the tears in her eyes. As she was standing on the other side of the door, Mildred said to herself, "They are so happy. She does seem to be the right one for him. I want to know why her and not me, Lord?"

Mildred went to Dr. Lands' office and let him know that the patient was awake. Then she went to the water closet and cried for her loss, finally realizing that although she had a strong desire for Garrison, he had no desire toward her at all.

CHAPTER 58

Dr. Lands came into the room while Garrison and Camila were still in an embrace. "Okay, you two stop this fooling around. You both are going to have to take it easy for a while." Seeing the puzzled look on his patient's face, the doctor smiled and said, "You need more time to recover, and your wife has been away for a while. She needs time to get used to being back here again."

After he examined Garrison, Dr. Lands gently led Camila from the room.

Seeing the puzzled look on his patient's face, Dr. Lands looked at Camila with a concerned expression and softly asked, "You haven't talked to your husband about your condition yet, have you, Mrs. LaRue?"

She shook her head slowly. "No, Doctor, not yet."

"Well, don't wait too long, or it won't be a surprise," the doctor admonished her jokingly.

As the days went by, Garrison became impatient and restless. "I don't want to be here anymore. I want to go home," he said to the doctor every day after his checkup, and the doctor would reply, "Just be patient. It's important that you recover completely, so stop pushing it."

Being immobile was difficult for Garrison. He wanted to get out of the bed and move around. "But I'm feeling pretty good, Doc. This bed is getting to me. I need to move around."

Garrison's face was drawn and pale, and his temper was getting short.

He continuously insisted that he could get up and walk around, but Dr. Lands repeated, "You stay in the bed."

Seeing the stubborn look on his patient's face, the doctor repeated his orders.

"Listen, young man, you are not going to get out of this bed until I say you can get out. So settle yourself down and stop upsetting your wife."

For the next few days, Garrison managed to hold his temper when the children were around, but when his parents finally took them to their ranch, he ranted about anything and everything. Camila managed to hold her tongue and would even leave the room when he was in a bad mood.

It was at the end of the third week of his recovery time in the hospital when Dr. Lands finally let Garrison go home to the weekend house to begin the next phase of his recovery. And after all that time of being confined to the bed, he was ready to yell and throw things.

One night, he woke up in the middle of the night from a fitful sleep, feeling like something was wrong. Everything seemed to be fine, but he thought he heard Camila sniffing. She was across the room in the large chair with her feet on the footstool.

"Are you okay over there?" he asked. "What's going on?"

She threw back the blanket she was covered with, stood, and walked to the bed. "Do you need something? Are you hurting?"

Garrison frowned at the raspy sound of her voice, but when he voiced his concern for her, she said, "I'm fine, just a little tired. Don't you worry about me. Get some sleep. I'll see you in the morning. We can go for another walk to the backyard."

Then she kissed him on the temple, but before she could return to the chair, he reached out and took her arm. "Lay here with me, please. I know that chair has to be uncomfortable."

When she climbed into the bed, he pulled her over to him so that her body was lightly touching his side.

When Garrison awoke again, it was just after daybreak. He thought he heard another noise, and the space beside him was empty. This time, he was sure he heard Camila in the water room, and it sounded like she was retching.

By the time he had the covers thrown back and had worked his legs off the bed so that he was sitting with his feet touching the floor, Camila was returning to the bedroom with a basin of warm water.

Smiling, she said, "You're awake. How are you? Let's get you ready for the day."

As she was helping him with his sponge bath, he spoke his concern for her. "Camila Rose LaRue, I heard you earlier. If you're sick, we need to have the doctor stop by to see you. You're working too hard taking care of me. You look tired, and you've lost weight."

She helped him into a fresh nightshirt, and as he was sitting back down on the side of the bed, she told him, "I've already seen a doctor back in Checotah, and she said that I'll probably be tired off and on throughout the day and a little sick to my stomach most mornings for just another month or so."

Garrison looked alarmed. "You *are* sick. What is it? Are you going to be okay?"

He had taken her hands in his and could feel them trembling as he pulled her between his legs and rested her head on his shoulder.

Breathing deeply and holding her firmly to his upper body, he demanded, "Camila, talk to me! What is going on with you?"

After a pause, she leaned back to look into his eyes. "Garrison, I'm . . ." A sob escaped her lips as she continued, "You're going to be a father again. I'm going to have a baby."

Without thinking, Garrison followed his natural instinct and pulled her back to his chest and held her there, kissing the tender side of her soft neck. "Did you just tell me that my wife is having a baby?" he asked, and he felt her nod her head before he heard her say, "Yes."

When she lifted her face, he cupped it in his hands he asked, "When?"

"In just a little over six months."

They stared at each other for a few moments, then he kissed her forehead and gingerly pulled her back down to his chest.

On Friday afternoon, three weeks after being at the weekend house, Dr.

Lands released Garrison, letting him go home to the ranch house. But he admonished him, "You are to stay in the bed more than you stay on your feet, or I'm bringing you back to my place!"

CHAPTER 59

It was a pleasure to sit on the back porch of his ranch house wrapped in a heavy quilt, watching his parents as they stood laughing at and playing with their grandchildren, who were running around in the backyard. He could hear the sounds of the animals as they were fed, ridden, prodded, and just milled around.

The ranch hands were busy going about their daily chores, and his wife was getting on his nerves, buzzing around him like a worker bee.

"Are you comfortable? Can I get you some coffee? Are you hungry?"

She was tired, but she wanted to make him comfortable before she sat down. Because once she was down, she didn't want to have to get up again too soon. It had been a task these past two months taking care of her husband and dealing with the symptoms of pregnancy, but Camila wanted him to know, really know without a doubt, that she was there for him.

Without a word to her, he threw open his covering, reached out, wrapped his hands around her expanding waist, pulled her down, and rested her beside him. Then, rewrapping the quilt around both of them, Garrison kissed her and said, "It's time for you to sit down. I heard Dr. Lands tell you to stay off your feet as much as possible when he was here the day before yesterday. So let's sit here and rock for a while."

Camila lay her head on his shoulder, and he felt her body relax. Holding her close, he smiled.

"I love you," he said. "You know that, don't you?"

Without raising her head, she said, "Yes, I know."

He placed his hand on her rounding abdomen. "I want you to know that I appreciate that you came back. When I was shot, all I could think about was that I wasn't going to ever see you again. And I'm glad that you are here to take care of me. But I want to ask you something."

Camila raised her head and looked into his eyes. "What do you want to ask me?"

"I need to know. Are you going to go back to your home in Oklahoma, or will you stay here with me? With us? I need you. The children need you . . ." He couldn't finish his thought.

Camila sat up and put her hand on his cheek. "Garrison LaRue, don't you know by now that being here with you and our children means that I am home?"

"If you are so happy, then why did you want to leave? And why did you tell me that you were home when I came to Checotah to get you?"

"At that time, I felt like . . . Why should I stay where I'm not wanted? Garrison, you couldn't find it in yourself to share your true feelings with me. I thought I was wasting my time."

When Garrison attempted to say something, Camila rubbed her thumb over his lips.

"No, wait,." she said. "You asked me why I wanted to leave, so give me the opportunity to give you my complete answer."

Garrison lifted his eyes, looking into hers, and nodded his head.

"We'd been married for four years," Camila said, "and up until then, you never told me you loved me, you never wished me a happy anniversary, you didn't even share my birthdays with me. What was I supposed to do? You wouldn't even accept my love for you. My heart was broken, and for a while, I tried to hold out to see if you would open your heart to me, but you were so hard. I didn't think that you even liked me or wanted me around. All I wanted was to be loved, not just by your body, but from your heart."

Garrison looked at his wife with sad eyes. "Well, you don't have to worry about that anymore, because I love you. I have given myself permission to accept your love, and I'm offering you all the love you could ever need and want from now on."

Over the next three months, Camila's body began to show stronger evidence of her condition. She was happy, and Garrison was overjoyed. He was looking forward to the time when he would be the one passing out the cigars and getting pats on the back.

It was Wednesday evening, and Garrison had just finished making his rounds. He'd been back to work full time for almost six weeks, and he was glad. The only drawback to his returning to work was that he had to leave his very pregnant wife.

He remembered kissing her when he left this morning, and like every morning, he rubbed her belly, but this morning she'd felt tight, and for the past week she seemed to be waddling a little more than usual. But when he offered to stay home with her, she quickly shooed him out the door and promised him that she would go back to bed as soon as he left.

Just as he was taking the keys from his desk to check on Jensen Jenkins, the town's resident drunk, the office door opened and in stepped Hank, holding Jensen's dinner tray and grinning like he had a secret.

"Hank," Garrison said, "you're a little early, and why are you so happy?"

Hank said, "I'm happy for you, brother."

Garrison quickly asked, "Why?"

"Oh, 'cause, Todd just came to get Tessa to take her to LaRue Crossing. And he gave me a message to give you from your momma."

"What? Wait? Is . . . is it time?"

Hank stood holding the tray, grinning and nodding his head. "Yep. You need to get going, man. Don't worry, I'll take care of everything here. Just go, man. Git!"

Roy, Thad LaRue, GJ, and Ella Grace were waiting in the side yard when Garrison arrived. "Here," Roy said, taking the horses' reins, "I got this. You jus' git yo'self inside."

When Garrison looked at his children, Thad added, "I got these two, now go on, boy, your wife needs you."

Anna Wolf was in the summer room. "Well, I see you made it." She stood and hugged her son and, pointing to the housekeeper's quarters, said, "You need to get in there, she's scared."

Garrison stepped from the summer room into the kitchen on his way to his wife's side.

"Hello, Sheriff," Dr. Lands, who was scrubbing his hands, said. "Glad you made it. Hope you're ready for this."

Three hours, several gallons of sweat, and ten chewed-up fingernails later, Emery Thaddeus LaRue's wails could be heard throughout the entire house. Much to his father's relief. After letting GJ and Ella Grace get a good look at their little brother, Garrison let them go off with their grandparents.

When she had finished feeding their brand-new son, Camila handed him to his father to be burped and placed in the cradle. Returning to the bed, Garrison kicked off his slippers and gingerly sat beside Camila, pulling her close to his side. He kissed her tenderly and hugged her gently.

"I'm so proud of you. It's only been a few hours since our son was born, and you look so beautiful. I love you so much," he said and kissed her again.

"Thank you," she said, smiling. "You are quite an amazing man yourself, you know? Most men don't stick around and help their wives with the delivery, but you did. So thank you. I love you too."

Garrison spent two nights at the ranch helping Camila adjust to being a new mother, but Friday morning found Sheriff LaRue in town passing out cigars, accepting pats on the back and declaring that his wife and his very handsome, healthy, nine-pound, twenty-four-inch son were both doing just fine.

ABOUT THE AUTHOR

G. Louise Beard was born in Baltimore, Maryland. The second of five children, she earned a B.S. in Special Education from Coppin State College. She and her family relocated to Ogden, Utah, where she earned an M.Ed. in Secondary Education from Weber State University.

An avid reader, she spent her early years dreaming of becoming a writer, however the necessities of life—marriage, raising a family, teaching, becoming a minister/pastor's wife—took priority and kept the dream at bay.

Now in retirement, she is taking advantage of the opportunity to fulfill her dream of becoming a published author. Her first book, *Right Next Door*, was published in 2021.